KT-546-498

DEATH OF A CELEBRITY

A HAMISH MACBETH MURDER MYSTERY

M.C. BEATON

CONSTABLE

CONSTABLE

First published in the United States in 2002 by Grand Central Publishing,
a division of Hachette Book Group USA, Inc.

First published in Great Britain in 2009 by Robinson,
an imprint of Constable & Robinson Ltd.

This edition published in Great Britain in 2018 by Constable

13 5 7 9 10 8 6 4 2

Copyright © M. C. Beaton, 2002, 2009

The moral right of the author has been asserted.

*All characters and events in this publication, other than
those clearly in the public domain, are fictitious
and any resemblance to real persons,
living or dead, is purely coincidental.*

All rights reserved.
No part of this publication may be reproduced, stored in a retrieval
system, or transmitted, in any form, or by any means, without the
prior permission in writing of the publisher, nor be otherwise
circulated in any form of binding or cover other than that in which
it is published and without a similar condition including this
condition being imposed on the subsequent purchaser.

A CIP catalogue record for this book
is available from the British Library.

ISBN: 978-1-47212-453-1

Typeset in Palatino by Photoprint
Printed and bound in Great Britain by
CPI Group (UK) Ltd, Croydon CR0 4YY

Papers used by Constable are from well-managed forests and other
responsible sources.

Constable
An imprint of
Little, Brown Book Group
Carmelite House
50 Victoria Embankment
London EC4Y 0DZ

An Hachette UK Company
www.hachette.co.uk

www.littlebrown.co.uk

To Benjamin Wiggin of
Honington Hall, Warwickshire
With affection

Chapter One

The fault, dear Brutus, lies not in our stars,
But in ourselves, that we are underlings.
— William Shakespeare

Hamish Macbeth did not like change, although this was something he would not even admit to himself, preferring to think of himself as a go-ahead, modern man.

But the time-warp that was the village of Lochdubh in northwest Scotland suited him very well. As the village policeman, he knew everyone. He enjoyed strolling through the village or driving around the heathery hills, dropping in here and there for a chat and a cup of tea.

The access to Lochdubh was by a single, twisting, single-track road. It nestled at the foot of two huge mountains and faced a long sea loch down which Atlantic winds brought mercurial changes of weather. Apart from a few tourists in the summer months, strangers were few and far between. The days went on much as they had done for the past century, although sheep prices had dropped like a stone and the small farmers and crofters were feeling the pinch. From faraway Glasgow and Edinburgh, authoritative voices suggested the crofters diversify, but the land was hard and stony, and fit only for raising sheep.

So Hamish felt the intrusion into his world of a newspaper office was unsettling. The owner/editor, Sam Wills, had taken over an old Victorian boarding house on the waterfront and, with the help of a grant from the Highlands and Islands Commission, had started a weekly newspaper called *Highland Times*. It was an almost immediate success, rising to a circulation of nearly one thousand – and that was a success in the sparsely populated area of the Highlands – not because of its news coverage but because of its columns of gossip, its cookery recipes, and above all, its horoscope. The horoscope was written by Elspeth Grant and was amazingly detailed. Startled Highlanders read that, for example, they would suffer from back pains at precisely eight o'clock on a Monday morning, and as back pain was a favourite excuse for not going to work, people said it was amazing how accurate the predictions were.

But Hamish's initial disapproval began to fade although he thought astrology a lot of hocus-pocus. There were only three on the editorial side: Sam, and Elspeth, and one old drunken reporter who somehow wrote the whole of the six-page tabloid-sized paper among them.

He did not know that the larger world of the media was about to burst in on his quiet world.

Over in Strathbane, the television station, Strathbane Television, was in trouble. It had been chugging along, showing mostly reruns of old American sitcoms and a few cheaply produced local shows. They had just been threatened with losing their licence unless they became more innovative.

The scene in the boardroom was fraught with tension and worry. Despite the No Smoking signs, the air was thick with cigarette smoke. 'What we need,' said the head of television features, Rory MacBain, 'is a hard-hitting programme.' Over his head and slightly behind him, a television screen flickered showing a rerun of *Mr. Ed*. 'People come to the Highlands but they do not stay. Why?'

'That's easy,' said the managing director, Callum Bissett. 'The weather's foul and it's damn hard to make a living.'

As a babble of voices broke out complaining and explaining, Rory leaned back in his chair and remembered an interesting evening he'd had in Edinburgh with a BBC researcher. He had met her at the annual television awards at the Edinburgh Festival. He had been amazed that someone so go-ahead and with such stunning, blonde good looks should be only a researcher. He had been even more amazed when she had taken him to bed. He had promised her that if there was ever any chance of giving her a break, he would remember her.

He hunched forward and cut through the voices. 'I have an idea.'

They all looked at him hopefully.

'Our biggest failure,' he said in measured tones, 'is the *Countryside* programme.'

Felicity Pearson, who produced it, let out a squawk of protest.

'The ratings are lousy, Felicity,' said Rory brutally. 'For a start, it's all in Gaelic. Secondly, you have a lot of old fogies sitting at a desk pontificating. We should start a new series, call it, say, *Highland Life*, and get someone hard-hitting and glamorous to present it. Start off by exploding this myth of the poor crofter.'

'They *are* poor now,' protested Felicity. 'Sheep prices are dreadful.'

Rory went on as if she had not spoken. He said that although people did not like to live in the Highlands, they liked to see programmes about the area. With a glamorous presenter, with a good, hard, punchy line, they could make people sit up and take notice, and the more Rory remembered the blonde charms of the researcher – what was her name? Crystal French, that was it – the more

4

convincing he became. At last his idea was adopted. He retreated to his office and searched through his records until he found Crystal's Edinburgh phone number.

After he had finished talking, Crystal put down the phone, her heart beating hard. This was the big break and she meant to make the most of it. She would be glad to get out of Edinburgh, glad to get away from being a mere researcher. Researchers worked incredibly long hours and had to kowtow to the whims of every presenter. Who would have thought that a one-night stand with that fat little man would have paid such dividends? And she had just been coming around to the idea that a woman can't really sleep her way to the top! She did not realize that her past failure to move on had been because of her reputation for doing just that thing. There were a lot of women executives in broadcasting these days who had got to the top with hard work and brains and did not look kindly on any of their sisters who were still trying the old-fashioned methods, so when her name had come up for promotion there had always been some woman on the board who would make sure it was turned down flat.

Rory, when he met her at the Strathbane Station, was struck anew by her looks. Her long blonde hair floated about her shoulders, and her slim figure was clothed in a business suit, but with a short skirt to show off the beauty of her excellent legs. Her eyes were very large and green, almost hypnotic. Crystal kissed him warmly. She had no intention of going to bed with him again. He had done his bit. He was only head of features. If necessary, she would seduce one of his superiors.

Hamish Macbeth did not watch much television. But he did read newspapers. He was intrigued to read that a new show called *Highland Life* was to start off with an investigation into village shops in the Highlands. He decided to watch it. He expected it to be a series of cosy interviews.

The show was to go out at ten o'clock that evening. He was about to settle down to watch it when there was a knock at the kitchen door. He opened it to find with dismay that he was being subjected to a visit from the Currie sisters. It had started to rain, and the sisters, who were twins, stood there with raindrops glistening on their identical plastic rain hats, identical glasses, and identical raincoats. 'Our telly's on the blink,' said Nessie, pushing past him. Jessie followed, taking off her plastic hat and shaking raindrops over the kitchen floor. 'I was just going to bed,' lied Hamish, but they

6

hung up their coats and trotted off into his living room as if he had not spoken.

Hamish sighed and followed them. The Currie sisters were unmarried, middle-aged ladies who ruled the parish. Jessie had an irritating habit of repeating everything. 'We're here to see that new show, that new show,' she said, switching on the television set. 'Don't you have the remote control, the remote control?'

'I need the exercise,' said Hamish crossly.

'A cup of tea would be grand,' said Nessie.

'I'll get tea during the ads,' snapped Hamish.

'Shhh,' admonished Nessie. 'It's on.'

The presenter was walking down a village street. 'That's Braikie,' hissed Nessie, recognizing a nearby village. Crystal's well-modulated voice could be heard saying, 'People deplore the decline of the village shops. The thing to ask yourself is, would you shop in one? Or do you drive to the nearest large town or supermarket? If you do, what are you missing?'

'That's old Mrs Maggie Harrison's shop she's going into, going into,' said Jessie. 'Oh, look at Mrs Harrison's face. It hasnae been rehearsed, rehearsed. She's fair dumfounert.'

'We're here from Strathbane Television,' Crystal was saying, 'and we are just going to have a look on your shelves.' She picked up a basket. 'That skirt is hardly covering her bum,' exclaimed Nessie.

'What have we here?' Crystal held up a tin of beans. 'Why are so many of these cans bashed?' she asked. She winked saucily at the camera. 'I don't think there is one unmarked tin in this shop.'

'It's because she gets them cheap,' muttered Nessie. 'But she sells them cheap. They're fine. How else is the poor old biddy going to compete with the supermarkets?'

'And this?' A packet of biscuits. 'This is past it's sell-by date.'

And so on and on Crystal went, seemingly oblivious to the fact that Mrs Harrison was trembling and crying.

Hamish felt great relief when this horrible blonde stopped the torment, but it turned out she had moved to Jock Kennedy's general store in Drim, and Jock Kennedy was having nothing to do with her disparaging remarks. 'Get the hell out o' here, you nasty cow,' he roared. And so it went on, from shop to shop.

'So you see,' said Crystal, summing up against a tremendous background of mountains and heather, 'the decline of the village shop is because they cannot possibly offer the same goods at the same prices as the supermarket. Why mourn their passing? Good riddance to bad rubbish, is what I say.'

The Currie sisters sat stunned. 'Well, I never, I never,' said Jessie.

'There's one good thing,' said her sister, 'there'll be so many complaints that the show will be taken off.'

8

Hamish privately thought that the show would get the response it had set out to get. Infuriated viewers would tune in the following week just to see how nasty it could get, and ratings would soar. There had been very few advertisements, but they would get more.

He switched off the television set and saw the Currie sisters on their way. They were too upset to notice that he had not given them any tea.

Viewers and locals, moved by the humiliation of Mrs Harrison, flooded into her shop during the following week to buy goods and commiserate with her. Newspapers interviewed her. Elspeth wrote a savage critique of the show and a flattering article about Mrs Harrison and her shop. The Highlands were rallying behind the underdog and forgetting that Mrs Harrison sold some quite dreadful goods and that her local nickname had been, before her appearance on television, Salmonella Maggie. Despite Elspeth's writing a further article telling people not to watch the next show because low ratings were the only thing that would get it taken off, everyone in Lochdubh, and that included Hamish Macbeth, switched on for the next airing of *Highland Life*. This episode was called 'The Myth of the Poor Crofter'.

Her first interview was with The Laird. The Laird was not a laird at all, but a crofter called

Barry McSween, who had earned his nick-name by farming several crofts, so instead of having a croft, which is really a small holding, he had quite a good-sized farm. But the drop in sheep prices had crippled him and his tem-per had suffered. Sheep were expensive to slaughter because, according to government regulations, the spine had to be removed and that added tremendously to the cost. Hoping that things would get better, he had bought himself a new Volvo, and the camera focused on its new licence plate and gleaming glory before moving in on his red, round face.

At first Crystal wooed him, cooing that things were bad and how was he surviving? Barry, like a lot of people, had privately nursed dreams of being on television. He invited her into his croft house, which in the palmy days had been extended. The camera panned over the expens-ively furnished living room and then into the large airy kitchen, which had every labour-saving device. Happily Barry bragged about his possessions while Crystal smiled at him and led him on. Elated, Barry preened and volunteered that he had a good voice and would she like a song? Crystal would. Hamish prayed that the unwitting Barry would sing a Scottish song, but he sang 'I Did It My Way', in an awful nasal drone during which the camera moved to Crystal's beautiful face, which was alight with mocking laughter.

When he had finished and was sprawling

back in his leather sofa with a smug grin on his face, Crystal started to go in for the kill. She said that in the south particularly, people heard a lot about the poor crofter and were not aware that someone like Barry owned so much land and lived in such luxury. Too late did Barry realize the way the interview was going. He blustered about how he could hardly make ends meet. Crystal went remorselessly on. Barry ended up by ordering her out of his house. It was unfortunate that just at that moment, Barry's wife, who had been ordered to stay away because he wanted the show to himself, should come driving up in her Jaguar. It was an old Jaguar and Barry had got it cheap. But his wife kept it gleaming and well-cared-for and it looked extremely rich.

Had Crystal left it at that, the reaction to her programme might not have been so violent, because Barry was not popular, but she picked on another crofter, Johnny Liddesdale, a quiet little man. The extension to his croft house he had built himself over the years. The furniture inside he had made himself. He stammered and blushed during the interview while Crystal made him look like a fool, and a lying fool at that. How could he plead poverty when he had such a beautiful home? Hamish could not bear to watch any more and switched off the set.

Half an hour later, there was a knock at the kitchen door. The locals never came round to the front of the police station. He opened it and recognized Elspeth Grant.

'Come in,' said Hamish. 'What brings you? Stars foreboding something or other?'

'As a matter of fact they are,' said Elspeth calmly. It was early autumn and the nights were already frosty. She was wearing a tweed fishing hat and a man's anorak. She removed her hat and put her coat over the back of a chair. She had a thick head of frizzy brown hair and sallow skin, gypsy skin, thought Hamish, but it was her eyes that were remarkable. They were light grey, almost silver, sometimes like clear water in a brook, sometimes like quartz, and emotions and thought flitted across those large eyes like cloud shadows over the hills on a summer's day. Her soft voice had a Highland lilt. Hamish disapproved of her. He thought her astrological predictions were making clever fun of the readers.

'Coffee?' asked Hamish.

'Please.'

'It isn't decaff.'

'That's all right. Did you think I would mind?'

'Yes, I thought you were probably a vegetarian as well.'

She leaned her pointed chin on her hands and surveyed him. 'Why?'

'Oh, astrology and all that.' He filled two mugs from the kettle that he kept simmering on top of the wood-burning stove.

'You are a very conventional man, I think.'

Hamish gave her a mug of coffee and sat down opposite her. 'Did you come round here at this time o' night to give me my character?'

'No. Did you see that programme?'

'The one with Crystal French?'

'That's the one.'

'What about it?'

'Someone's going to kill her,' said Elspeth calmly.

'Whit! Havers, lassie. Her nasty programme will run one series. Then there'll be another and the novelty will hae worn off and she'll either sink without a trace or go to London.'

'I don't think so. I think she'll be killed.'

'See it in the stars?' mocked Hamish.

'You could say that. It's something about her. She's *asking* to be killed.'

'And who's going to do it?'

'Ah, if I knew that, maybe I could stop it.'

'I am afraid in the world of television, the wicked can flourish like the green bay tree,' said Hamish.

'Quoting the Bible, Hamish? You?'

'Why not? I am not the heathen. Let's see, you have come here late at night to tell me you haff a feeling.' Hamish's Highland accent always became more pronounced when he was upset. 'And yet you seem a sensible girl. I don't trust you. I think you came along here to have a private laugh at my expense.'

And although Elspeth's face was calm,

Hamish had a feeling that somewhere inside her was a private Elspeth who found him a bit of a joke.

She drank her coffee. Then she put on her hat and swung her anorak around her shoulders. 'Don't say I didn't warn you,' she said.

He leaned back in his chair and looked up at her. 'And just what wass I supposed to do about this warning? Phone up my superiors and say I have a *feeling* her life's in danger?'

'You could say you had received anonymous calls from people threatening to kill her.'

'Oh, I should think those sort of calls are already arriving at Strathbane Television.'

She gave a little shrug. 'Well, I tried.'

And then she was gone. She left so quickly and lightly that it seemed to Hamish that one minute she was there, and in the next, she had disappeared, leaving the door ajar.

He tried to dismiss the whole business from his head, but he felt uneasy.

Rory MacBain was basking in Crystal's success. The first two programmes were to run on national TV followed by the subsequent ones. The switchboard had been jammed with angry calls. The mail bag was full of threatening letters. And that *was* success. Reaction was success. He was disappointed that Crystal kept rejecting his advances, but the praise he was receiving for having thought up the idea more than compensated for any disappointment.

There would be more money, much more money for the next series. This one had been thought up on the hoof, with less than a week from the idea to the filming. On Monday, the topic was decided. 'Behind the Lace Curtains' was to be an exposé of what really went on in Highland villages. Researchers burrowed through old cuttings, digging up scandals that people had hoped were long forgotten.

Crystal, who had little to do, as the research was all done for her and scripts written for her, although she preferred to put her own comments into them at the last minute, decided to head out from Strathbane and cruise round various villages. Her path was about to cross that of Hamish Macbeth and on the very day he felt his world had come to an end.

Yesterday morning, he had read his horoscope, Libra, in which Elspeth had written, 'You will receive news on Monday which will make you feel your heart has been broken. But remember, no pain, no gain. This is not the end. This is the beginning of a whole new chapter.'

'Rubbish,' muttered Hamish. He fed his dog, Lugs, and was just getting ready to go out when the phone rang. It was Mrs Wellington, the minister's wife. 'I don't suppose you know,' she said. 'Do you read the *Times*?'

'No,' said Hamish.

'I thought not. It was in the social column four days ago and it's all round the village. I said someone's got to tell Hamish, but then I decided that, as usual, it would have to be me.'

'Tell me what?' asked Hamish patiently.

'Priscilla Halburton-Smythe is getting married . . . Are you there?'

'Yes.'

'It was in the social column. She's marrying someone called Peter Partridge.'

'Thank you.' Bleakly.

Hamish put down the receiver and sat staring blindly at the desk. Lugs whimpered and put a large paw on his knee. Priscilla Halburton-Smythe, daughter of the colonel who owned the Tommel Castle Hotel, had at one time been the love of his life. They had even been engaged. She might have told him. He told himself that he had got over her long ago, but he still felt sad and bereft.

He remembered his horoscope and suddenly got angry. Elspeth would have heard the gossip, Elspeth heard all the gossip. She must have found out the date of his birthday. She must have found it very amusing.

He patted Lugs on the head and said, 'Stay, boy.' He would go out on his rounds as usual, he would work as usual. Life would go on.

He was just getting into his police Land Rover when a bright green BMW did a U-turn on the harbour and raced along the waterfront,

16

well over the speed limit. He jumped in the Land Rover and with siren blaring and blue light flashing, and holding the speed camera gun, that was fortunately on the front seat, out of the window with one hand, trained on the fleeing car, he set off in pursuit.

The BMW stopped abruptly on the hump-backed bridge that led out of Lochdubh. Hamish stopped behind it and climbed down. He leaned down and looked into the BMW and Crystal French looked back.

Chapter Two

For in the sterres, clerer than is glas,
Is written, God woot, whoso koude it rede,
The deeth of every man.
                    — Geoffrey Chaucer

Now, Hamish had always despised policemen who took out the miseries of their personal life on members of the public, and chances were that, in his usual way, he might have given Crystal a stern caution, but her first words, delivered insolently, were, 'Don't you know who I am?'

'You are a motorist who has just been speeding at a dangerous rate. Papers, please.'

'Look, I haven't got them with me . . .'

'Deliver them within a week to your nearest police station – that is, registration of ownership, MOT and insurance. Driving licence, please.'

'I am Crystal French.'

'Thank you for that information, miss. Driving licence, please.'

She scrabbled in a large leather handbag and then held it out. 'Shouldn't you be out catching criminals, instead of harassing law-abiding citizens?'

'Speeding is breaking the law.' He checked her licence and handed it back. 'Please step out of the car.'

'Why?'

'I am going to breathalyze you.'

'Don't be so silly.' Crystal switched on the engine.

'If you drive off without taking a breathalyzer test then you must follow me to Dr Brodie's and allow a blood sample to be taken.'

Crystal thrust open the door of the car with such violence that Hamish had to jump back to avoid his legs being hit. She glared up at the policeman with the flaming red hair and snapped, 'Well, get on with it.'

He breathalyzed her and found with some regret that she had not been drinking. 'Wait here,' he said.

He went back to the Land Rover and checked the speed camera. Then he came back. 'You already have six points on your licence for speeding,' he said. 'The camera shows that you were driving at sixty-five miles per hour in a thirty-mile area.'

Crystal stared at him in dismay. She knew she would more than likely be banned from driving for three years. She changed tack and smiled at him. 'Look, Officer . . . what is your name?'

'Hamish Macbeth.'

'I am sure we could find something better to do than stand here arguing.' She moistened her lips and put her hand on his arm.

He picked her hand off as if it were an insect. 'You will hear shortly when you are to appear in court,' said Hamish evenly.

Crystal was beginning to feel desperate. The BMW was a new purchase and she adored driving around in it. She reached into the car and brought out her handbag. She opened it and took out her wallet, opened the wallet and riffled through the notes. 'You can't earn much as a village bobby,' she said, smiling slyly at him.

'Nonetheless, I do not take bribes and unless you want a further charge, I would advise you to put that wallet away.'

Crystal lost her temper. 'I wasn't trying to bribe you, you village idiot.'

And Hamish lost his temper as well. 'Just because you are a television celebrity and go around making people's lives a misery doesn't mean you can risk the lives of the villagers of Lochdubh by reckless driving.' Women, damn them, thought Hamish as his voice rose. 'Chust get the hell out o' here.'

'What is going on?' asked a cool voice.

Hamish swung round. Elspeth was standing there. She was wearing a ragged T-shirt under a baggy cardigan, corduroy trousers, and sneakers. 'I represent the *Highland Times*,' said Elspeth to Crystal. 'You are the famous Crystal French. My, you are every bit as beautiful in real life as you are on television.'

Hamish surveyed them both with disgust. 'See you in court,' he said to Crystal. He climbed into the Land Rover and drove off to the police station where he sent a report to Strathbane.

Then he resisted driving up to Tommel Castle Hotel to find out more news about Priscilla. It was over. It was done.

He put Lugs on his leash instead and went to visit Angela Brodie, the doctor's wife.

'Come in,' said Angela, her thin face lighting up with pleasure. 'Will Lugs bother my cats?'

'He's too lazy,' said Hamish, and sure enough Lugs padded into the kitchen, ignored the cats, and slumped down in a corner and closed his eyes, his odd large ears spread out like wings.

'So what's new?' asked Angela.

Only to Angela would Hamish talk about Priscilla. 'Mrs Wellington phoned me with the news about Priscilla's engagement,' he said.

'I should have told you myself,' said Angela sadly. 'It was all round the village. Then I heard Mrs Wellington say to Elspeth Grant that she was going to tell you herself in a few days' time if no one else did and Elspeth asked when your birthday was.'

'I thought that was the reason for my horoscope,' said Hamish.

'So how do you feel? Devastated?'

'I was hurt and upset. Right now, I don't know what I feel. She might have told me herself. Anyway, I went and lost my temper with that awful woman Crystal French.' He told her the story of Crystal's speeding.

'Bet you're asked to drop it,' said Angela.

'Why?'

'Callum Bissett is a Freemason. He's the managing director of Strathbane Television.'

'So?'

'Well, so is Peter Daviot, your boss.'

'Come on, now. They wouldn't dare.'

'They might try when Strathbane Television's lawyers get on to them.'

Sure enough, Hamish got a call from Peter Daviot that afternoon. 'I wish you had just let her go,' said Daviot. 'I've had Callum Bissett on the phone asking me to drop the case. You say you recorded her on a speed camera?'

'Yes, sir.'

'Oh, well, you'll have to go through with it. But this is bad, very bad.'

'It's a straightforward case of speeding through a built-up area.'

'It's not just that. Crystal French is to do an in-depth report on policing in the Highlands, finishing with an interview with you.'

23

'I do not need to agree.'

'Oh, yes you do,' snapped Daviot. 'And that's an order. We must show we have nothing to hide.'

'Very well,' said Hamish reluctantly. He had been demoted twice from sergeant and he knew that Crystal's researchers would dig up every detail they could to use against him.

'The interview is to take place at two o'clock next Monday afternoon.'

'Must I?'

'Must I, what?'

'I mean do I have to, *sir*?'

'Yes.'

'Do you know, she attempted to come on to me and when that didnae work, she attempted to bribe me?'

'Any witnesses?'

'No.'

'Well, there you are. Just get on with it.'

After he had rung off, Hamish sat staring at the phone. Maybe Elspeth had witnessed something. How long had she been standing there? He picked up the phone and dialled the number of the *Highland Times* and asked to speak to Elspeth, only to be told by Sam that Elspeth was covering the Highland Games at Braikie.

Hamish put Lugs in the Land Rover and set off for Braikie. He was due there on duty in the afternoon anyway.

The Highland Games at Braikie was a small affair, not like the big ones at Drumnadrochit or Balmoral. But an Indian summer was holding well and mellow sunlight shone down on the events and sideshows.

Hamish had thought somehow it would be easy to find Elspeth. He had vaguely assumed that she was telling fortunes in one of the booths. Then he remembered that Sam had said she was reporting on the games. He headed for the press tent. He recognized a couple of the local reporters, drinking beer at one of the rickety tables.

'Anyone seen Elspeth Grant?' he asked.

'She's just left,' said one. 'Caber tossing.'

Hamish headed for the main ring where the caber tossing was in progress. A burly man was staggering around, trying to throw the huge caber. 'He shoudnae even ha' tried,' said one disgusted spectator. Hamish looked around the crowd. There was no special section for the press but he knew they usually herded together to compare notes. He saw a television camera and went in that direction. At first he did not recognize Elspeth because she was wearing a grimy baseball hat with her hair tucked up under it. But she turned and looked back and he saw those odd eyes of hers.

She smiled at him and he called, 'A word with you.'

Elspeth joined him. 'How long had you been standing there when I was talking to Crystal French?' asked Hamish.

'Less than a minute.'

Hamish was disappointed. 'So you didn't see her trying to bribe me.'

'No, but I'll say so if it'll help.'

'You are not going to lie for me!'

She shrugged. 'The offer's open. You might need it.'

'By the way, that was a nasty trick you played on me.'

'What?'

'Thon horoscope,' said Hamish angrily. 'You found out my birthday, you found out about Priscilla's engagement and that Mrs Wellington was going to tell me, so you put in that rubbish about no pain, no gain.'

'Why would I do that? Libra horoscopes are not just for you.'

'You know I'm Libra. You found out because you asked Angela Brodie when my birthday was.'

'Do you mind?' Elspeth turned back to the games. 'I'm supposed to be reporting this. Fascinating watching men chucking tree trunks around.'

'Chust stay away from me,' said Hamish furiously.

She turned back. 'You approached me, I didn't approach you.'

Hamish stalked off like an outraged cat.

As he officially reported for duty at the police caravan and then toured the show, he found he was worrying about the forthcoming court case where Crystal had been charged with speeding. He had the evidence on camera. Surely there was nothing to worry about. But he kept feeling that because of his upset, he had slipped up somewhere.

Three days passed by and he was beginning to relax. He had just locked up his hens for the evening when, as he was approaching the kitchen door, he saw Elspeth strolling towards him. To his surprise, she was wearing a smart business suit and high heels. 'Been to see the bank manager?' he asked.

'I've been down at Strathbane Television, doing a profile on Crystal French.'

'I'm surprised she agreed to see you after you trashed her show in your paper.'

'She hadn't read it . . . fortunately.'

'Well, I'm going to get my supper and I haven't forgiven you for that horoscope. So be on your way.'

'What a prickly sort of man you are! I came to tell you about the speeding case.'

'What about it?'

'What about inviting me in?'

Hamish hesitated. But that little worry at the back of his brain was still there.

'All right. Come in.'

She followed him into the kitchen. Hamish took down the whisky bottle from the kitchen cupboard along with two glasses and set them on the table. 'Will you be having a dram?'

'A small one, yes, but no water. Just straight.'

He poured two measures and they sat down. 'Now what is it?'

'Crystal's got some hotshot lawyer to trash you in court.'

'What on earth can he do? The woman was speeding and I've got the record on speed camera.'

'That's the problem. The speed camera.'

'What about it?'

'You drove with one hand and held the speed camera out of the window with the other, stretching across the front seat and holding it?'

'Yes, so what?'

'You don't read as many newspapers as I do Hamish. There have been cases of people arrested because they've taken one hand off the wheel to use a mobile phone. One woman was even charged for taking out her powder compact and dusting her nose while waiting at traffic lights. You see what he's going to say. *You* are going to be held up as a danger to the public, not her.'

'But that's daft.'

'Nonetheless, that's their case. And just to put the frights into the judiciary, Crystal has announced that she is going to do a programme on Scottish sheriff courts, and the sheriff at Strathbane is a rabbit of a man.'

'Damn.' Hamish took a drink of whisky. 'Wait a minute. She's coming to interview me next Monday and I've been ordered to give her the interview. She shouldn't be seeing me if we're going to be in court.'

'I gather she can get round that. You don't talk about the speeding case and neither does she. She's still insisting on the interview. And she's put off the "Behind the Lace Curtains" show to do it.'

'I'll have my own lawyer,' said Hamish.

'A good lawyer might run rings around her, but you're police and you'll be represented by Boozy Burroughs.'

'Oh.'

'Oh, exactly. If he's even awake, it'll be a miracle. So I'm here to tell you, I'm prepared to go into court and say I saw her trying to bribe you.'

'But you didn't.'

'I've suddenly remembered I did.'

'No, I cannae be having that. I can get witnesses among the locals to say they saw her speeding, but someone might come forward and say you didn't come up to us until the last minute.'

'You might get a witness to say they saw her trying to bribe you.'

Hamish ran his fingers through his thick red hair. 'She took out her wallet and riffled

29

through the notes and said something like I couldn't earn much money as a village policeman. But no one was close enough to hear that. She could simply say she was looking through her wallet for car papers.'

Elspeth drained her glass of whisky and stood up. 'Maybe she'll die.'

'Maybe pigs will fly.'

'Oh, someone will kill that one, sooner or later.'

He looked sharply at her, but those odd eyes of hers were unreadable.

'She's a Scorpio, which is no surprise to me,' said Elspeth, heading for the door.

'You surely don't believe that rubbish.'

'Oh, I do. See you.'

When she had gone, Hamish decided to phone Peter Daviot at home. Crystal would not mention the speeding case during the interview, but he knew she would try to make him look like an officious fool. And she would certainly try to get him to betray his dislike of her.

He did not mention anything about the speed camera to Daviot but outlined the dangers of an interview with Crystal before the court case. But Daviot would not be moved. 'It's just a television interview,' he said, 'and if we refuse her, she'll think we've got something to hide.'

When Hamish put down the phone, defeated, he marvelled again at the power of television. Had it been a newspaper interview, then he would not have been forced to go through with it, but everyone always went on as if television were some sort of government enforcement agency. People who would not speak to the press let television cameras and reporters into their homes.

He thought about Elspeth. It was good of her to offer to lie for him. On the other hand, that horoscope had been cruel. Lugs gave a short, sharp bark from the kitchen and then rattled his food bowl.

Hamish sighed and went through to the kitchen. 'You've been fed already,' he said crossly. Lugs gave a pathetic whimper as Hamish lifted a casserole out of the oven. 'Oh, well,' said Hamish weakly. 'Just a little bit. What am I going to do about that wretched woman, Lugs?'

But Lugs was eyeing the casserole with his bright blue eyes, his mind only on food.

On the following Monday, Hamish awoke with a heavy heart. Somehow he would get through the interview. He would be bland and smiling, no matter what skeletons from his past Crystal let out of the cupboard. His complimentary copy of the *Highland Times* rattled through his letter box. He made a cup of coffee and spread the paper out on the kitchen table. He turned to the horoscope to make sure

31

Elspeth had no more nasty messages for him. He read that those born under the sign of Libra would find that a problem that had been haunting them had been forcibly removed. Death would solve all problems. He stared at it and then his eye travelled to Scorpio. Had the girl gone mad?

'All the trouble and strife you have caused will come back to haunt you and violently, too. Don't leave home on Monday. Lock the doors and close the curtains and do not even answer the phone. If you go out, then something terrible will happen to you.'

What on earth was Elspeth up to? Did she think that Crystal would read her horoscope and cancel the interview? He reached for the phone to ring her and then decided against it.

He went about his chores, fed his hens, checked on his sheep, repaired a broken section of fence, and then, after a light lunch, sponged and pressed his uniform and put it on.

At precisely two o'clock, there was a knock at the front door of the police station. He opened it. Four people stood there. They introduced themselves. A thin nervous woman, Felicity Pearson, researcher; a fat, smooth man, Harry Jury, cameraman; a thin bearded man, Tom Betts, director; and a cross little man, John Leslie, sound.

'Where's your boss?' asked Hamish.

'Should be here any minute,' said Harry. 'If you don't mind, we'll just start getting set up.'

'Come in,' said Hamish reluctantly. He led them into the police office.

'Right,' said the director, Tom Betts. 'You just sit behind your desk while we get the light right.'

What an age of preparation it seemed to take! Hamish waited patiently while a microphone was fitted to his tunic, while bright lights shone in his face, while he had to speak several times until the sound was adjusted. Felicity sat crouched in a corner studying a sheaf of notes.

'Are those the questions?' asked Hamish. 'Can you give me some idea of what I will be asked?'

''Fraid not,' said Felicity. 'Madam does not like anyone to be prepared. She likes the interview to be natural. Then we have to rush it back. It goes out tonight.'

Hamish looked at the clock. 'It's now three o'clock,' he said. 'When is Miss French going to arrive?'

They all looked puzzled. 'Should be here by now,' said Harry.

Felicity gave a nervous giggle. 'She was upset by her horoscope.'

'In the *Highland Times*?' asked Hamish sharply. 'I thought she wouldn't read it.'

'Oh, some girl from the paper interviewed her and then talked about horoscopes. Crystal is very keen on horoscopes. She sent me out this morning to buy a copy of the *Highland Times*.'

Hamish sent up a prayer that the absent Crystal should turn out to be superstitious.

Tom took out a mobile phone and rang Strathbane Television. When he rang off, he said, 'That's odd. They say she left in plenty of time. In fact she left at eight. Said she wanted to cruise around Lochdubh and get a feel of the place.'

'Unhitch me from this microphone,' ordered Hamish. 'I'd better drive around and look for her. She may have met with an accident.'

The sound man removed the microphone. Hamish was heading for the kitchen door when it was thrust open and Angela Brodie stood there, her face quite white.

'It's awful, Hamish. Come quickly. She's dead.'

'Who's dead?'

'Crystal French.'

Chapter Three

Lady, the stars are falling pale and small.
                    – G. K. Chesterton

'Where is she?' cried Hamish.

'Up on the back road, I think it's suicide.'

Hamish started to run, his long legs going like pistons. He raced along to Patel's grocery store, up the lane at the side, up to the narrow, grassy road, little used.

The green BMW stood there, a bright splash of colour against the purple of the heather on the flanks of the hillsides. The engine was still running. A hose led from the exhaust and in the top of one window. He seized the door handle. Locked. He grabbed a rock and smashed the window on the passenger side, reached in and unlocked the door, climbed in, and leaning round Crystal's body, switched off the engine. Crystal French was slumped over the wheel. Taking out a handkerchief and holding it over his nose to protect himself from the fumes, Hamish felt Crystal's neck for a pulse. Nothing.

Dr Brodie came along in his car. 'Leave her to me, Hamish,' he called. 'Phone for an ambulance.'

'I think it's too late for that.' Hamish got out of the car. He retched and coughed and then reached back into the dashboard and picked up Crystal's mobile phone. He phoned for an ambulance and then called police headquarters. Dr Brodie had Crystal's body out on the ground and was fixing an oxygen mask over her face. 'I brought the oxygen tank the minute Angela told me,' he said, 'but man, it's no good, no good at all.' He looked up and then shouted, 'Show some decency, for God's sake.'

Harry had arrived with Tom and Felicity and John, and Harry was busy filming the scene.

Harry reluctantly put down his camera. Hamish walked round to where Crystal was lying and knelt down by her body. Her once-beautiful face was a ghastly pink. He felt with his long fingers, probing her neck and then the back of her head. 'There's a lump here,' he said to Dr Brodie.

Dr Brodie crouched down beside him. 'Where?'

'Feel there, just at the back.'

'Aye, there's a bit of a lump. I may as well take the mask off. She's well and truly dead, Hamish.'

A crowd was gathering. They stood silently, a little distance away. Hamish saw Elspeth among the onlookers. He would need to have a word with her.

He seemed to wait a very long time before he heard the ambulance coming.

The police arrived at the same time as the ambulance. Heading them was not Detective Chief Inspector Blair, who was on leave, but his replacement, a tall, thin man, Detective Chief Inspector Carson.

Hamish reported briefly how he had found the car with the engine still running.

'Thank goodness it seems a straightforward case of suicide,' said Carson.

'As to that,' said Hamish cautiously, 'she's got a lump on the back of her head.'

Carson had a long face, a long, thin nose and drooping eyelids over pale eyes. Those eyes raked Hamish up and down. 'Are you a qualified medical examiner?'

'No, sir. But . . .'

'But nothing. You will say nothing about this until the experts have done their job. Go back to your station, type out your report, and then question the people in the village to see if there are any witnesses to her arrival, see if anyone saw anything.'

Hamish saw Detective Jimmy Anderson eyeing him sympathetically. As Hamish walked past him, he whispered, 'Get the whisky ready. I'll try to drop in later.'

When he got back to the police station, the phone was ringing. He picked up the receiver. Daviot's voice came down the line, sharp and anxious. 'What's happening?'

Hamish described how he had found Crystal. 'It's a blessing in a way,' said Daviot. 'Nice, neat little suicide. Wraps it up. No fuss, no scandal.'

'There is one thing, sir,' said Hamish. 'She's got a lump on the back of her head. Someone could have socked her and then faked the suicide.'

'You must be mistaken. A lot of people have bumpy heads – naturally, I mean. These television people are often prone to depression. It's the life they lead. What does Carson say?'

'At the moment, he is of the opinion it's suicide, but to my mind that's wishful thinking.'

'Carson is a good man and a highly experienced officer. Anyway, if it were murder, guess who would be the first suspect?'

'Who?'

'You,' said Daviot nastily and slammed down the phone.

Now, I could look at it this way, thought Hamish, sitting down in front of his computer. I could go along with it and do a report and not mention that bump. If I mention it, they'll need to do something about it. They all want it to be suicide. She was investigating the methods of the Highland police, finishing with me. On the other hand, this is my parish and there's a murderer out there. I'm sure of it. Someone as vain and egocentric as Crystal

French would never commit suicide, but on the other hand, a lot of people must have wanted her dead.

He began to type. He wrote about how he had found the car with the engine still running, and that from the colour of Crystal's face, she had died of carbon monoxide poisoning. But he had felt the back of her head and found that lump, and in his opinion, she could have been stunned and a suicide faked.

He worked steadily and then sent the report off to Strathbane. Now, he thought, I'd better have a word with our astrologer.

He walked along to the *Highland Times*. There was no receptionist. The street door led straight into the editorial room. Sam Wills looked up as he entered. 'Grand story, Hamish,' he said. 'Pity it hadn't happened later in the week. It'll be old news by the time the paper comes out next Monday.'

'Pity that,' said Hamish sarcastically. 'Your astrologer about?'

'Elspeth's still out. Great girl that. Can turn her hand to anything.'

'What about murder?' asked Hamish and walked out leaving Sam staring after him.

He saw Elspeth walking towards him along the waterfront. When she came up to him, he said, 'I want you to come with me to the police station. There are a few questions I want you to answer.'

39

Once at the station, he led her into the office and said curtly, 'Sit down.'

'What are those television lamps and cables doing here?' asked Elspeth.

'I was supposed to give Crystal an interview. Now, I read your horoscopes this morning . . .'

'Another fan?'

'Be serious. You knew Crystal was a Scorpio. I think all that stuff about not going outdoors was directed at her. And Libra? Death was going to solve my problems?'

Elspeth looked guilty. 'I thought it was worth a try. I thought I was doing you a favour.'

'How?'

'Well, Crystal was fascinated to find out I was an astrologer. She believes all that stuff. She said she would get the paper today. I thought she might stay home and let you off the hook.'

'Why should you do that for me? You don't even know me.'

'I was sick of that trouble-making bitch. I just wanted to give her a fright.'

'Someone did more than that.'

Elspeth's eyes widened. 'You mean it isn't suicide?'

'I didn't say that.'

'But you said . . .'

'Forget it.'

There came a tentative knock at the kitchen door and then Harry, Tom, John and Felicity came into the office. 'We'll just pack this stuff up,' said Harry, 'and be out of your way.'

'I would like to ask you a few questions,' said Hamish. 'That will be all, Miss Grant. I'll be speaking to you again.'

He waited until she had left and then he said, 'Was Miss French depressed in any way?'

'Not that I could see,' said Harry. 'What about you, Tom?'

The director shrugged. 'She has a new director each week. I've been brought up from Manchester. I didn't even speak to her. The producer would know more about it.'

'Who is the producer?'

'Alistair Campbell.'

'And he doesn't come out with you?'

'No,' said Tom, 'that's the job of the director. I take the film back and the producer looks at the rushes and does the editing. He picks the directors as well.'

Hamish turned to Felicity. 'Would you say she was depressed?'

'Well ... she was very edgy lately. She'd been getting a lot of nasty letters. I think they were getting her down. No one wants to be that hated.'

'Had she been married?'

'No,' said Felicity. Her pale, weak features seemed to tighten. 'Although rumour has it she was having an affair with the head of features and that she'd moved into the bed of the managing director.'

'Names?'

'Callum Bissett's the managing director and Rory MacBain is the head of features.'

'And are both men married?'

'Yes,' said Felicity. 'You mean, that might have made her depressed? Only being able to attract married men?'

'No, I didn't mean that at all. Are you her usual researcher?'

'I'm really a producer,' said Felicity. 'I'm between shows. Just helping out. I did the village shop one, but Amy Cornwall did the crofter thing.'

'If you could all leave your extension numbers at Strathbane Television, I would like to speak to you all again.' He passed over a notepad and they all wrote their numbers on it.

'Where did Crystal French come from?'

'Edinburgh,' said Tom.

'And what did she produce there?'

'She was only a researcher,' said Harry. 'It was Rory who brought her up and promoted her to presenter. At first we could see his point. She was a real stunner, and we don't have any of those around Strathbane Television. But what a bitch! The minute the show went national, she demanded a bottle of champagne to be put in her dressing room every day. She queened it around the place. I don't think there was one person she was nice to.'

'If she was having affairs with these two men, she must have been nice to them.'

'Oh, she was nice to anyone she thought could be useful,' said Harry.

They packed up their gear and left.

Hamish sat down at the computer again. He typed out all the gossip they had given him about Crystal and sent it off. Then he set off around the village, looking for witnesses, but non one seemed able to help him until Mrs Wellington volunteered the information that Willie Lamont, formerly a policeman and now working at the Italian restaurant, often walked his dog along the back road. Hamish headed for the restaurant.

Willie was there, scrubbing the floor. The delight of Willie's life was cleaning.

'It's yourself, Hamish,' he said, throwing the scrubbing brush into a pail of soapy water.

'Have you heard about Crystal French's death?'

'Aye, a bad business. I mean, no one'll miss her, but it's bad she had to choose Lochdubh to commit suicide in.'

'I'm told you usually walk your dog up the back road. Did you see anything or anybody?'

'Fact is, I didnae take the beast a walk this morning. Just let it out into the garden.'

'Why was that?'

Willie looked uncomfortable. Then he said sheepishly, 'I'm a Scorpio.'

'You mean that rubbish about not going out of the house?'

'There could have been something in it.'

'I'm surprised you even turned up for work!'

'Lucia made me go.' Lucia was his Italian wife and a relative of the owner. 'She said it

43

was a lot of rubbish. But I'll bet thon Crystal was Scorpio.'

'Let me know if you hear anything, Willie. I'm going back up there.'

'Blair handling the case?'

'No. Thank God the scunner is away, although I think his replacement is going to be every bit as nasty.'

That evening, Detective Chief Inspector Carson was studying Hamish's reports. He sent for Jimmy Anderson. 'Tell me about this Hamish Macbeth,' he said, tapping the reports.

'Oh, he's a clever one is Hamish,' said Jimmy. 'Matter of fact, I was just about to go over to see him. He picks up things the ordinary copper misses.'

'I want to think this was suicide,' said Carson. 'But Macbeth said she had a lump on the back of her head. He seems to think someone stunned her unconscious and then faked the suicide.'

'Aye, that's Hamish for you. Always pointing out something no one wants to believe, and it always turns out to be right.'

'I haven't had the pathologist's report yet.' Carson sat frowning. 'Did Macbeth get on well with Blair?'

'Not always. Hamish's methods are a bit unorthodox.'

'I've a feeling we might need an unorthodox

mind on this one. Go over and have a chat with him and find out what else he knows.'

'It might have been someone she knew,' said Hamish that evening, pouring Jimmy a generous measure of whisky.

'How d'ye figure that out?'

'Of course someone could have hidden in the back-seat of her car, waiting for the right moment. But it's more likely she gave a lift to someone.'

'But if she was slugged on the back of the head, it would need to be someone behind her. I mean, if she gave a lift to someone, then that someone would surely sit in the passenger seat.'

'True. But wait a bit. I wish we had that pathologist's report. She could have been socked on the head somewhere else and driven to a quiet spot, like that back road.'

'She left Strathbane Television in the morning, so it wasn't done in the dark,' said Jimmy. 'I mean, it's taking an awfy risk, to set up a suicide in broad daylight. Anyone might have come along.'

'Willie Lamont often walks his dog there, but he was too feart to go out.'

Jimmy's foxy face was a study. 'Why?'

'He read his horoscope in the newspapers, warning Scorpios not to go out.'

Hamish bit his lip and wished he had said nothing about the horoscope. Elspeth had tried to do him a favour.

But Jimmy's blue eyes were surveying him. 'I don't suppose our Crystal was a Scorpio?'

'As a matter of fact she was.'

'Now, there's a thing. Got that horoscope?'

Hamish wanted to say he had thrown the paper away, but Jimmy would simply go and buy one. The damage had been done.

He reached a long arm behind him and handed the newspaper to Jimmy.

The detective flipped through the newspaper and then read aloud. '"All the trouble you have caused will come back to haunt you and violently, too. Don't leave home on Monday. Lock the doors and close the curtains and do not even answer the phone. If you go out, then something terrible will happen to you."'

Jimmy put down the newspaper. 'Who wrote this?'

'Lassie called Elspeth Grant.'

'Did you ask her why she wrote this? There was nothing in your report.'

'Look, don't tell Carson. She was trying to help me.'

'You mean get you out of the interview?'

'Aye. She knew Crystal was a Scorpio and she knew Crystal believed in horoscopes. Forget about her for the moment, Jimmy. Did Crystal tread on any toes at Strathbane Television?'

'A lot, I should think. But for the moment, they're all saying what a darling she was, including Felicity Pearson.'

'Why do you mention her?'

'She was producer of the *Countryside* programme. It was bumped to make way for Crystal's show and she was reduced to researching for Crystal.'

'There's also the husbands,' said Hamish.

'Husbands?'

'I put that in the report.'

'I just skimmed over it.'

'Crystal was having affairs with Callum Bissett, managing director, and head of features, Rory MacBain, and both men are married.'

'Could be true. Could be spite.'

'I don't think so. Felicity was badly shaken. I suppose she and the cameraman, the director, and the sound man have been interviewed as to their movements.'

'Harry Jury and Tom Betts, camera and director, John Leslie, sound. Well, Felicity came on her own. She was supposed to go around looking for a villager who would criticize you and she couldn't find one. Sound, camera and director all came over in time for two o'clock in the television van.'

'And where was Felicity just before two o'clock?'

'There's a whole list of villagers she visited. I've got it back at the station. At twelve noon, she finished talking to Mary Hendry. Who's she?'

'Widow. Keeps a craft shop. Highland stuff. Tommel Castle is not pleased. They feel she's taking trade away from their gift shop.'

'Newcomer to the village?'

'No, she's been in the village for as long as I can remember. She just started up the business last year. Her husband died two years ago. He'd been tight with money. Crofter and ghillie. But he must have scrimped and saved all his life, for he left her a good bit of money.'

'How did her husband die?'

'Fell in the river, drunk. Went over the waterfall and was bashed to pieces on the rocks. Anyway, she confirms Felicity was with her until noon. Then Felicity went to the Italian restaurant, ate and read a book right up until two o'clock. But I'm telling you this, Hamish, I've a feeling we'll have too many suspects. There's that crofter, Barry McSween, for starters. He isn't popular.'

'No, he is not,' said Hamish, 'and a lot of the locals would be pleased he made a fool of himself on television.'

'Aye, and there was an anonymous call saying that Barry had been heard threatening to kill her. Then there's Mrs Harrison.'

'What about her?'

'She was heard the other day telling the customers that something really nasty was going to happen to Crystal.'

Hamish groaned. 'I wish I knew where to start.'

'I think you're going to have more freedom on this one than Blair would have given you. Carson was impressed with your reports. I'm going to interview the errant husbands at Strathbane Television in the morning. Care to come along?'

Hamish brightened. 'Wouldn't Carson mind? It's out o' my territory.'

'I'll square it with him. I'll see you outside the television building at ten in the morning. But I'll be talking to that astrologer friend of yours. By the way, what does Angus Macdonald think of the competition on his patch?'

'I don't know,' said Hamish thoughtfully. Angus Macdonald was the local seer. 'But I think I'll pay him a late visit and find out.'

Angus Macdonald lived in a small, white-washed cottage above the village with a long winding path leading up through green fields to it. It looked from a distance like a cottage illustrated in a fairy story. Hamish left the Land Rover at the foot of the path.

He knew it must be nearly eleven o'clock at night and hoped the seer was still awake. As he approached, the cottage door opened and Angus stood there, looking as usual like one of the minor prophets with his shaggy grey hair and long beard.

'It iss yourself, Hamish,' he said. 'Bad business.'

'It is that. How's yourself, Angus?'

'Fair to middling. What have you brought me?'

'I havenae brought you anything,' said Hamish crossly. 'You can't expect folks to bring you presents the whole time.'

'It helps the spirits,' said Angus portentously.

'The only spirits that help you, you auld moocher, are the ones that come in bottles, and I don't mean genies either.'

'I do not like your attitude,' said Angus loftily, 'and you will not be enjoying the hospitality of my house.'

Hamish sighed and caved in. 'I've a nice Dundee cake at home that Mrs Wellington gave me. You can have it.'

'Then go and get it,' said Angus and slammed the door.

Hamish was tempted to forget about him, and yet he knew Angus heard and noticed a lot more than other people. He went home and collected the cake and returned.

'Come in, come in,' said Angus cheerfully, taking the cake and going on as if it were the first time he had seen Hamish that day.

Hamish ducked his head and walked in. He always thought Angus kept his cottage looking as antique as possible to impress visitors. A peat fire smouldered on the hearth with an old blackened kettle hung on a chain over it.

Angus went through to the kitchen in the back and placed the cake on a shelf, already stacked with groceries.

He returned. 'You'll be having a wee dram?'

'No, Angus, I've had enough and I'm driving. Let's get down to business. You hear and see things. I'm desperate to find out if this Crystal woman was murdered or whether it was suicide.'

Angus gave him an evil look. 'So why don't you ask your wee friend, the astrologer, to look in her stars?'

'Come off it, Angus. You know she makes it up.'

'Aye, but that one has the sight and one day it iss going to surprise her.' By the sight, Angus meant the second sight, a gift that meant whoever had it could sometimes tell the future.

'It's not the future I'm interested in,' said Hamish, 'but the past.'

Angus put one bony finger on his forehead, like a Tenniel illustration of the Dodo in *Alice in Wonderland*. Then he shook his head.

'I havenae got a thing.'

'That's unlike you, Angus. I mean, even if you don't know anything, you usually make something up.'

'I tell you what, Hamish, I will ferret around and work night and day for ye.'

'And what do you want in return?' asked Hamish suspiciously.

'Your dog.'

'No, neffer, absolutely and finally, not. Why did you even ask?'

'I haff neffer seen a wee dog wi' thae blue eyes afore.'

From that, Hamish surmised that Angus thought Lugs would be an added attraction.

'No,' he said again.

'Then,' said the seer waspishly, 'I suggest you go to Elspeth Grant for help. She probably did it herself.'

Hamish rose and made for the door. 'Why?' he asked over his shoulder.

'Her predictions are so daft, she decided to commit murder to make one o' them come true,' said Angus spitefully.

What a waste of time, thought Hamish grumpily, as he strode down the hill to his Land Rover.

There was nothing more he could do that night. Tomorrow, he would go to Strathbane Television and see what he could find out.

Chapter Four

Tempt not the stars, young man, thou canst not play
  With the severity of fate.

— John Ford

When Hamish met Jimmy outside Strathbane Television, the detective said, 'Carson's already in there. They've given us a room for the interviews. He says you can sit in on the questioning.'

'Makes a change from Blair.'

'He's ambitious. He thinks you might have brains. He don't know you like I do.'

Hamish followed Jimmy into the building and through long corridors and then up two flights of stairs. Jimmy pushed open the door.

Detective Chief Inspector Carson rose to meet them. 'Sit yourself over in that corner, Macbeth,' he said. 'I just want you to observe.' Then he turned to a policewoman who had been making coffee and said, 'Show in our first. Let me see. That will be the managing director, Mr Bissett.'

Hamish studied the executive as he came in. He looked in his middle forties, dressed in a charcoal-grey business suit, silk tie and striped shirt. He had a fleshy face and thick lips, small brown eyes, and an open-pored large nose. His brown hair was flecked with grey.

Callum Bissett sat down and said, 'Let's get this over with. I've got a lot to do.'

'And so have we,' said Carson. 'I have the preliminary pathologist's report. Miss French died of carbon monoxide poisoning.'

'Poor girl,' said Callum, shaking his head. 'She had everything to live for.'

'There is one difficulty,' went on Carson. 'She had been struck a blow on the back of the head prior to her death. In our opinion, she could have been stunned and a suicide faked.'

Callum's face registered shock. 'Are you sure? I mean, she might have hit her head on something at home.'

'That might be the answer,' said Carson, 'but until we can be sure, we'll need to go on and ask questions. What were your relations with Miss French?'

'I hardly knew her. I mean, it was Rory MacBain's idea to bring her up from Edinburgh. Of course, I called her in after the success of the first show to congratulate her and tell her it was going national.'

'Did she ask for more money?'

Callum looked shifty. 'Well, let's say she didn't have to. I offered.'

Carson's cold eyes bored into those of the managing director. 'Did she have any leverage on you?'

'What are you talking about?' Callum blustered.

'There is a rumour that you were having sexual relations with Miss French.'

'Bollocks! I'm a married man.'

Carson shuffled his notes. Callum took out a handkerchief and mopped his brow.

'Ah, here we are,' said Carson. 'Miss French's flat is opposite an all-night garage. My men are currently studying the videos. The security cameras sweep the forecourt of the garage and also cover the entrance to the building where Miss French had a flat. Do you want to tell us anything now, or do you want to wait until we have viewed all the film on the security cameras? I must warn you, if you are found to have been lying to the police, then we can charge you with obstruction.'

Callum gave a very false, expansive smile. Wouldn't ever have qualified for a job on the other side of the camera, thought Hamish. 'I did visit her at her flat several times,' he said. 'I know it looks bad, but I merely went along to discuss business and have a quiet drink.'

'I hope for your sake that is true. Our forensic team is still going over her flat. But I can tell you they found a vase with a dozen red roses and on the florist's card that came with it is a message. It reads, "To my blonde goddess from your devoted Callum."'

Callum leaned forward and looked earnest and sincere. Going to tell a real whopper, thought Hamish.

'I see I must explain the world of show business to you,' said Callum. 'We're the luvvies. We pay each other exaggerated compliments.' He spread his hands. 'Okay. I did butter her up. I gave her flowers and champagne. And why not?'

'We'll leave it for the moment,' said Carson. 'Now, as to her state of mind: How did you judge it?'

'I must admit I was worried about her. She was very strung up, very nervous. I wondered at one point whether she might be on drugs – speed or something like that.'

'Indeed? We'll look into that.'

'Is there anything else? I really need to get to work.'

'Not for the moment. Send Rory MacBain in.'

Callum put his head round the door of Rory's office. 'Your turn with the fuzz. Look, tell them the damn woman was on the verge of a breakdown.'

'Why should I do that?'

'Like working here?'

'Of course, I –'

'Then tell them. If you ask me, it was straightforward suicide and now they're sniffing around a murder. And guess who they'll have their eye on?'

'Who?'

'You, of course. You brought her up from Edinburgh. You were diddling her.'

'Who told you that?'

'She did. Now get along there and do your bit.'

When Rory walked into the interviewing room, Hamish thought he looked a bit like his boss; heavy-set, well-groomed, paunchy and fleshy, but with thin mousy hair combed over a pink scalp.

Carson started right away. 'Sit down, Mr MacBain. Describe your relations with Crystal French.'

'We met at a television conference in Edinburgh . . .'

'When?'

'Last year. At the Edinburgh Festival.'

'Which hotel?'

'The George.' A bright little memory flashed across Rory's frightened brain, that of leading Crystal out of the bar and up to his room. But there had been no staff in the corridor outside. Play it cool.

'Did you have sexual relations with her?'

'How dare you!' shouted Rory. 'I'm a married man.'

Carson turned to the pathologist's report. 'There are two disturbing things here. It appears she may have been stunned with a blow to the head and then a suicide faked. Secondly, she had sexual intercourse recently. We will be taking DNA samples.'

Wasn't him anyway, thought Hamish, watching the flicker of relief in Rory's eyes.

Carson leaned forward. 'I urge you to be honest, Mr MacBain. I ask you again: Did you have sexual relations with Crystal French?'

Rory sat with his head down. Then he said, 'If I tell you, can you keep it from my wife?'

'Unless you are guilty of murder, I see no reason why Mrs MacBain should know.'

'I did, then, but that was down in Edinburgh. Just the one night at the George. I'll come clean. I would have resumed the relations when she came up here, but she kept putting me off, saying, wait till I get settled. Then she was a success and could snub me as much as she liked.'

'You mean you were prepared to use your position to seduce an employee?'

'Oh, get real,' snapped Rory. 'She seduced me.'

'What was her state of mind recently?'

'I was worried about her,' said Rory. Better actor than his boss, thought Hamish. 'She was given to emotional tantrums, but, well, in this business, you get used to that.' Callum's had a word with him, thought Hamish. Rory was going on. 'As a matter of fact, I suggested she might try therapy.'

'When was this?' asked Carson.

'Just last week.'

'And what did she say?'

'She said she was all right. But you know what they say, if you're mad then you're the last to know.'

'Was she depressed?'

'Yes, she was distressed and frightened. You see, we were getting bags of hate mail and death threats.'

'Death threats? You didn't report those.'

'Oh, television stations always get death threats. Lots of nutters out there. But it was getting to Crystal. I told her to just look at the size of the mail bag. That's what counts. Poor thing. Committing suicide like that.'

'As I said, we are not sure it was suicide.'

'I don't believe it. I'm telling you, that poor girl's state of mind was a mess.'

He was asked several more questions and then allowed to leave.

'I think we should have this Felicity Pearson in,' said Carson. 'She seems to be a fund of gossip, to judge from what she told Macbeth.'

'I'm afraid, sir, that by now she won't have much to tell us,' said Hamish.

'Why?'

'I think she'll be told to keep her mouth shut. They might even have offered her her old show back.'

Carson consulted his notes again and then raised his eyes and looked at Hamish

'You think so? So what would you do?'

'The three others were with her when she was talking to me – I mean Harry Jury, Tom Betts and John Leslie. I would question them all together.'

'Right, we'll try it your way.'

'Although,' said Hamish, 'I suppose they've all been warned by now.'

The policewoman was sent to fetch the four. They shuffled in together. The policewoman arranged four chairs in front of Carson's desk. Hamish eyed her sympathetically and wondered what she thought about being given all this dogsbody work, from making the coffee to arranging the furniture.

'I'll get right to the point,' said Carson, changing tack. 'This is now a murder inquiry.' Felicity gave a little gasp.

'Now before you all tell me what an emotional mess Crystal was and how she was ripe for suicide, I must urge you to tell the truth.'

Before anyone could speak, the door opened and a man popped his head round it. 'Just wondered if you wanted to see me.'

'And who are you?'

'I'm Alistair Campbell, the producer of Crystal's show.'

'We'll get to you later,' said Carson.

'Right.'

'Wait a minute!' Hamish shouted to the

60

producer's retreating head. Alistair Campbell reappeared. 'Did you just get to the office?' asked Hamish.

'Yes, just got in. The girl at reception told me where you were and I thought I'd get any questions over with before I start work.'

Hamish turned to Carson and said, 'I think Mr Campbell should answer questions first, as he hasn't had time to see anyone.'

Carson studied Hamish for a long moment and said, 'Do come in, Mr Campbell. Another chair please.'

Hamish crossed the room and said to the policewoman, 'I'll do that.'

She flashed him a grateful smile and returned to her position by the door.

'So, Mr Campbell,' said Carson. 'I'll start with you.' Hamish noticed Felicity's hand reaching out to tug Alistair's jacket and said sharply, 'Miss Pearson!'

She flushed and put her hands on her lap.

'What was your impression of Crystal French?' asked Carson.

The producer was a tall, thin man in his mid-thirties with a long mobile face and horn-rimmed glasses. He leaned back in his chair and grinned. 'Can I talk ill of the dead?'

'As long as it is the truth.'

'I don't believe it was suicide,' said Alistair. 'She was a downright bitch and one of the worst people I've worked with. She had an ego the size of Mount Everest. She made every-one's life a misery.'

'Would you say she was depressed?'

'Anything but. She seemed to think her role in life was to make other people depressed.'

'That is interesting. Your managing director and your head of features claimed she had gone mad, that she was nervous and strung out.'

'They did? Well, they knew her better than I did.' He winked. 'Know what I mean?'

Felicity could contain herself no longer. 'You should not talk about your bosses.'

'I can say what I like,' said Alistair easily. 'I'm finished here. I've got a job with the BBC in Glasgow.'

Carson stared at Felicity. 'You said to Constable Macbeth that Crystal French was depressed.'

'All I meant,' said Felicity shrilly, 'was that the letters she got were getting her down.'

'And you said,' Carson ploughed on, 'that she was having affairs with Callum Bissett and Rory MacBain.'

Felicity turned white. 'I didn't mean that. I was upset by her death.' She clasped her hands together. 'Oh, don't tell Callum I said so.'

She stared at them, stricken. Callum had called her in an hour ago and promised her the *Countryside* show back again. He had said that he relied on her loyalty to him and everyone else in the station.

Carson turned his attention to Tom Betts. Felicity's heart sank.

Tom confirmed that what Hamish had reported them all saying, including Felicity, was correct. He stated that he hadn't started work with Crystal yet and didn't know her.

Carson asked more and more questions. When he had finished, Hamish spoke up. 'Miss Pearson, you were doing research for Miss French. As she was about to interview me, I am sure you were told to go about the village and try to find something against me.'

'Yes, but I couldn't get anything. I wish we had done the village one first, you know, what goes on behind the lace curtains. But Crystal was furious about her speeding case and meant to get even with the police.'

'Who was doing the research on the village one?' asked Hamish.

'Amy Cornwall.'

Hamish said to Carson, 'I think we should see her.'

'Why?'

'There may be someone somewhere in the Highlands who didn't want an old scandal raked up again.'

'Good point,' said Carson. He looked at the policewoman. 'Get this Amy Cornwall in here.'

'And I would keep these people here until she arrives,' said Hamish.

Carson looked at him with a flash of irritation. He knew Hamish meant that Felicity would tip off Amy as to what to say, but he didn't like the way Hamish was taking over the course of the interview.

'Very well,' he said.

They waited in silence for Amy Cornwall. When she arrived, the others were told to leave. Amy sat down and smiled saucily all around. She was a contrast to Felicity. She was in her twenties and had a mop of golden curls over a cheeky face.

'I gather your job was to dig up some dirt on villagers for Miss French's show,' said Carson.

'Yes, that's right. I hated doing it, but success is all that counts in the television business.'

'And how did you go about it?'

'Newspaper cuttings. Old scandals.'

'Like what?'

'I hadn't got around to many people. Just made a few phone calls, setting up interviews.'

'I'll need a list of the people you were going to see.'

'Right.'

'How soon?'

'Have it right here.' She opened her handbag and produced a grubby list. Carson eyed it with disfavour. 'What happened to computerized reports?'

'I have it on my computer. You can have my written notes for now.'

'Now, my detectives have already taken statements from some of the television people about where they were on the day of Miss French's death.' He didn't ask, thought Hamish, and then realized that Jimmy Anderson and others would have already done preliminary interviews. 'Where were you on Monday?'

'I was doing research for the motor show. Nice easy stuff. I was down in Inverness at the Rover dealer arranging for our presenter to test drive the new car. I left early in the morning and didn't get back till six in the evening.'

'A long day to set up one interview.'

'Well, I went shopping. I was in no mood to hurry back. You see, I didn't know of Crystal's death.'

'Meaning you didn't like her,' said Hamish suddenly.

'Exactly. I thought if I came back early and showed my face in the office, she would find work for me to do, and I hated working for her.'

'Why?'

'She was thoroughly nasty, that's why. Always complaining and bullying. Very spiteful woman. I'm surprised she took her own life. Couldn't believe it.'

'There is a chance it could be murder and that the suicide was faked.'

'That figures,' said Amy cheerfully. 'I could have killed her myself.' She laughed. 'Just as well I have an alibi.'

'I am surprised at your lighthearted approach to this unfortunate death,' said Carson reprovingly.

'I never was a hypocrite and I don't intend to start now,' said Amy.

'That will be all,' said Carson.

When she had left, Hamish asked, 'Who's on that list?'

'Who's on that list what?'

'Who's on that list, sir?'

Carson was tempted to refuse. He thought Hamish Macbeth was not showing him due respect, but he passed it over.

Hamish raised his eyebrows as he saw that the first name on the list was that of Barry McSween, the crofter. Then there was Mrs McClellan, the bank manager's wife who lived in Lochdubh; Mrs Harrison, she whose shop in Braikie Crystal had trashed; Finlay Swithers, who owned a fish and chip shop in Cnochan; and Maisie Gough, also of Cnochan.

'Why them?' asked Carson.

'There was something way back about Barry McSween,' said Hamish slowly. 'Mrs McClellan at one time was a kleptomaniac and was charged with shoplifting, two people once brought a charge of food poisoning against Mrs Harrison, Finlay Swithers was once charged with wife beating, and Maisie Gough is new to me. Amy must have phoned or approached these people with a view to interviewing them.'

'I don't think any of them would have granted an interview,' pointed out Carson, 'particularly McSween and Harrison. They

66

would feel they had suffered enough from television.'

'She probably meant to arrive unheralded on their doorsteps and get some really nasty confrontations with frightened people,' said Hamish.

'Go and see all these people anyway,' said Carson, 'and find out where they all were on the day of the murder. So many people and not one obvious motive.'

'There's adultery,' said Jimmy.

'Yes, so there is, but having seen the two gentlemen, I feel their respective flings with Crystal were probably by no means their first.'

'I think Felicity Pearson had the best motive,' put in Hamish.

'Why?' demanded Carson, wishing at the same time that this village constable would remember his place.

'Until Crystal came, she had a show of her own, she was producer of that show. Because of Crystal, her show was axed and she was demoted to researcher for Crystal, and Crystal no doubt made her life a misery.'

Carson shuffled through his papers. 'But we have here reports that cover her activities for Monday.'

'There may be a loophole,' said Hamish. 'It's impossible to pinpoint the exact time of death.'

The phone rang. Carson picked it up. He listened carefully and then replaced the receiver. 'That was the pathologist. He says that yes, the lump on the back of the head was caused by a severe blow, a blow hard enough to stun. So it seems, gentlemen, we have a case of murder.'

Jimmy and Hamish left the television station in the late afternoon. Carson had interviewed everyone all over again. The only difference was that the fiction that Crystal had been depressed had been dropped. 'I'm starving,' said Jimmy. 'You'd think he might ha' stopped for lunch.'

'I thought you only had a liquid lunch,' said Hamish.

'Oh, I've been known to eat. There's a café over there. We can get a sandwich or a pie.'

'Right.'

They walked together into the café. Hamish ordered ham sandwiches and tea, and Jimmy a mutton pie and chips. 'What made you say you thought it was Felicity?' asked Jimmy.

'Just a hunch.'

'I think it was a man. You were out at the toilet when Carson let fall another gem from the pathologist and from the forensic report.'

'What was that?'

'They think that Crystal was killed just after breakfast. Her bacon and eggs were barely digested. They think she was stunned somewhere else and brought to Lochdubh. Also her hair had been brushed straight out of its style – when she was seen leaving in the morning, she had it pinned up – but there were some little bits o' heather in it as if she'd been laid somewhere in the heather before being put in the car.'

'Odd, that,' commented Hamish.

'Aye, that it is. So can you see a lassie like Felicity bashing someone and having the strength to arrange that person in the car?'

'Yes, I can, somehow. Don't ask me why.'

'You'd best forget about her for the moment. You've got Barry McSween and the others to check up on. Going to start this evening?'

Hamish shook his head. 'No, I'll have a go at them all tomorrow.'

When Hamish finally got back to the station, he got a rapturous welcome from Lugs. Hamish had phoned Angela earlier to beg her to feed and walk Lugs. The dog then rattled his food bowl.

'Don't kid me,' said Hamish. 'I know Angela would feed you well.'

Lugs whimpered and banged the bowl even harder.

Hamish sighed. 'I'm not cooking anything for you. It's dog food or nothing.' He filled the bowl with hard dog food, which Lugs stared at and then turned away from, but somehow in the dog's mind, some sort of code of honour had been satisfied and he lay down on the floor and soon he was asleep.

There was a knock at the door. Hamish opened it. Elspeth stood there. 'I wanted to know how the case was going,' she said.

The evening was chilly, and Elspeth's clothes seemed to be a lumpy mixture of odd grey and brown garments.

'If you want anything for the newspaper,' said Hamish, 'you'll need to phone police headquarters.'

'I've done that,' said Elspeth. 'Can I come in?'

'Don't be long. I'm tired.'

'I could be of help to you,' she said. She leant against the stove. 'This stove is cold.'

'Of course it is. I just got back. Move aside, lassie, and sit at the table. I'll light it.' Hamish raked it out and put in paper, wood, fire-lighter and peat and lit it. Then he joined her at the table.

'Why did you say someone was going to kill her?'

'Just a feeling. She was causing so much trouble.'

'But you were so emphatic about it.'

'We have these feelings sometimes.'

Hamish gave her a cynical look. 'I thought you'd dropped the all-seeing astrologer act with me. Anyway, how could you help me?'

'I'm good at finding out things.'

'I wish you could find out if anyone saw Crystal yesterday morning at any time at all.'

'I'll try. What about Sean Fitzpatrick?'

Hamish looked at her in surprise. 'I'd for-

70

gotten about him.' Sean was a recluse who lived out on the Glenanstey road. Although he seemed to have no friends or to converse much, he had an amazing knack of observing things and picking up gossip. 'I'll go and see him now.'

'I'll come with you,' said Elspeth.

'I cannot be taking you in a police vehicle.'

'Meaning you don't want me. I've seen you giving people lifts before, copper. But I've got my own car outside and I can follow you.'

'As you wish,' said Hamish grumpily. 'But don't be writing anything without asking me first!'

Although they could see a light in Sean's cottage, they waited and waited after Hamish had knocked, wondering if the recluse was going to answer the door or not.

Just when Hamish was raising his hand to knock again, the door opened. Sean looked at them wearily. Sean Fitzpatrick was stooped and old, but with intelligent blue eyes in a tanned and seamed face. 'What is it?' he demanded. 'I was just going to bed.'

'It's about the death of Crystal French. Did you see anything of her? I mean, before she died. She was driving a green BMW.'

'Come in.'

They followed him into his book-lined living room. 'Sit down,' he ordered. 'I'm not going to

71

offer you anything. I want to make this short. Yes, I saw a green BMW.'

'Where? When?' asked Hamish eagerly.

'It would be about nine-thirty. It stopped a little while on the road out to Glenanstey. I had been stooped over in my front garden, but when I heard the car, and then heard it stop, I straightened up. I thought someone might not be sure of their way. I opened my gate to walk towards the car. It did a U-turn and roared past me in the direction of Lochdubh.'

'Did you see who was driving?'

'No, just a glimpse. Large hat, dark glasses.'

'Man or woman?'

'Couldn't say.'

'Have you heard anything?'

'You know how it is, I never talk to anyone, so when I go to Patel's for my groceries, folk talk in front of me as if I'm invisible. Before her death, they were all vowing vengeance, but I was down today and there wasn't a murmur. I can't tell you any more.'

'The figure in the car,' pursued Hamish, 'fat or thin?'

'Thin, I would say.'

'What colour was the hat?'

'Brown, I think. But the head was down over the wheel. I didn't look very closely. I mean, if I had known it was the car a murdered woman was going to be found in later on, I would have looked more closely.'

'Murdered? Why do you say murdered?'

72

'I saw her television show. Cocky bitch and loving every minute of making people's lives a misery. I would be amazed if she'd killed herself.'

'I want you to let me know if you hear anything,' said Hamish.

'What's in it for me?'

'Public duty. You're as bad as Angus Macdonald.'

Sean's bright eyes turned on Elspeth. 'And who is this?'

'I'm right sorry. I forgot to introduce you. This is Elspeth Grant, who works for the local newspaper.'

'You're the astrologer. Angus Macdonald is fed up about that. He feels he should have been asked to do it.'

'I'm a reporter as well,' said Elspeth. 'I'm tired of the astrology thing. I might ask Sam if he'd consider employing Angus.'

Sean looked amused. 'Angus would try to be a proper astrologer and no one would like it. They like your daft predictions – you know, at five o'clock on Tuesday you will have a severe headache.'

'I'll report what you have said.' Hamish got to his feet. He was tired. He had put the news of Priscilla's engagement to the back of his brain but now it flooded his mind.

'And I was desolate and sick of an old passion,' said Sean suddenly, as Hamish was making for the door.

73

His back stiffened. He swung round, his eyes blazing. 'What did you say?'

'Just quoting,' said Sean mildly. 'I read a lot of poetry. Ernest Dowson.' He leaned back in his chair and half-closed his eyes.

'"I have forgot much, Cynara! gone with the wind,
Flung roses, roses, riotously, with the throng,
Dancing, to put pale, lost lilies out of mind."'

'Come on!' snapped Hamish at Elspeth. 'Leave him to his babbling.'

Carson was working late. 'Report from Hamish Macbeth, sir,' said a constable, putting a printed sheet of paper on his desk.

Carson read it and then said, 'Is Detective Anderson still in the building?'

'Yes, sir.'

'Then get him up here.'

When Jimmy entered, Carson said, 'I have just had a report from Macbeth. Someone called Sean Fitzpatrick who lives on the road between Lochdubh and Glenanstey saw a green BMW at nine-thirty in the morning. Read it.'

Jimmy read the report and let out a soundless whistle.

'What I want to know is why it was left to Macbeth to find this out,' said Carson.

'It's his beat, sir.'

'Ordinarily, yes. But I've had officers and detectives going from door to door and yet they've missed this. Tomorrow, make sure they all go over the area again.'

'Macbeth has a way of finding out bits that others miss,' said Jimmy.

'He is only a village constable, not Sherlock Holmes. I want no more lapses like this.'

'Do you want Macbeth to go round the village again as well?'

'No, he's got that list to follow up. Leave him.'

Chapter Five

Look at the stars! look, look up at the skies!
O look at all the fire folk sitting in the air!
           – Gerard Manley Hopkins

Next morning, Hamish reluctantly made his way to the bank manager's house at a time when he knew he would be at work in the bank.

Mrs McClellan answered the door. 'I don't need to ask you why you've come,' she said wearily. 'It's a nightmare.'

'So the television company did contact you?'

'Yes, some girl called Amy Cornwall. I'm haunted by this, Hamish. Do you remember when that awful dustman was blackmailing me over this? It never came out then and I thought it was all over. But this girl had got hold of that old newspaper cutting that said I had been charged with shoplifting. Remember I told you that we'd moved here because my husband felt the scandal deeply? I refused an interview and she said that they would talk about it just the same and that I should put my side of the story. I still refused. Now Crystal's dead. Has she been murdered?'

'We believe so.'

'And that blackmailing dustman was murdered. It's a nightmare all over again. Will this get in the newspapers?'

'Unless you killed her, no. My bosses will have the cutting about you from the newspaper so I can't keep it quiet from them but they'll have no reason to tell anyone. I must ask you what you were doing on Monday from early morning up till three o'clock.'

'I worked in the garden all morning. Then I got lunch ready for my husband. Oh, dear, if you ask him to confirm this, he'll wonder why.'

'I'll just tell him we're asking everyone in the village for their movements and that's pretty much the case. With any luck, you won't need to say anything. You're not the only one.'

Hamish next drove to Braikie and parked outside Mrs Harrison's shop. The reason her dingy shop still kept in business was because she let those on social security benefits run up a bill until their next government payment. Hamish walked in. The shop was empty except for Mrs Harrison and an old-age pensioner who was paying for a meagre supply of bashed tins. Hamish waited until the customer had left and then asked, 'Did Strathbane Television contact you about that old food-poisoning case?'

'That they did,' she said furiously, 'and I chust told them that if they dared to show their faces here again, it would be the worse for them.'

'What could you do?'

'My two sons would be here to protect me. Persecuting an old widow woman like me. The case was years ago. They said it was my mutton pies. Havers! But I haven't sold a mutton pie since.'

'I must ask you what you were doing on Monday morning and early Monday afternoon.'

'You know what folks are saying?' she demanded, her face twisted with spite. 'They're saying that chust because thon Priscilla got engaged to someone else, you're taking it out on everybody.'

'Chust answer the question ... *you horrible auld crone.*' Hamish had added the last part sotto voce, but she heard it.

'I'm not going to answer any of your questions.'

'Then I must ask you to accompany me to the police station.'

They glared at each other, and then Mrs Harrison began to sob. Hamish stood helplessly wondering what to do until he saw those eyes behind the tears watching him sharply, as if to gauge his reaction.

So he waited, unmoved and apparently immovable, until she took out a grubby paper tissue and wiped her eyes.

'Ochone, ochone.' she said. 'What's a frail old woman to do?'

'Answer my question. Where were you last Monday?'

'I was here.'

'Witnesses?'

'Ask about. Folks'll tell you, I'm always open on a Monday.'

'Thank you. That will be all for now.'

Hamish left the shop. He walked up and down the street, questioning various people, until one woman said, 'Yes, she was open on Monday as usual. Except for around ten-thirty in the morning. I needed some milk, but she had a sign on the door. Back Soon, it said.'

Hamish returned to the shop. Questioned again, Mrs Harrison said she had merely gone home to get her cigarettes. Hamish mutely stared at the packets of cigarettes behind her and Mrs Harrison countered shrilly by saying that she did not normally smoke but the fuss about the television show had upset her nerves and she didn't want to start a new packet. Hamish knew her to be mean and judged this seemingly improbable explanation to be true.

He warned her again that he would be back. Now for Barry McSween.

Barry McSween was not at home and his wife, red-eyed with recent weeping, volunteered that he was probably down in the pub in Lochdubh. Hamish found him there, sitting at a corner table, moodily drinking whisky.

He sat down opposite and Barry looked at him dully. 'Folks are saying I killed that woman,' he said. 'But I didnae. I wanted to. She brought shame on me.'

'Don't let it get to you,' said Hamish. 'She brought shame to a good few people. In a few weeks' time, it'll all have blown over and they'll have something else to talk about. Now where were you on Monday?'

'That's easy. Drinking.'

'Where? Here?'

'No, I was upset. I didn't want to see any of the locals. I went to the bar at the Tommel Castle Hotel. I drank there until about two, when Mr Johnston said I'd better go home and asked for my car keys.' Mr Johnston was the manager. 'I had to walk home. I went straight to bed. Jeannie'll tell you.' Jeannie was his wife. 'I didn't wake until early evening, and I walked back to the hotel to pick up my car. That's when I heard about the death. And I was glad. I'm sorry she committed suicide.'

'It hasn't been in the papers yet, Barry, but we think it was murder.'

McSween's normally ruddy face turned a muddy colour. 'That cannae be true. Folks say she was found in her car and a pipe had been stuck in the exhaust and into the window of the car.'

Pipe, thought Hamish. I wonder where that length of pipe came from. I wonder if they've traced it.

Aloud he said, 'I think that puts you in the clear, but I'll need to check your story.' He pointed to the whisky glass. 'How many of those have you had?'

'This is the second.'

'Make it the last. I don't want to add to your troubles by charging you with driving over the limit.'

Hamish made his way reluctantly to the hotel, which, since he had learned of Priscilla's engagement, he had been hoping to avoid. He wondered, not for the first time, why memories of Priscilla should still hurt. He finally decided that once you had been in love, it was like contracting an infection and a bit of the disease would always linger.

Mr Johnston gave him a warm welcome and led him into the hotel office. 'Coffee, Hamish?'

Hamish nodded. The manager poured him a mug and set it in front of him. 'What brings you? The murder?'

'Aye, I've got to check Barry McSween's story. He says on Monday he was up here drinking.'

'That's right. The barman warned me he was getting drunk and I took his car keys away from him.'

'Did he make a fuss?'

'No, staggered out, quiet as a lamb.'

'I'm glad,' said Hamish. 'I don't like Barry, but, man, she did make a fool of him.'

'If you ask me, he made a right fool of himself. Any idea who did it?'

'We don't know. So many suspects.'

There was a silence. Hamish drank his coffee. 'Must have been a shock to you,' said Mr Johnston at last.

'The murder?'

'No, Priscilla.'

'Yes, it was. I thought she might have warned me. Who's the fellow?'

'Some stockbroker in London. Lots of money. Parents are delighted.'

'Still, she might have told me. When's the wedding?'

'Sometime in the spring.'

'Here?'

'No, London.'

That's a mercy, thought Hamish. He couldn't bear the idea of her getting married in Lochdubh.

He left the hotel and drove over to the village of Cnothan. He called at Police Sergeant

Macgregor's house to explain his presence on the other's beat. 'I don't know why they sent you,' said Sergeant Macgregor. 'I'll put in a complaint about it.'

'You do that,' said Hamish amiably. 'Now, the television researcher was going to dig up old scandal for a programme. On the list were Finlay Swithers and Maisie Gough. Finlay Swithers, well, it was probably that charge of wife beating, but who is Maisie Gough?'

'Poor wee mouse of a woman. Got accused a few years back of pinching the Mothers Union funds. Fact is, she's a bit absent-minded and she'd given them to her friend, Mrs Queen, for safekeeping and forgotten about it. Mrs Queen was on holiday when she was accused. Comes back from holiday. Horrified to learn about Maisie. Charges dropped.'

'So why her?'

'Fault of the local papers. Charge reported but nothing when it was dropped. Word got around, of course, of her innocence, but anyone looking up the cuttings would still see the charge.'

'Funny how they still talk about the cuttings,' said Hamish. 'It's probably all on computer discs these days. Where will I find her?'

'Down by the loch. Waterside Cottages, number six. And when you're finished, get out o' my parish.'

'Gladly,' said Hamish, who hated Cnothan.

He walked down the drab, grey main street

84

towards the black loch. It was one of those lochs artificially created by the Hydro Electric Board. No trees grew at its edge. No birds sang. Bleak, dreary, with a great dam at one end.

He found Waterside Cottages and knocked at the door of number six. He waited. There was a chill feel of approaching autumn and a smell of peat smoke in the air.

He frowned at the closed door. He sensed there was someone inside. He tried the door handle. The door swung open. He smelled gas and his heart began to race. He went into the kitchen. A small, grey-haired woman was lying with her head on a cushion inside the oven. Hamish switched off the gas and threw open the window. Then he lifted her gently out. 'Miss Gough,' he said, raising her tear-stained face. 'It iss not the coal gas. It iss the North Sea gas. You cannot be committing suicide with the North Sea gas.'

'I cannae dae anything right,' she moaned and burst into tears. Hamish sat beside her on the floor, cradling her in his arms, and rocking her backwards and forwards as if soothing a hurt child. He waited patiently until she had finished crying, took out a clean handkerchief, and dried her face. He then lifted her up and placed her in an armchair next to the stove. 'I'll wait till the gas clears and make us a cup of tea. Was it because of the television people?'

She nodded dumbly.

'But you were innocent.'

'It would all come out again. The shame. The fright. Even if people knew I was innocent, they'd think I was mad, not even remembering I'd given the money to Mrs Queen.'

'But it's over. The woman's dead. There won't be any show.'

She gave a pathetic little hiccup. 'I thought they'd send someone else.'

Hamish looked at her elderly crumpled figure, the hands crippled with arthritis, the tear-stained wrinkled face, and thought in that moment, if Crystal had been alive, he could cheerfully have killed her himself. 'Is Mrs Queen your friend?' he asked.

'Yes, we're very close.'

'Would you have her phone number?'

'It's there, on a pad over the phone. I forget things these days.'

'One of the problems of getting old,' said Hamish. He phoned Mrs Queen and talked rapidly, then put the phone down. 'She'll be right round. You need someone with you.'

He waited until Mrs Queen arrived. She was a heavy-set matron with a round, kindly face. 'You leave Maisie to me,' she said.

I didn't ask her what she was doing on Monday, thought Hamish. He drew Mrs Queen out into the narrow passage that ran from the front door to the back, off which the rooms led. He wondered if it was still called the lobby in Scotland. A song his mother used to sing to him, a relic of the Second World War

86

when sausages were filled with all sorts of
junk, came back to him and rang in his head:

I love a sausage, a bonny Highland
sausage,
I put one in the oven for ma tea,
I went into the lobby, to fetch ma Uncle
Bobby,
And the sausage came after me.

'I didn't ask Miss Gough what she was doing
on Monday,' he whispered, 'and I didn't want
to upset her further by asking her now. Do you
know?'

'She was with me all morning. We were
cleaning the church. Oh, why didn't the poor
soul say anything about her worries?'

'Never mind. Look after her. But keep telling her it's all over. Nothing to worry about
any more.'

It was hard on the older generation, thought
Hamish as he walked away and eyed a group
of youths lounging by the waterfront: white,
pinched faces, gelled hair, dead eyes. Respectability was all. They'd kept themselves decent
all their lives and done their bit for the church.
The generations that came after couldn't give
a toss. He sighed and made his way to the fish
and chip shop. It was closed. He looked at the
opening hours. Didn't open until five in the
afternoon. He saw there was a flat above
the shop and a door beside the plate glass

window, which probably led to the upper premises. He rang the bell and waited. Then he heard footsteps clattering down the stairs. The door opened. A thin little man stood there, his face a mass of bad-tempered wrinkles and broken veins. 'Mr Swithers?' asked Hamish.

'Aye, what d'ye want?'

'I'm making inquiries into the death of Crystal French.'

'What's that to do with me?'

'Can we go inside?'

'I suppose. Place is a mess, mind.'

He scampered up the stairs and Hamish followed him. A door at the top of the stairs led into a living room that made the word 'mess' seem like a euphemism. Overflowing ashtrays lay about, empty bottles, dirty clothes, greasy plates. Hamish lifted a pile of smelly clothes off a chair, sat down, and pulled out a notebook.

'Where were you on Monday?' he asked.

'Here. Why?'

'Crystal French's researcher contacted you with a view to doing a piece on you.'

'So she did. I told her to get stuffed and slammed the phone down.'

'Was it because you were charged with wife beating?'

'That was years ago and Ruby, the wife, dropped the charges.'

'And where is your wife?'

'Left me right after. Silly cow. Down in Inverness with her mother.'

'So where were you on Monday?'

'Like I said, here.'

'Any witnesses?'

'None. I slept late. Got up about noon and started getting things ready for the evening trade. More work these days. Not happy with just the fish and chips any more. Deep-fried pizza and chips, Mars Bars and chips. I'm telling you, changed days.'

'So no one can give you an alibi?'

'Why would I need an alibi? I wasn't going to have anything to do with those TV people anyway. But you can ask the locals. I've lost my driving licence and the only way for me to get to Lochdubh is on the bus and the bus doesn't run on Mondays.'

Hamish drove slowly back to Lochdubh. His thoughts turned to Felicity Pearson. He would ask Jimmy Anderson if it was possible for him to interview her.

Jimmy was waiting for him at the police station. A mobile police unit had been set up outside the village on the back road where Crystal's body had been found, and Hamish could see uniformed policemen going from house to house.

Jimmy followed Hamish into the police station and held out a chocolate biscuit to

Lugs, who turned his head away. 'What's up wi' your dog?'

'If he eats chocolate he gets his teeth cleaned, and he doesnae like getting his teeth cleaned. So what's new, Jimmy? What about that hose that was in the car? They trace it?'

'They are trying. It was ordinary garden hose. Could have come from anywhere.'

'I've been thinking, Jimmy, am I still in Carson's favour?'

'As far as I know. I mean, I don't think he approves of you, but he's sharp enough to want to pick your brains. Why?'

'I would like permission to interview Felicity Pearson.'

'Why her? And didn't you interview her already, when you sat in on Carson's interview?'

'I've a funny feeling about her. I'd like to know more about her.'

'I'll see what I can do. Did you get anywhere with the people on the list?'

'Och, not a hope.'

'You'd better send over your report.'

'I'll do that.'

'Just a wee word of advice. You've got your mind so set on Felicity Pearson, it could stop you looking hard enough at other suspects.'

Hamish looked at him haughtily. 'I do not haff the closed mind. When did I effer haff the closed mind?'

Jimmy knew by the sudden sibilance of

Hamish's accent that he was seriously annoyed. Jimmy, who knew about Priscilla's engagement, thought that the news of that was turning Hamish's mind away from its usual clear logic.

'Tell me about the others,' he said.

Hamish went over what they had all said, leaving out only the attempted suicide of Maisie Gough. If Sergeant Macgregor learned of that, it would be all over Cnothan.

'Those two sons of the Harrison woman,' said Jimmy, 'Iain and Jamie, now they're a bad lot. They've been in trouble a couple of times for drunk and disorderly.'

'So have an awful lot of people in the Highlands.'

'But you must admit, they're brutal and devoted to their mother. Did you have a word with them?'

'No.'

'Why not, Hamish?'

'Because I feel the further we get away from the television people, the further we get away from solving the murder.'

'Hamish Macbeth, you forget you are supposed to be the village bobby, conscientious and plodding. Before you put your report in, I would suggest you go and see them.'

'Is that an order?'

'I'm just covering your back for you, man.'

Hamish sighed. 'I'll go now.'

* * *

As he drove to Braikie, he turned over what Jimmy had said, and his common sense told him that he was in danger of letting things slip. The Harrisons' croft lay out on the far side of Braikie. As he was driving along the main street, Ian Chisholm darted out in front of the Land Rover and waved to Hamish to stop. Ian Chisholm ran the garage in Lochdubh but had recently opened up a launderette in Braikie.

Hamish stopped and opened the window. 'It's them gypsies,' panted Ian. 'Look over there.' He pointed to the launderette. Spray painted in red on the window was the legend: THE MACHINES IN THIS LAUNDERETTE ARE ALL BROKEN DOWN LIKE THE SILLY OLD FART WHO OWNS THEM.

Hamish bit back a smile. 'Are you sure it's the gypsies?'

'Who else? I caught them fiddling with the dials with a screwdriver, trying to get free washes.'

'Why didn't you report it?'

'You take on one gypsy and you take on the lot.'

'I've got to see someone first and then I'll have a word with them.'

Iain and Jamie Harrison were both sitting in the kitchen of their croft house when Hamish drove up. They went out to meet him. They were both squat burly men, both bachelors, both truculent.

Hamish climbed down from the Land Rover and faced them. 'I would like to know where you pair were last Monday.'

'Why?' demanded Iain.

'A woman was murdered, or didn't you hear?'

'Oh, the television lassie. Good riddance to bad rubbish,' said Jamie. 'What's it got to do with us?'

'Your mother had a hard time at her hands. You both had a reason to hate her. So where were you?'

'Mending dry stone walls. Sheep knocked down a length over the back field.'

'I'll have a look.'

Hamish strode off, his regulation boots squelching in the soggy grass. Trails of misty rain were drifting over the mountains and a curlew set up its mournful call from the heather. The air was balmy and sweet with the smells of wild thyme and heather. He came to the wall. Sure enough, a long stretch of it showed signs of repair, but who could say they had done it on Monday?

He returned to where they were still waiting. 'Any witnesses to the fact that you were working on that wall on Monday?'

'Matt Soutar ower the next croft came by for a crack and to ask us if we'd do one o' his walls. He was with us most of the morning.'

Hamish left them and called on the next croft, where Matt Soutar confirmed the Harrisons' story. Hamish studied the crofter's face as he talked, knowing that Highlanders could be accomplished liars, but Soutar seemed honest enough.

Now for the gypsies, he thought.

Chapter Six

Go, and catch a falling star,
Get with child a mandrake root,
Tell me where all past years are,
Or who cleft the Devil's foot.
                                — John Donne

The gypsies had loaded up their sideshows and rides. There was bustle everywhere. They were preparing to move on.

Hamish had dealt with them many times before, complaining about squint sights on the rifles at the shooting gallery, coconuts glued down at the coconut shy, and blocks of wood under the prizes at the hoopla stand that were just that clever fraction too big, to ensure that no hoop would fall cleanly over the prize. The senior member of the gypsies was John Grey. Hamish headed for his trailer.

John opened the door to him. 'I wisnae there,' he said immediately, 'and I've got twenty witnesses to the fact.'

'I'm sure you have,' retorted Hamish wearily. 'But I'm sure we can both save a lot of time. You do what I tell you, and then I don't need to turn this camp over for a can of red spray paint or haul you into the police station for questioning. You will go to the launderette and wash that paint off the window.'

'It wisnae me.'

'It was one of you. There's a lot of police in Lochdubh because of this murder. I can get them over here to turn every single place over.'

They stared at each other. John Grey's eyes, Hamish noticed for the first time, were an odd silvery colour. They reminded him of Elspeth's eyes. What had she said? We have these feelings sometimes. We? He had never asked Elspeth where she came from.

John Grey nodded. It was enough. Hamish knew that headquarters would have been furious if he had taken their manpower away. He turned away and then turned back. 'Know anyone called Elspeth Grant?'

A sort of cloud veiled John Grey's eyes – a sure sign, Hamish knew of old, that the man was about to lie. 'Cannae say I've heard of her.'

Hamish walked away. He would ask Elspeth where she came from.

As he drove back to Lochdubh, he noticed the nights were beginning to get dark early. Soon there would only be a little light during the day as the long northern winter set in. The stars were blazing overhead. His stomach rumbled. He had forgotten to get anything to eat.

Back at the police station, he fed Lugs and himself and then phoned Jimmy Anderson. 'Did you ask whether I could interview Felicity Pearson?' he asked.

'Aye, and I've set up an interview for you. She'll see you at her place in the morning.'

'Where's that?'

'Thon flats on the Inverness road, number twenty-five, flat two A.'

'What time?'

'Nine o'clock. She's due at work at ten.'

'Grand, Jimmy. One thing. That hat and glasses that Sean Fitzpatrick saw the driver of the BMW wearing. Any places been searched?'

'Everyone's home has been searched, including the managing director.'

'And what about the video camera at the garage? Get any film of her leaving?'

'Yes. Getting in her car, but no hat and glasses and with her hair up.'

'So she wasn't attacked at home. Thanks for the chance of the interview.'

'I think you're barking up the wrong tree, Hamish. She's just a faded wee thing. I don't think she could swot a fly.'

'I'll let you know how I get on.'

'You'll do more than that. You'll come round here afterwards and type out a report.'

'Aye, I'll do that.'

As Hamish put down the receiver there was a knock at the kitchen door. When he opened it, Elspeth was standing there. Instead of her usual rag bag of thrift shop clothes, she was wearing a cherry red dress under a smart black coat. Hamish wondered if she had dressed up for him. 'You're looking smart,' he said, ushering her into the kitchen.

'I've just got back from a charity fashion show in Inverness.' She swung off her coat. I might have known, thought Hamish. No woman's going to go to the trouble of dressing up for me. The red dress clung to her, revealing that she had an excellent high-breasted figure.

'So what brings you?' asked Hamish.

'Friendly call. How's it going?'

'Dead ends everywhere.'

'I've been thinking. I can't believe Crystal would wear a large hat and glasses. She liked everyone to recognize her.'

'Well, they think she was stunned outside the car. So there's a good chance the murderer was the one in the hat and glasses. Where are you from, Elspeth?'

'Here and there.'

'Now, that's not an answer to be giving a policeman. If I was nosy enough I could find out.' He lifted a bottle of whisky down from the cupboard. 'Jimmy hasn't left much but there's enough for a dram. Are you a gypsy?'

She coloured slightly. 'What makes you say that?'

'Just an idea.'

'I'm half a one. My mother was a Grey but broke with them to marry a plumber down in Inverness. He went off and left her after I was born, but she had a lot of pride and wouldn't go back to her family. She said she was sick of moving the whole time. She was bright. She worked as a secretary and put me through school. I was going to go to university, but she got ill with cancer, so I got a job in Inverness in a factory out on the industrial estate and nursed her till she died.'

'So where did you get your journalistic experience?'

'I didn't. I haven't. I was doing secretarial work like my mother, but it was boring. I saw a small item in the *Inverness Courier* about Sam starting a paper up here. I travelled up and asked him for a job. I suggested the astrology and the recipes and the home hints. He asked me to produce examples, and I had several articles already written. He was impressed so he employed me. I got a room in the village, so here I am.'

'And do you enjoy it?'

'Oh, yes. Something different every day. One day a baking competition, another, a murder.'

'Thinking of getting a job on one of the nationals? There were a few reporters from the big papers around the village right after the murder.'

'I shouldn't think so. Sam lets me be my own boss.'

'So is Angus Macdonald going to take over the astrology column?'

'No. Sam says that people like my way of doing it.'

'And have you heard anything that might interest me?'

'Not a whisper.'

They sipped their whisky in companionable silence for a while. Lugs put his head on Elspeth's knee and gazed up into her face with his blue eyes. 'What an odd dog,' she said. 'Some of the villagers are a bit afraid of Lugs. They think he's someone who's come back, because of those eyes of his.'

'There's still a good few of them around here that still think folks come back as seals,' said Hamish.

'And do you?'

'No, though mind you I've seen seals out on the rocks that look like some of the villagers.'

'I can't imagine, say, the Currie sisters as seals.'

'I can. They would organize the whole colony. In no time at all, those seals would be fund raising for charity and turning up at church.'

'So what's your next move?'

'In this case?'

'Yes.'

'I'm going to interview Felicity Pearson tomorrow.'

'The researcher?'

'Herself.'

'Which means you suspect her,' said Elspeth. 'Why would a mere village bobby want to go to Strathbane to interview someone not on his beat?'

'I have a feeling about the lassie.'

'Why her? Why not one of the others? Her bosses, for example. She was having affairs with both of them.'

'How did you hear that?'

'Word gets around.'

'So why did you tell me you had heard nothing?'

'I knew you would know.'

'How?'

'I cannot reveal my source, Officer. I'd best be getting home.'

She put on her coat and Hamish walked her to the door. She turned and looked up at him. Those silver eyes of hers seemed to suddenly grow larger. He found himself saying, 'Perhaps we might have dinner one evening?'

'Yes, that would be fine. Shall we say Sunday at eight?'

'Yes,' said Hamish.

Her eyes suddenly seemed to diminish to their normal size. 'See you,' she said cheerfully and swung out into the dark night where the blazing stars above were reflected in the black waters of the loch.

Felicity had a flat in what had once been a manse. Church ministers were expected to have many children in the last century, so the Victorian building had provided ample space for modern flat conversions.

Hamish pressed the bell marked 2A and was buzzed into an entrance hall. Felicity opened a door on the left. 'I hope you are not going to take up too much of my time,' she said. 'I'm busy.'

'And so am I,' rejoined Hamish. 'Murder takes up a lot of a policeman's time.'

The living room looked like a shrine to what Felicity considered the days of her success. There were photographs of her in studios, on sets, out in the countryside with a camera crew, at television parties, laughing loudly and showing as many teeth as Cherie Blair.

It was a bleak room, because it had the Victorian height of ceiling, and it was cold.

Hamish removed his cap and set it on a coffee table. 'I don't really know what more I can say that I haven't already,' said Felicity. 'I mean, everything's been checked.'

He studied her. She was wearing a pale blue lambswool sweater and a string of cultured pearls with a tweed skirt. Her hair was scraped back in a knot. Her eyes were light, no colour, and restless.

'The BMW that Crystal was supposed to have been driving . . .'

'What do you mean?' demanded Felicity shrilly. 'Of course she was driving it!'

'Well now, that is the strange thing,' said Hamish. 'The car was spotted on the Drim road, but the driver was wearing dark glasses and a big hat. We have a video security camera film from the garage opposite her place and it shows her leaving in the morning, without the hat and glasses and with her hair up, so what does that tell you?'

'That she had a hat and glasses in the car and put them on later.'

'No. Whoever attacked her did it outside the car. At one point she was lying in the heather. An attempt had been made to disguise that fact. Her hair had been brushed down but a couple of tiny little bits of heather were still caught in it.'

'She was probably driving with the windows open and some bits of heather got blown in on it,' said Felicity. 'Then she knew she was going to be on camera soon, so she probably brushed her hair out herself.'

'My, you do have the answers, Miss Pearson. Tell me about yourself. How did you get started with Strathbane Television?'

She glanced impatiently at a clock on the wall, but she said, 'I came to Strathbane

103

Television ten years ago. I was secretary to Rory MacBain. He gave me a chance of being a researcher, then a director, and then he gave me my own show, *Countryside*. It was my idea to have a Gaelic show.'

I wonder if she had an affair with Rory, thought Hamish.

'How did you feel, Miss Pearson, when your show was axed?'

'Well, it was a bit of a blow, but Rory told me it was only temporary, that they would find something else for me. I thought, mind you, that he would at least have suggested I direct one of Crystal's shows instead of making me a researcher.'

'And what was it like working for Crystal French?'

She smoothed out a pleat in her tweed skirt with a careful hand, her head down. 'You know how it is, one just goes with the flow.'

'No, I don't know how it is. From what I have learned of Miss French's character, I would have thought it would have been very humiliating indeed.'

'Well, it was a bit,' she mumbled. 'When she learned that she was there to replace my show, she asked to see a video of it, and then she trashed it in front of me and everyone. She ordered me around like a slave, getting me to do her shopping for her and making her appointments at the hairdresser.'

'Were you having an affair with Rory MacBain?'

Colour flooded her face. 'Of course not! How can you even suggest such a thing? I will report you to your superiors.'

'Just doing my job.' Hamish consulted his notes. They had been sent over that morning by Jimmy Anderson. 'You talked to Mrs Wellington, the Currie sisters, Mrs Brodie, people in Patel's grocery store, and finished with Mary Hendry. You went to Mrs Hendry at eleven and did not leave until twelve noon. Why so long?'

'I was tired of the job. I knew I wouldn't get anyone to say anything bad about you and that Crystal would be furious. Mary was sympathetic. We had tea and talked a long time.'

'About what?'

'Chit-chat. Life in general. It's been checked.'

'So I see.'

'I don't know why you're questioning me again,' said Felicity. 'What about all the other people who must have wished her dead? There was that crofter . . .'

'Barry McSween. He's got a good alibi.'

'Not him. Johnny Liddesdale.'

'Why him?'

Felicity bit her lip. 'I'm not supposed to tell you. He phoned up after the "Myth of the Poor Crofter" show. He said he would kill her.'

'Why has no one been told about this?'

105

'There were a lot of calls like that. I can't remember the other ones. I remembered him because the others were just members of the public. He was the only one who had been interviewed.'

'So why weren't you supposed to say anything?'

'Rory said it couldn't have been him because he's just a wee crofter and if it came out, it would look bad for the television station, I mean riling someone decent like that.'

'Is there anyone else you're not telling me about?'

'No, I think that's it. Can I go? I'm running late.'

'Are you getting your show back again?'

'They said I would. But they've changed their minds.' She stood up and picked up her handbag.

'I'll see myself out,' said Hamish, getting to his feet. 'But I may need to question you again.'

Hamish went straight to police headquarters and typed out his report. When he had finished, Jimmy Anderson said, 'I'll take that up to Carson. You wait here.'

Carson read the report and then read it again. He raised his eyes. 'Have you seen this?'

'No, I haven't read it. I brought it straight up.'

'Macbeth says that Felicity Pearson, in his opinion, had been possibly having an affair with Rory MacBain, and that would be another reason for her hating Crystal. There's something else. That crofter, Johnny Liddesdale, who was on one of the shows, phoned up and threatened to kill Crystal. I don't know how Macbeth does it, but couldn't any of my detectives have found this out before? Is all detection to be left to a village policeman? I shall see Rory MacBain myself. Tell Macbeth he's to go and talk to this crofter.'

'Yes, sir.'

Jimmy rattled back down the stairs. 'Hamish, you're to go and talk to the crofter.'

'I might have a word with Carson before I go,' said Hamish. 'I mean, I think Felicity Pearson's flat should be searched.'

'We already searched it for the hat and glasses, along with everyone else's home.'

'You see, we weren't looking for hairpins,' said Hamish. 'Crystal French had her hair up, so she would use blonde hairpins. Felicity Pearson would have dark ones.'

'Carson's just gone out,' lied Jimmy. He felt Hamish had gained kudos enough.

'All right. I'll maybe see him later,' said Hamish.

As Hamish left police headquarters, he glanced up at the windows and then stiffened. He could see Carson, his back to the room,

107

looking as if he were dictating letters. Now why did Jimmy ...?

His hazel eyes narrowed. He went back into the building, not to the detectives' room but to the general operations room, and said to the policewoman who had been there at the television interviews, 'Can I borrow your computer, just for a few moments?'

She nodded. Hamish typed busily and printed it out and then ran up the stairs to Carson's office. Jimmy was waiting outside. 'What are you doing here?'

'Just putting in a further report about these hairpins.'

'You'd better get off and see that crofter. I'll take it in to him.' Blue eyes met hazel for a long moment. Then Hamish suddenly jerked open the door to Carson's office. 'Hey!' shouted Jimmy. 'You can't just walk in there!'

'Don't you knock?' demanded Carson wrathfully.

'I've got a further report, sir,' said Hamish meekly. 'Awfy sorry to bother you.'

He laid it on Carson's desk and walked out, closing the door quietly behind him. Jimmy was no longer waiting. Hamish grinned and walked down the stairs, whistling.

Johnny Liddesdale, he thought, as he parked the car outside the croft house. Couldn't be him. But then the seemingly meek, he had discovered in the past, could be frightening when roused.

The crofter answered the door to him. He was a small, neat man with thick grey hair carefully parted and brushed, grey clothes, greyish skin. 'It iss yourself, Hamish,' he said. 'Come ben.'

Hamish walked into the kitchen, admiring, as he had done before, the beauty of the ladder-backed chairs that Johnny had made himself. 'Will you be taking a dram?'

'No, I'm driving.' Hamish put his cap on the kitchen table and sat down. 'Tea would be nice, though.'

'I wass chust making a pot.' Hamish waited until Johnny placed teapot and cups on the table.

'Now, Johnny,' said Hamish gently. 'I've heard a report that you phoned Strathbane Television and threatened to kill Crystal French.'

'Yes, I did indeed, Hamish. I wass that upset. Oh, man, she made such a fool o' me and worse. Times are hard, Hamish. I've got cousins and nephews all over the place. I neffer married, as you know, but I've got four sisters and lots of aunties. They've been phoning me up asking for money, saying they saw the programme and I wass the millionaire and not letting them know. And me worried sick about money.'

'I'll have to ask you, Johnny, what were you

doing on Monday? Don't panic. I'm asking everybody.'

'I wass doing the usual jobs, mending fences, moving the sheep to the upper field, cutting logs, stacking peats.'

'Anyone see you?'

'I don't know if they did. You can ask at the next croft, that's Bert Mackenzie. He may ha' seen me out and about.'

'I'll check that. Not like you to threaten to kill anyone.'

'It wass chust wan o' those things you say when you're overwrought. You know me, Hamish, I wouldnae hurt a fly.'

Hamish's eyes wandered to an open copy of the *Inverness Courier* spread out on the table. He saw the headline, AMERICAN STAR VISITS INVERNESS. Jolene Carey, a famous country and western singer, was touring Scotland on holiday. He suddenly remembered seeing a news item about her bidding for Shaker furniture. He looked thoughtfully at Johnny's beautifully crafted chairs.

'Would you sell your furniture if you got an awful lot of money for it, Johnny?'

'I'd sell masell if anyone would pay me a lot. Times are bad. I'm living on potatoes.'

'I've got an idea. Could you put one o' your chairs in the back o' the Land Rover?'

'I'll do that. What are you up to ?'

'Just an idea.'

* * *

110

As Hamish drove down to Inverness, he realized he hadn't checked out Johnny's alibi with Bert Mackenzie. Oh, well, he would do it later.

Once in Inverness, he parked at the Caledonian Hotel and asked to see Miss Carey. 'Who is asking for her?' asked the receptionist.

'Police,' said Hamish.

She picked up the phone, dialled a number, and then Hamish heard her say, 'There's a policeman here to see Miss Carey.'

The voice at the other end squawked, and the receptionist said, 'You're to go up,' and gave him the room number.

A middle-aged secretary answered the door to him and invited him in. Jolene Carey was sitting on a sofa. She rose to meet him. He had imagined her to be almost as tall as himself, having seen her wearing stiletto heels on television, but it was a diminutive blonde in flat shoes who stood in front of him.

'So what's up?' she demanded with a nasal twang. 'Speeding?'

'Nothing like that,' said Hamish. 'I have a chair outside in the police Land Rover that might interest you.'

Her eyes, which were very large and green, goggled at him. 'A chair?'

Hamish shuffled his large boots. 'I heard you were interested in fine furniture. There is a man up north who makes chairs like you have never seen before.'

111

She studied the tall policeman standing shyly in front of her, twirling his cap in his hands, from the top of his flaming red hair to his large boots. Then she began to laugh. 'I don't know what you're up to, but I may as well have a look.'

Out in the car park, Hamish opened the Land Rover and gently lifted Johnny's chair down. 'This is the finest Highland workmanship, very rare,' he said.

She studied it, her head a little on one side. 'Got more like it?'

'Up at his croft. But it's a good bit away, over on the coast. I'll be straight with you, Miss Carey. He's never sold anything before, but don't be trying to get them cheap. His chairs are unique.'

'You drive and I'll follow.' She turned to her secretary, who had followed her down. 'Mary Ann, get the car.'

Johnny Liddesdale stood nervously while Jolene examined the rest of his chairs. Her eye fell on a rocker in the corner. 'This is your work, too, isn't it?'

Johnny nodded. She sat down at the table and took out a chequebook, pen and notepad. 'Here's what I'll do,' she said. 'I'll take the six chairs and the rocker, and I like this table. I'll have that as well. I'll pay you ten thousand pounds for the lot, provided we do a deal.'

Johnny began to stammer, so Hamish stepped forward. 'What's the deal?'

'I'll get this lot shipped back to the States. And then I want you to start making furniture exclusively for me. My manager will explain the arrangements for shipping and delivery. He will arrange for the shipping to be paid for. My lawyers will draw up a contract. You work only for me.'

Hamish suddenly remembered that Jolene owned a chain of restaurants and a theme park.

'One thing,' he said, for Johnny still seemed struck dumb. 'You're going to sell them in the States?'

'Yes, I'll keep this lot, and sell the ones he makes next.'

'I think,' said Hamish cautiously, 'that you should arrange in the contract to give him a good percentage of the sales. You see, if they catch on and you make an awful lot of money, he should benefit. Ten thousand pounds is not much for such superior craftsmanship.'

'I'll take it, I'll take it, Hamish,' blurted out Johnny, finding his voice.

'Well, all right, Johnny, but I want to see the contract and we'll go over it together.'

Jolene eyed him shrewdly. 'And what's your cut?'

Hamish looked at her haughtily. 'Nothing.'

Her eyes crinkled up with amusement. 'I'm hungry. Why don't we all go for dinner?'

* * *

113

They caused a minor sensation when they entered the dining room of the Tommel Castle Hotel. Johnny was still too shy to speak much, but Jolene entertained them with funny stories about her life, pausing only to sign autographs.

The phone in the hotel office rang. Mr Johnston answered it. It was Priscilla. 'I've been trying to phone Hamish at the police station, but all I get is the answering machine.'

'Oh, he's here.'

'Can I speak to him?'

'It's not convenient at the moment, Priscilla. He's having a romantic dinner with Jolene Carey.'

'You're pulling my leg. Do you mean the country and western singer, the one with the blonde hair and the big boobs?'

'That's the one. Hamish is fair smitten with her.'

'I won't interrupt him, then,' said Priscilla coldly. 'Tell him I called.'

'No, I won't,' muttered Mr Johnston after he replaced the receiver.

After Hamish and Johnny had waved Jolene goodbye, Johnny stammered out his thanks. 'Imagine getting paid for something I love,' he said. 'I'll neffer forget this, Hamish Macbeth. Neffer.'

Hamish clapped him on the shoulder. 'Glad to be of help.'

He followed Johnny back to his croft and then travelled on to the next croft. To his relief, Bert Mackenzie said he had been out in his fields on Monday and had seen Johnny, off and on, for most of the day.

When he drove back to the police station, a reproachful Elspeth was waiting for him. 'You might have told me Jolene Carey was here. By the time I got the news, she had left the hotel and she was halfway to Inverness by the time I caught up with her for an interview. You might have told me she was an old friend of yours.'

'Is that what she said?' So she doesn't want anyone else to know about Johnny's chairs, thought Hamish.

'Yes, and so you knew she was coming up here and didn't say anything.'

'She landed in out of the blue,' said Hamish mildly. 'There wasn't time. I was on my way with Johnny to the hotel for a drink when she arrived. So we had dinner.'

'How did you meet her?'

With the lying ease of the true Highlander, Hamish said, 'She was up here, oh, about four years ago but it wasn't in the papers. She called at the police station for directions and we got friendly.'

Those odd eyes of Elspeth's sharpened. 'She says you wrote her a fan letter once that was so nice that she looked you up last time she was in Scotland.'

'That's the truth,' said Hamish. 'But don't be putting that in your story. Wouldnae want people to know I wrote fan letters. A policeman,' he added virtuously, 'has a certain appearance to keep up.'

Chapter Seven

When stars are in the quiet skies,
Then most I pine for thee;
Bend of me, then, thy tender eyes,
As stars look on the sea!
— Baron Lytton

Hamish decided the following morning to visit Mary Hendry's craft shop. He knew she had been interviewed by police detectives, but he wanted to talk to her himself.

She had made a successful business out of the craft shop, stocking tourist items in the summer and moving on to Christmas presents in the winter: toys, scarves, and jewellery.

She was a small, plump, dark-haired woman with large dark eyes. Hamish thought that she reminded him of a bird. She was in her middle fifties but with few wrinkles on her smooth, thick skin.

She greeted Hamish with her usual friendly manner and said with a twinkle in her dark eyes, 'I suppose you'll be ready for a cup of coffee.'

'That would be grand.'

It was another thing about Mary's craft shop that had irritated the Tommel Castle Hotel. Customers to their craft shop were offered coffee, and they thought it mean of Mary to pinch the idea.

'I came to ask you about Felicity Pearson,' he began, after she had served him a mug of coffee.

'I've been questioned and questioned about that poor lassie.'

'Why "poor lassie"?'

'I was right sorry for her. She was a nervous wreck. She said that Crystal woman was making her life a misery. The shop was quiet so I got her to talk about it. She was bitter at losing her programme – you know, the Gaelic-speaking one. I told her that there's not many people around who speak the Gaelic these days. A lot of Scottish Nationalists down in the cities take courses but when it comes to television, the biggest audience is English-speaking. She said she had been trying to introduce a bit of culture. I said I didn't think folk were interested in culture anymore. They want real-life dramas, cop shows, Oprah Winfrey, things like that. She said Crystal was treating her like a slave. She went on and on and I just listened. Then I asked her if she had eaten any breakfast and she said she hadn't. I suggested she go to the Italian restaurant and get herself a good meal. And she said she would do that.'

'I'll ask you this straight,' said Hamish. 'Did she look like someone who had just committed murder or was about to?'

Mary laughed. 'No. She's too weak. Too frightened of her own shadow, that one. It would take more guts than she has to murder someone.'

Hamish could feel all his conviction that Felicity was the murderer slipping away.

And that conviction received a further blow when he returned to the police station. Jimmy Anderson phoned.

'You're in deep shit, laddie,' he said. 'We got a search warrant and searched Felicity Pearson's flat. Nothing in the way of hairpins. Not one. Then Callum Bissett comes down like a ton of bricks on Daviot and says that this is police harassment and demands an apology. Daviot chews up Carson. Carson says he should never have listened to you and you're to get on with your regular policing and leave the murder case to the experts.'

Hamish frowned at the receiver. Then he asked, 'Not *one* hairpin?'

'Not the one.'

'Wait a minute. When I interviewed her, she had her hair in a bun and there was a dark hairpin sticking out of it. You mean no hairpins at all?'

'I told you. No.'

119

'So what did you say when you asked her what had happened to her own hairpins?'

Silence.

'Jimmy?'

'We didn't ask her,' said Jimmy.

'Maybe I should drop a report to Carson suggesting it.'

'Let it alone, Hamish. You've got a bee in your bonnet about that girl. We're checking out Crystal's background in Edinburgh. She philandered around a lot, usually with married men. Could have been someone from her past. Just leave it alone.'

Hamish put down the phone, feeling frustrated. And yet Mary Hendry had been so sure that Felicity was innocent.

He wondered what Priscilla would make of this case, and then wished in the same moment he hadn't thought of her. Still, he had dinner with Elspeth to look forward to. He felt suddenly weary. He would go about his usual chores, walk Lugs, talk to the villagers, and let Strathbane get on with it.

On Sunday, Hamish found he was looking forward to his dinner with Elspeth even more. He could not quite figure her out and that was intriguing, and it would take his mind off his failure to impress Carson.

He took Lugs out for a good long walk first. Any time the dog sensed Hamish was going out somewhere for food and leaving him behind, he sulked like a child and looked miserable, so Hamish wanted to leave a tired and well-fed dog behind.

The weather was still dry and chilly. The old-fashioned street lamps along the waterfront cast a greenish glow, and above them in the dark sky stretched the Milky Way.

He met Angela walking home from the church. She was wearing a checked shirt, jeans, and cowboy boots. 'Line dancing?' asked Hamish.

'Yes, I thought I might as well join in. It's all Mrs Wellington's idea. She's bought herself a Stetson.'

Hamish laughed. 'That must be a sight worth seeing.'

'It gets better. The Currie sisters have joined. To see them dancing to "All My Exes Live in Texas" is a sight to behold. How's the case going?'

'It's not. Not for me that is. I got this fixed idea that Felicity Pearson was the culprit. Suggested they do a thorough search of her flat.'

'What were they supposed to find?'

'Hairpins.'

'What?'

'You see, it looks as if someone stunned Crystal when she was outside her car, combed out her hair to get bits of heather out of it, for she was wearing her hair up when she left her flat in the morning. Now, there wasn't a hairpin in that car. So I thought it was a chance

121

that Felicity had put them in her pocket and got rid of them at home. They didn't find a single hairpin, which I think is odd, because Felicity used them herself. But the television station came down like the wrath of God on police headquarters, screaming harassment, so I'm off the case.'

'But didn't they think it peculiar when they didn't find even one pin? I wore my hair up last summer and the house is still full of pins. They seem to get everywhere. What did she say when they asked her why she didn't even have any pins of her own?'

'They didn't. I wanted to put in a report suggesting they do just that but Jimmy Anderson told me to forget about it.'

'Not like you to drop a case whether or not you've been told to, Hamish.'

'Well, I'll leave it for a bit. I've got a nagging feeling now that I made a mistake, thinking it was her. I'll wait until the police do some more ferreting around in Crystal's background and then winkle the information out of Jimmy. I'd best be going, Angela. I've got a date.'

'With Elspeth Grant?'

'Yes, how did you guess?'

'She's been seen calling at the police station. Attractive girl. Take your mind off . . .' Angela bit her lip. 'Bye, Hamish.'

He stood for a moment watching her hurrying away along the waterfront through the round pools of light cast by the lamps. 'The trouble with living in a village, Lugs,' said Hamish, 'is that everyone knows your business. 'Member that tourist from New York? He said we were lucky up here because in the cities, you could live next door to someone and never know him. He didn't know how lucky *he* was.'

Hamish decided as he entered the restaurant and saw Elspeth sitting there that she could not be romantically interested in him. She was wearing a washed-out black T-shirt under a droopy wool cardigan and a shapeless skirt. He had put on his one good suit, striped shirt and silk tie, and his newly washed red hair gleamed in the candlelight.

'You look very grand,' said Elspeth. 'You'll need to forgive my outfit. I came straight here from the sheep sales.'

'Prices bad?'

'Really rotten. But there's one mystery. Johnny Liddesdale is getting rid of all his sheep. Practically giving them away. The other crofters told him to hold on, that the government was coming up with subsidies, but he said he was going into the carpentry business full-time and couldn't be bothered with sheep.'

'He makes good furniture. Probably found a buyer,' said Hamish, and then, anxious to change the subject, he went on. 'Why is it always you that's out reporting? I thought there was that reporter.'

'Malcolm Dinsdale? He didn't last long. Sam sent him to a rehab in Inverness to dry out. It's only a weekly paper, so Sam and I can do all the work ourselves with the help of freelancers.'

'You seem to have long hours.'

'I enjoy it. It's a hobby as well as work. So how's the case going?'

'It isn't,' said Hamish, and told her the latest.

'This feeling you've got about Felicity. Have you had these hunches before?'

'Sometimes. But never as strong as this.'

'And are you always right?'

'Most of the time.'

'And are you still sure it's her?`

'Frankly, no. I'll bide my time for a bit and see if something comes up.'

She looked steadily at him. 'Like another murder?'

Hamish gazed at her, startled. He opened his mouth to speak, but Willie Lamont bustled up with menus and stood over them until they had made their choice.

When he had gone, Hamish said, 'You're making me feel uneasy. Why did you say another murder?'

'Just a feeling. I sometimes think that for every one who commits a murder, there's at least one person who knows something about it, and that person could be in danger.'

'Your psychic powers tell you?'

'My common sense tells me.'

'Don't you get lonely up here?'

'Away from the bright lights of Inverness? No, I'm too busy to be lonely.'

'What about boyfriends?'

'None . . . yet.'

'Don't tell me you never had any!'

'A few, in the Inverness days. I was even engaged to be married.'

'So what happened?'

'We went away on holiday together and he got on my nerves. He was keen on diets. We were in Italy, in Tuscany, and the food was marvellous, but each restaurant meal was a nightmare. I had to wait while he combed through the menu for what he considered non-toxic food. It was when he started ordering the same lousy food for both of us without consulting me that I told him it was off.'

'Women!' said Hamish bitterly.

She looked at him in surprise. 'You mean I should have married someone like that?'

Hamish blushed and fiddled with his fork. 'Well, no, not exactly.'

'You should not inflict your own bad experience of women on me, Hamish Macbeth.'

Fortunately for Hamish, at that moment their food arrived.

'So what's in my stars tomorrow?' asked Hamish.

'I forget,' said Elspeth.

'Now why do I get the feeling you haven't forgotten at all?'

'I don't write Libra horoscopes just for you.'

'We'll see,' said Hamish. 'What's your star sign?'

'Gemini.'

'Is Angus upset at not getting the job?'

'Yes, he came to the office and told Sam I was a charlatan.'

'He can be nasty.'

'So I gather. To get back to the murder and forgetting Felicity for the moment, you must be wishing it turns out to be someone in Strathbane.'

'Why?' asked Hamish.

'You wouldn't want it to be someone in the village. Who else could have done it?'

'This is all off the record,' said Hamish sharply. 'I don't want to see everything I've said to you published in the *Highland Times*.'

'I promise it's all off the record.' Elspeth smiled at him. 'It's a weekly paper, Hamish, not a big national. By the time I get it in the paper a week on Monday, all sorts of other things could have happened. Someone could have been arrested. So who else do you think could have done it?'

'It would be easier for me to make guesses if I'd spent more time at the television station. She'd been having affairs with a couple of bosses, but somehow I can't think it's one of them. They both look like serial philanderers.'

'But what about the wives?' asked Elspeth. 'Maybe one of them philandered just that once too often and one of the wives cracked.'

'What I'm really worried about is that it might turn out to be the sort of person who won't get found out.'

'And what sort of person is that?'

'Oh, just someone who works in the canteen or one of the cleaners, some psycho she snarled at who suddenly decided in a fit of madness to get rid of her.'

'You know what I think?' said Elspeth. 'I think you've all been forgetting that behind-the-lace-curtains programme.'

'No, I got the list from the other researcher, Amy Cornwall, and checked them all out.'

'I can't think a bully like Crystal would use just the one researcher and leave the other in peace.'

'She didn't. She had Amy working on one programme and Felicity on the other.'

'But the police programme was a last-minute decision,' said Elspeth eagerly. 'What if Felicity had a list as well?'

Hamish sat back in his chair and looked at her in surprise. 'You may have something there,' he said slowly. 'Och, if I suggest anything to do with Felicity again, they'll tell me to get lost.'

'You forget, there's me!' said Elspeth triumphantly. 'I'll ask her. And I'll be sympathetic about the police searching her flat and I can ask her about the missing hairpins.'

'You could do that,' said Hamish cautiously. 'But remember, it could be dangerous.'

After the meal, Hamish walked her to her flat. She turned in the doorway and smiled up at him. 'Thank you for a lovely evening, Hamish.'

Her eyes glowed like starlight. He suddenly wanted to kiss her but stopped himself in time. He was fed up making mistakes where women were concerned.

The following morning, he opened his copy of the *Highland Times* and turned to the horoscope. Libra. He read: 'You are a shrewd and clever man when it comes to business, but you fail in romance because you never see what is under your nose. This will be a quiet week for you, but you will have a headache on Saturday due to an over-indulgence of whisky the night before.'

He looked at Gemini and read: 'You are chasing after a man who is on the rebound. It's a waste of time. It is probably no use telling you this, because Geminis are impetuous and will not listen to reason in matters of the heart. This will be a busy week. Do not kill your sheep or sell them cheap. Government subsidies will soon be coming if you can hang on.'

Am I the man on the rebound, thought Hamish, or am I just like everyone else and think Elspeth's daft predictions apply to me?

The phone rang. It was Ian Chisholm to say that the machines in his launderette had been broken into and all the money taken. Hamish headed for Braikie. At least it was something to take his mind off murder.

On Friday, Bessie Macpherson, a girl in the village, was getting married, which meant the whole village was invited. Hamish had heard nothing from headquarters. He had heard nothing from Elspeth. So he put on his good suit in the afternoon and headed for the church.

He met Elspeth and Sam on the church steps. Sam was holding a camera. Hamish drew Elspeth aside. 'Did you find out anything from Felicity?'

'Not much. I'll tell you after. Here comes the bride. You'd better take your place in the church.'

Hamish sat at the back of the church with the other villagers. Bessie came up the aisle on the arm of her father. She was a plump little girl of no great beauty, but she looked so excited and happy in her white gown and veil that she seemed to carry up the aisle with her a sort of radiance. Her groom in full Highland dress stood at the altar.

As women around him began to sob, Hamish's mind drifted back to the murder case. Ian's problem hadn't taken up much time. Two schoolboys had been seen late at night, fiddling with the machines. He had arranged with the parents that the stolen money be returned to Ian and that they wash the launderette floor twice a week. He had not charged them, having a reluctance to condemn two schoolboys to the juvenile court for a first offence.

When the service was over and everyone filed out after the bride and groom to walk the short distance to the church hall where the reception was to be held, he searched for Elspeth and then saw her. Sam was taking photographs and Elspeth was noting down names. A local paper did its best to get in as many photographs and names as possible, knowing that it would boost sales.

There was a buffet meal. Hamish queued up with the rest and helped himself to a plate of food. May as well eat something until Elspeth was free.

Then there were speeches and then it was announced that the Lochdubh line-dancing group would entertain them. Hamish stared as the men and women emerged headed by the massive figure of the minister's wife, Mrs Wellington, wearing a fringed skirt, checked shirt and a large white Stetson. Then came the Currie sisters, in identical cowboy boots, shirts and jeans. And then, leading the rest, came the diminutive figure of fisherman Archie Maclean, with two toy six-shooters at his belt.

'Yee-haw!' yelled Mrs Wellington as the music started. Hamish could feel laughter bubbling up inside him. He stumbled to his feet and fled out of the hall and rolled on the grass outside, shrieking with laughter.

'Hamish, Hamish,' chided a voice above his head. He sat up and looked into the laughing face of Elspeth.

'I couldnae believe it,' said Hamish, taking out a handkerchief and mopping his eyes. 'Do they know what they look like?'

'They all think they look like real western dudes, even the Currie sisters. It's the best fun they've had in ages.'

Hamish stood up. 'I can't go in there again until they've finished or I'll disgrace myself. So what about Felicity?'

'Well, I interviewed her and then took a few photographs. She said she had only been working on the police programme, not the other.'

They walked down to the waterfront and leaned on the wall. A pale sun was glinting on the waters of the loch.

'And what about the hairpins?'

'That bit was tricky. She's now got her hair cut short. But she said that when the police arrived, any hairpins she had were in her head.'

'Damn, and they wouldn't even think to ask her to take her hair down to look for blonde pins. And she's got thick hair. She could have buried them in there somewhere.'

'Hamish, you're getting carried away. If she committed the murder, she'd have taken out those pins and thrown them in the heather, anywhere between Strathbane and Lochdubh. But I've got one little thing for you.'

'What's that?

'The minute I brought up that business about the hairpins, she went off me. Up till then, she was delighted to be interviewed. But immediately she had explained about the pins in her hair, she said sharply that she was busy and terminated the interview. Up till then, she could have talked all day, she was so happy to be in the limelight.'

'I'm going to put in a report,' said Hamish. 'I don't care what Jimmy says.'

'You do that. But it's a wedding. I've finished my work. We should go and have fun. Will you dance with me?'

'Of course. Is the line dancing over?' He cocked his head to one side. He could hear an accordion band playing the strains of an eightsome reel. 'Yes, the dancing's started. Come on.'

Earlier that day, Felicity Pearson received a phone call. She listened to the voice in utter amazement, her heart beating hard. Then she said, 'Yes, I'll meet you. Where?' She scribbled something down on a pad.

When she rang off, her eyes were glowing. Success was coming her way at last. Rory had said they had decided to give her a break as a presenter. They were going to start a new series of *Highland Life*, and as some of the research on the lace-curtain programme had been done, they would start with that. The voice on the phone had promised to talk about something dramatic, and if Felicity got that person in front of the camera, it would mean she would be on national television.

She debated whether to tell Rory and then decided against it. What if this person did not turn up?

Hamish checked that he had remembered to lock up his hens for the night and refused Lugs food, for the dog had already been fed before he went out. He felt restless. Did Elspeth fancy him? Should he bother? He walked over to the waterfront wall and looked down the loch. He could feel a puff of dampness in the light wind against his cheek. He looked up at the sky. A thin veil of black cloud was crawling in from the west to cover the stars.

Hamish shivered suddenly. There was something in this murder case that he had missed. He had a bad feeling.

Then he laughed. An evening with Elspeth was making him superstitious and fanciful.

He turned and walked back to the police station.

Felicity Pearson parked her car outside what used to be Dock Number Two, edged her way between the high rusty gates, now never closed, and walked towards where she had to meet her informer.

Empty warehouses stood behind her as she walked towards the sea, mute testimony to the days when Strathbane had been a prosperous port. The wind had sprung up, and somewhere a loose bit of metal clanged with the monotonous regularity of a tolling church bell. The sea heaved in great oily swells, covered in filthy debris.

She had not heard anyone approaching and jumped nervously when a voice said, 'There you are.'

Felicity swung round eagerly. 'What have you got for me?'

'This.'

The shotgun blast at close range blew a hole in Felicity's chest. Seagulls wheeled and screamed, and then there was silence again apart from the sound of the clanging metal and the sound of brisk, retreating footsteps.

Chapter Eight

As some divinely gifted man,
Whose life in low estate began
And on some simple village green:

Who breaks his birth's invidious bar,
And grasps the skirts of happy chance,
And breasts the blows of circumstance,
and grapples with his evil star.
— Alfred, Lord Tennyson

No one from police headquarters phoned Hamish to tell him of Felicity's murder. He was cruising out of Lochdubh the next morning to check that Ian Chisholm was all right and had experienced no more trouble when he heard it on his police radio.

At first he simply couldn't believe it. Then he swung the Land Rover round and headed for Strathbane.

He checked at police headquarters and learned that Jimmy Anderson was with Carson down at Dock Number Two.

When he arrived at the dock, an ambulance was just leaving. Forensic men in white suits were combing the dock for clues. Carson, followed by Jimmy, other detectives and policemen, came walking towards him. Carson scowled when he saw Hamish.

'What are you doing here, Officer?' he demanded.

'I heard about it on the radio. What happened?' asked Hamish.

'Firstly, you will address me as "sir" at all times. Secondly, your place is back on your beat, and I suggest you get there before I suspend you for dereliction of duty. If it had not been for your mad ideas, sending us off in the wrong direction, then that woman might still be alive. Get along with you.'

If I were a dog, thought Hamish, my tail would be between my legs. He meekly went off. He felt he deserved the reprimand. What on earth had caused him to focus all his attention on Felicity?

He drove round by police headquarters, hoping to see a friendly face, and then saw the policewoman who had been present at the television station when Carson was interviewing everybody. He screeched to a halt and waved her over.

'I'm sorry to bother you,' said Hamish awkwardly, 'but I wondered if you could fill me in on this murder.'

She looked beyond him down the long street

and saw Carson's official car turning the corner. 'I can't now,' she whispered. 'I'll drive over to Lochdubh this evening and tell you.'

'Grand. What's your name?'

'Maggie. Maggie Fleming. And you're the infamous Hamish Macbeth. Get along with you.'

'Eight o'clock,' said Hamish hurriedly. 'At the Italian restaurant. Dinner's on me.'

'I'll get away when I can. Off with you. Here they come.'

Hamish sped off.

His mind was full of questions. He hoped that when he got back to the police station Jimmy would phone, but thought it unlikely. He knew he had put Jimmy's nose out of joint before with the hairpin business.

All he could do was wait anxiously for the evening and hope to learn as much as he could from Maggie Fleming.

Hamish had not really looked at Maggie properly and was surprised to see how attractive she really was.

She was not in uniform and was wearing a soft creamy satin blouse with a short skirt and high heels. She had a mop of glossy black curls, bright blue eyes and a generous mouth.

'This is very good of you,' said Hamish.

'I get tired of being treated like some secretary,' said Maggie. 'Just because I'm a woman,

I get to make the coffee, or, as you noticed, arrange the chairs.'

'Strathbane is a chauvinist part of the world. Let's order first and then you can tell me about it.'

Willie Lamont took their order. 'Here again?' he said to Hamish. 'You're getting to be a right caravanserai.'

'Casanova, Willie.'

'Aye, that's the man.'

'Willie, do me a favour, take our orders and crawl off.'

'It's all murder and mayhem,' said Willie, shaking his head. 'Someone's running about the Highlands, going bare sark.'

'Berserk, Willie. Just please . . .'

But Willie's eyes had fallen on a silver bracelet that Maggie was wearing. 'That bracelet of yours is getting a bit dim, miss,' he said. 'Now, there is nothing like old-fashioned rouge and a toothbrush for –'

'*Willie*,' Hamish roared.

'Oh, all right,' said Willie sulkily. He took their orders and departed.

'You'd never think that man used to be a policeman,' said Hamish.

'So why's he working in a restaurant?'

'He married a relative of the owner and fell in love with cleaning at the same time. Never mind him. What about this murder?'

'She was found on the dock this morning,' said Maggie. 'She had been killed by a close-range shotgun blast to the chest. A preliminary investigation suggests that she had been killed sometime during the night. She didn't tell anyone she was going down there. She was all excited because they were resuscitating *Highland Life* and she was to be a presenter, in front of the cameras this time instead of behind.'

'I gather she was going to start with that behind-the-lace-curtains programme, digging up old scandals?'

'Yes.'

Hamish thought about the bank manager's wife and that poor woman over in Cnothan.

'You know,' said Hamish, 'I can't figure out why I became so convinced that it was Felicity who murdered Crystal, despite her alibi.'

'Funnily enough,' said Maggie, 'I was thinking along the same lines. Good heavens, there's an odd-looking dog with big ears staring in the window at us.'

Willie had placed them at a window table, and sure enough, there was Lugs, standing upon his hind legs, paws resting on the windowsill, glaring at them accusingly.

'Ignore him,' said Hamish. 'It's my dog.'

'But how did he get out?'

'I got tired walking him. He always wants to go out. I figured this is a quiet village, he doesn't bite anyone or chase sheep, so I left the door open.'

'Your computer could be stolen.'

'Not in this village, and Lugs is a good watchdog.'

'Is that his name? Lugs? Scottish for "ears". But how can he be a good watchdog if he's wandering about the place?'

Hamish looked back at the window, but Lugs had gone. 'Never mind my dog. Tell me about Felicity.'

'I went into her background before, after Crystal's murder. She's from Glasgow. Respectable middle-class background. No scandals. No lovers. Parents dead. Only child. Went to Glasgow University and then began work at the BBC in Glasgow as a researcher. Applied for a job on Strathbane Television. Rory MacBain originally thought ... Hamish, do you think this window table a good idea? Now there's some odd girl in a fishing hat staring at us.'

Elspeth Grant looked in the window at Hamish and then slowly moved away.

Hamish found himself blushing with embarrassment while telling himself furiously that he had nothing to be embarrassed about. 'Go on, what were you saying?'

'Oh, about Rory MacBain. Yes, he liked the idea of a Gaelic show. Give the station a bit of tone. At first it went quite well. People were all saying it was a shame the Gaelic language should be allowed to die, and then gradually the novelty wore off and ratings slumped. It was well known Crystal gave Felicity a hard time. That other researcher, Amy Cornwall, she's tougher, and she said she felt Crystal wouldn't last, but she told me that one day she found Felicity in tears.'

'I would like to talk to Amy Cornwall,' said Hamish. 'But if Carson found out, I'd be in more trouble than I am already. He blames me for Felicity's death.'

'That's ridiculous.'

'He feels that my reports suggesting she did it took the focus away from the real killer.'

'But they haven't a clue who the real killer is!'

'Still, I can see his point.'

Their food arrived and throughout the meal they talked over the various points of the case.

Then Maggie said reluctantly that she had better be getting home. Hamish walked her outside. A thin rain was beginning to fall. Raindrops sparkled in her black hair.

She smiled up at him.

Then Elspeth appeared to materialize from nowhere and linked her arm in Hamish's. 'I'll walk you home, darling,' she said. 'I've got news for you.'

Maggie's face took on a closed look. 'Good night, Hamish,' she said abruptly.

When she had driven off, Hamish said angrily, 'What was all that "darling" business about?'

'Don't you want to hear my news?'

'All right,' said Hamish, but he was still angry with her. Lugs came panting up and walked on his other side. Hamish felt he was being firmly escorted by two jailers.

In the police station kitchen, he slammed a mug of coffee down in front of her.

He sat down opposite and stared at her, his hazel eyes hard. 'So what?'

'Amy Cornwall,' she said.

'What about her?'

'I talked to her. She said they hadn't got around yet to contacting people about the lace-curtains programme. I asked her if, on the one that Crystal was supposed to present, Felicity had been working on any of it. She said no.'

'I knew that already,' snapped Hamish, still angry with her.

'Wait. She said, however, that Felicity crawled to Crystal quite dreadfully and was always trying to please her, and Felicity put expenses in for a trip to Bonar Bridge.'

'Why there?'

'I checked back to see if there were any scandals associated with Bonar Bridge. There was one. Might have been it. A woman called Jessie Gordon had two babies that died of cot death. After the second one died, there was a big investigation.'

'I'll look into it. Thanks. I'll need to go over the others again, too.'

'Did you know that the bank manager's wife was once done for shoplifting?'

'Yes, and I wish to God it could be kept

quiet. She was a kleptomaniac and hasn't been in trouble since. If it all flares up again, it might ruin her marriage.'

'So how do you keep it quiet?'

'People round here don't know about it, so keep your mouth shut. If only I could find the murderer, that would be an end of her troubles.'

'Who was that girl you were with?' asked Elspeth.

'Just a friend and none of your business,' said Hamish stonily.

She looked at him thoughtfully. Lugs came up to her and rested his front paws on her knees, and Elspeth scratched his rough head. Hamish was suddenly reminded of his previous dog, Towser, of how when Priscilla had sat in this very kitchen discussing some case or other the dog would place his paws on her knees, just as Lugs was doing to Elspeth. A stab of pain shot through him.

'Oh, I see,' said Elspeth quietly.

'See what?'

'See that I must be on my way,' said Elspeth sadly. 'Good night, Officer.'

The following day was fine and unusually mild for the time of year. Hamish put Lugs's bowl of food and bowl of water out in the garden. 'I'll leave you to look after yourself,' he said. 'Come to think of it, I'd better lock up

143

the police station in case some stranger pinches my computer.'

Lugs watched Hamish get into the Land Rover. For the first time, the dog did not whine or bark.

Getting used to the new arrangement, thought Hamish. I should have let him out on his own before.

He drove over to Bonar Bridge and checked at the police station, where he learned that Jessie Gordon still lived in the town, on the council estate. Armed with the address, he went to her home.

A powerful-looking slattern of a woman answered the door. 'Mrs Gordon?'

'Yes.'

'Can I be having a word with you?'

'Come ben.'

He followed her into a messy living room. The homes of the poor, thought Hamish, always seemed to be damp and redolent of the smell of baked beans and urine. A three-piece suite, battered and stained, sagged in front of the television set, which was showing a commercial. The sound was off. The ornaments on the mantelpiece, dolls and cheap figurines, were dusty and dirty. One of the window-panes was cracked and had been clumsily repaired with brown masking tape.

'So what's this about?' said Jessie.

'Did you have a visit from Felicity Pearson of Strathbane Television?'

She shrugged. 'No point in denying it. All the neighbours could tell you. I threw her out, and I mean, I threw her out.'

'Was it about the death of your children?'

'Aye.' She sat down. Hamish removed his hat and sat down opposite her.

She pushed a lank lock of hair away from her forehead.

'Tell me about it,' said Hamish.

'She was going to rake up the whole business again. I couldnae believe it. It waud all come back, the gossip, the stares. I couldnae even mourn my ain bairns because o' the whispers and scandal.' Her accent thickened in her distress. 'My husband left me because o' it.'

Hamish caught a whiff of stale booze coming from her. Her eyes were red and bloodshot. 'I told her I was having naethin' to do with it. She said they would stand outside the house and do a commentary anyway. I was that upset, I was crying.'

'Did you attack her?'

'I said I'd kill her. It was then I saw she was enjoying hersel' and her wee bit o' power and I snapped. I got her by the scruff o' the neck and marched her out the door and shoved her on her face in the garden.'

'Do you have children?'

'Do I have children?' she screeched. 'Man, I couldnae bear to go through that again and got a hysterectomy. Now she's dead and I'm not one wee bit surprised. Muckraking, nasty bitch!'

145

'I think you'll understand when I ask you where you were on Sunday night.'

'I was right here with the telly on. I'm getting a bit deaf so it's loud. The walls are thin. The neighbours would have heard it.'

'But did anyone see you?'

'Them down at the grocery store. I went down to buy whisky at nine o'clock.'

'Do you have a car?'

'Do I hell.'

'That will be all,' said Hamish. He rose.

She rose, too, and grabbed his arm. Her grip was powerful. 'Will it all come out again?'

'I hope to God it doesn't,' said Hamish.

He left her and checked with the neighbours. They had heard her television set blaring. They said they had complained several times to her about the noise.

He then checked at the grocery store, where they confirmed that Mrs Gordon had bought a bottle of whisky. Hamish reflected that it was amazing how folks could buy drink around the clock in Scotland these days. The woman in the grocery store added that Jessie had been so drunk it was a wonder she could stand.

He was just driving out of Bonar Bridge when he saw an elderly figure in shorts and hiking boots striding out along the road. He recognized Professor Tully from Felicity's Gaelic programme and pulled to the side of the road and got down.

'Professor Tully!' he called.

The professor walked up to meet him. 'Bad business about that Pearson woman,' he said.

'You were on that programme she produced,' said Hamish. 'What was your impression of her?'

'Didn't much notice,' said the professor. 'I mean, all these television people seem alike to me. I miss the show. I thought we were doing well. There was me and Grace Witherington and Henry Thomson. We're all fine Gaelic speakers and all we had to do was to chat about things in the Highlands – sheep farming, about a plan to teach Gaelic in schools, stuff like that. I used to forget there was a camera on me. We were all friends and we would chat away as if we were at our own fireside.'

'Have you an address for Grace Witherington?'

'She lives in Strathbane. Let me see, it's one of those house conversions on the Inverness road.'

'Not the old manse where Felicity lived?'

'Come to think of it, that's the one.'

'I'll try her.'

'If there's any news of the show going back on the air, will you let me know?'

'Certainly.'

'I got some good shirts out of that show.'

'Shirts?'

'Well, one time, I'd got egg on my shirt collar and they said I could have a shirt from the wardrobe department, and then they said I

147

was to keep it. So after that, a few times, I'd deliberately spill something on my shirt so I could get a new one.'

Hamish waved goodbye. He decided to check on Lugs before going on to Strathbane. That was the trouble with dogs. They were like children. Cats you could leave to look after themselves.

When he got back to the police station, Lugs was asleep. His food bowl had not been touched.

He roused himself sleepily and stared at Hamish with a glazed look. 'I know it's dog food,' said Hamish. 'But you've got to eat it. I can't be cooking for you all the time.'

Lugs licked his hand and wagged his tail. Hamish looked at him doubtfully. But the animal looked healthy enough. Probably tired himself out chasing rabbits, thought Hamish.

He changed out of his police uniform and drove to Strathbane, but parked some distance from the Inverness road and started to walk. As he turned the corner into the road, he could see a mobile police van set up outside the house. If he were spotted, then Carson would hear about it and Carson would wonder what he was doing in Strathbane.

He knew from television what Grace Witherington looked like. He decided to lurk at the end of the road and see if he could spot her.

After an hour of diving behind a pillar box when he saw a police car driving past, he was about to give up when he saw Grace approaching, carrying a shopping bag. Like the professor, she was elderly, white-haired, and looked bright and intelligent.

He introduced himself and showed her his identification. 'I just wanted to have a word with you about Felicity Pearson.'

'Come to the house and we'll have some coffee.'

'I can't do that. I'll be honest with you. Strathbane is not on my beat, and I might be in trouble with my boss if I'm spotted, but I got talking to Professor Tully over at Bonar Bridge. He really didn't notice Felicity at all, but I thought a lady like yourself would have a sharper eye.'

She studied him for a moment and then said, 'There's a little café around the corner. We can go there.'

They walked together into the café. Hamish ordered coffees and found them a quiet table in a corner. 'You see,' he began, 'living in the same flats, you must have seen more of her than most.'

'I did at one time. She seemed a harmless, humourless girl. Then when the show was axed, she took to calling on me at all hours, whimpering and complaining. At first I was sorry for her, and sorry for myself, too, for the extra money had come in handy, although I get a bit from teaching Gaelic at night classes. But I value my privacy, and I got tired of her

149

turning up on my doorstep. She was completely self-absorbed and there was a mean and spiteful streak in her. Until she was murdered, I was sure she had killed that French woman.'

'Any proof?'

'No, I would have gone to the police right away if there had been. It was just a feeling. I thought she was paranoiac on the subject of Crystal.'

'Did you see any of the television people visiting her?'

'Rory MacBain used to call on her a few times.'

Hamish's eyes sharpened. 'At night?'

She looked amused. 'I see what you're getting at. Mostly in the evenings, and he would stay for a couple of hours.'

'Did she say anything about having an affair with him?'

'I asked her. She said pompously that she was still an important figure and that Rory liked to discuss ideas with her.'

'And did you tell the police this?'

'No, they didn't ask. I didn't volunteer the information. The reason I saw him was he was quite often arriving when I was leaving for my classes and leaving when I got back. I felt that to suggest to the police that they might have been having an affair might make me seem like an old gossip.'

'I think I should tell them this,' said Hamish.

150

'Do what you like, but how are you going to tell them if you're not supposed to be in Strathbane?'

Hamish looked at her in dismay.

'Look, tell them you met the professor by chance and phoned me. That should cover it.'

Hamish thanked her and drove back to Lochdubh. Lugs was still lying asleep beside his untouched food bowl.

That's it, he thought. The report can wait. Lugs is going to the vet. He loaded the sleepy, grumbling dog into the Land Rover and drove to the vet's house.

'I'm finished for the day,' said the vet crossly.

'Please,' said Hamish. 'I'm right busy with a case just now. I'm worried about Lugs. He sleeps the whole time and won't touch his food.'

'I'll tell you what the problem is,' said the vet with a smile. 'That there dog is stuffed.'

'Stuffed?'

'A severe case of pasta, ham and mozzarella cheese.'

'What?'

'It's the talk of the village. He's spent all day strolling along to the back door of the Italian restaurant where your friend Willie feeds him large plates of food. You'd better stop the animal or he'll die of obesity.'

'Thanks,' said Hamish, feeling foolish. He carried Lugs back to the Land Rover. 'I'll deal with Willie later,' he said. 'But first, I'd better do that report.'

Chapter Nine

I will make you brooches and toys for your
 delight
Of bird-song at morning and star-shine at
 night.
I will make a palace fit for you and me
Of green days in forests and blue days at sea.
I will make my kitchen, and you shall keep
 your room,
Where white flows the river and bright blows
 the broom.

— R. L. Stevenson

Carson read Hamish's report with great irritation. He had put Hamish down as some fool whose previous exploits in police work had been much exaggerated. But once again the village constable had come up with something important that they had missed.

He decided it was time he had a face-to-face talk with Hamish.

Unfortunately for Hamish, he was strolling back to the station in an old shirt and stained trousers, swinging an empty feed pail, when Carson arrived.

'Not in uniform, Officer?' demanded Carson.

'Well, no,' said Hamish with a blinding smile, a sure sign he was about to lie. 'It is my day off.'

'In the middle of an investigation of two murders, all leave has been cancelled.'

'Is that a fact?' Hamish put the pail down. 'And here's me thinking I had orders to stay off the case.'

Carson looked at him with irritation. Hamish was tall with a friendly face and hazel eyes fringed with thick eyelashes. His red hair gleamed like a beacon. Carson thought, illogically, that no decent policeman should have hair that fiery colour.

'I got your report, Macbeth,' said Carson. 'I would like to discuss it with you.'

'I've got some coffee keeping warm on the stove, sir,' said Hamish. 'We'll go in.'

Carson followed him into the kitchen. He sat down and looked about him. There was a smell of damp dog and woodsmoke. The table was covered with a red and white checked cloth. White painted shelves held glasses and crockery. There was a wood-burning stove sending out a pleasant heat. An old round clock tick-tocked on the wall near the door. Through the window, he could see sheep cropping the grass on a field at the back.

'Your sheep?' he asked.

154

'Aye,' said Hamish.

'Won't be bringing you anything these days.'

'That's the pity o' it.' Hamish filled two mugs with coffee and placed them on the table. Then he took a bottle of milk out of the fridge, emptied some of it into a jug, and then placed the jug along with a bowl of sugar on the table.

'The longer I keep those sheep,' said Hamish, 'the more they take on individual personalities. I am afraid they will stay out there until they die of old age.'

'You do not strike me as a sentimental man.'

'I'm a practical one, sir. No use slaughtering the beasts for a few pennies.'

Hamish sat down opposite Carson. Carson frowned. He should have asked permission to sit down, but then it was the man's own house, and Carson had come for a friendly chat.

'Can you tell me,' he began, 'why Grace Witherington, with a mobile police van outside her house, should choose to phone you with this information?'

'I had been chatting to Professor Tully. He was on that Gaelic programme with her. She said she felt more comfortable talking to me about it, because the police hadn't asked her, and she felt a bit uncomfortable relating gossip.'

'MacBain should have told us if he was having an affair with the girl.'

'What is Mrs MacBain like?' asked Hamish curiously.

'I went to see her myself. Hard, blonde, thin, fortyish. I didn't mention his affair with Crystal, or rather his one-night stand. She said she had phoned him at the television station on the day of Crystal's murder and they had a chat. There certainly is a record of that call on their phone bill, but then she could just have spoken to the switchboard. The girl who was on duty can't remember anything.'

'I thought all these television people had direct lines these days,' said Hamish.

'Not in Strathbane, they don't. Now, I would like to go over the first case with you from the beginning. I was angry with you for fixing your mind, it appeared, solely on Felicity Pearson. I was inclined to dismiss you as a fool. What made you so sure it was her?'

'It seemed so likely,' said Hamish. He stood up and opened the lid of the stove, shovelled in some peat, and sat down again. The clock ticked lazily, the coffee was delicious, and from outside the window came the faint bleating of sheep and cackle of hens. Carson began to have an idea why this odd policeman had either shunned promotion or sabotaged promotion. 'She had lost so much that was dear to her,' said Hamish. 'Rory would be running after Crystal. If he was having an affair with Felicity then that must have made her even more bitter.'

'But you did not know he was having an affair with her when you put in your initial reports.'

'True. Then it was because I sensed she was furious over losing her show. I was in her flat. All those photographs. A sort of shrine to Felicity Pearson. People always assume it's the beautiful who are vain.'

Suddenly in Hamish's head, he heard Professor Tully mourning the loss of his television job because it would mean no more free shirts.

Carson looked in sudden irritation at Hamish. The man was sitting as if he had been struck by lightning. His eyes were glazed and his mouth was open. Inbreeding, thought Carson sourly. Must be a lot of it in these villages.

'Wardrobe,' said Hamish faintly.

'What?' Carson half-rose to leave. Hamish Macbeth was obviously subject to mental seizures of some kind. Better humour him.

'I'm sure you do have a wardrobe. We all have a wardrobe.'

'No, no.' Hamish's eyes were sharp and clear again. 'The television station wardrobe.'

'What about it?'

'The hat and glasses that the person driving the BMW was wearing. Did anyone check the station's wardrobe department?'

'No,' said Carson. He looked at him in amazement. Then he said, 'Let's go. Now!'

'Aye,' said Hamish, heading for the door.

'Put on your uniform first. You look a disgrace.'

Hamish meekly went off to the bedroom to

put on his uniform. Carson helped himself to another mug of coffee. How was it that this village policeman could hit on things that the whole force had missed? A blinding flash of the obvious, he thought sourly. He should have thought of it himself.

A small, neat man called Derry Hunt was in charge of the wardrobe department. 'Yes,' he said. 'We've always got stuff on hand, even suits. Now Professor Tully, he turned up in a suit that strobed dreadfully, so we had to supply him with one. He wanted to keep it, but I said an odd shirt or two was all right, but a suit, no.'

'What we're looking for,' said Carson, 'is a floppy brown hat and dark glasses.'

'I might have those among the odds and ends.'

'Do you do all the wardrobe work yourself?' asked Hamish.

'No, I've got a wee girl who works for me. Does the ironing and mending, things like that.'

'Do you just hand over the stuff?' asked Hamish. 'Or is it logged somewhere?'

'Of course it's logged.'

'Can we see the records?' asked Carson.

Derry produced a large ledger. 'No computer for me,' he said. 'I wouldn't know how to operate one. Let me see, what day are you looking for?'

'The day Crystal French was murdered. Monday, twenty-eighth August.'

'Or the day before,' put in Hamish.

He ran a long forefinger down the page. 'Here we are. Brown hat, black glasses.'

'Who took them out?' asked Carson.

Hamish found he was holding his breath.

'Felicity Pearson.'

'You're sure?' snapped Carson.

'Yes.'

'And did she return them?' asked Hamish.

'Yes, took them out on the twenty-seventh, back on the twenty-eighth.'

'Have you got them?' asked Hamish.

'I'll go and look, but since they've been returned, they should be here somewhere.'

Carson drew a thin pair of gloves out of his pocket. 'Put these on,' he ordered. 'Lift them very carefully and bring them to us.'

They stood there impatiently, waiting.

Then Derry came back, carefully carrying a large floppy hat with a wide brim and a pair of dark glasses.

'Put them on the desk. Turn the hat up,' said Hamish. 'I want to look inside.'

Derry's gloved hands gently lifted the hat over. To his amusement, Hamish pulled a magnifying glass out of his pocket and studied the inside of the brim.

'You look like Sherlock Holmes,' said Derry, but Hamish was letting out his breath in a long hiss of excitement. He handed the glass to

159

Carson. 'Look there, sir. A hair. A brown hair. How soon can we get it compared to Felicity Pearson's hair?'

'As fast as I can arrange it. Got one of those envelopes?'

Hamish produced a cellophane envelope.

'Tweezers?'

'Forceps, scalpel?' said Derry cheekily, and Carson gave him a withering look.

Hamish found a pair of tweezers. Carson gently lifted the hair and put it in an envelope.

'How soon can we find out if that hair is Felicity's?' asked Hamish.

'I'll make them rush it,' said Carson. He turned to Derry. 'Is there some sort of plastic bag we can put the hat and glasses in?'

Derry went off and came back with a plastic shopping bag. 'Come with me,' said Carson to Hamish. 'We're going back to police headquarters.'

When they arrived and walked up to Carson's office, Jimmy Anderson was coming down the stairs and he stared in surprise at Hamish.

'Do you know what this means?' demanded Carson. 'If that hair should prove to have belonged to Felicity Pearson, then it's ten to one she murdered Crystal. So that will leave us with the unsolved murder of Felicity herself.'

'With your permission, sir,' said Hamish, 'I'd like to have a word with that researcher, Amy Cornwall.'

'Later. Wait until I get this stuff over to the lab.'

When he had finished making the arrangements, Carson called his secretary and asked her to send Jimmy Anderson in.

When Jimmy entered his eyes darted suspiciously to Hamish. With Blair around, there had been little chance of Hamish rising in the ranks, but with Carson, it was another matter.

'I want you to take a uniformed officer,' said Carson, 'and go over to Strathbane Television and bring Rory MacBain back here for questioning, and I don't care how busy he is.'

'Something new come up?' asked Jimmy eagerly.

'I'll fill you in later. Now get MacBain. We'll be using interview room number three.'

When Jimmy had gone, Carson said to Hamish, 'I'll be interviewing MacBain myself. Like to sit in on it?'

'Yes, thank you.'

Carson sighed. 'How many times do I have to tell you?'

'Yes, thank you, *sir*.'

Half an hour later, Rory MacBain, looking flustered and anxious, faced Carson and Hamish in the interviewing room. Policewoman Maggie was manning the tape recorder. She gave Hamish a chilly little smile.

Asked if he wanted a lawyer, Rory said,

161

'Why on earth should I want a lawyer? I haven't done anything. Just get on with it. It's a busy day.'

'We believe you were having an affair with Felicity Pearson,' said Carson.

Rory had not been expecting that, thought Hamish.

'Who says?' Rory tugged at his tie to loosen it.

'You were seen visiting her regularly at her flat.'

'Of course I did. And of course the neighbours saw me. I'm her boss. Television never stops. I called on her some evenings to discuss shows.'

'And yet you made her a researcher?'

Hamish gave an apologetic little cough.

'What is it, Macbeth?' demanded Carson.

'It can easily be cleared up,' said Hamish. 'All Mr MacBain has to do is give us a DNA sample.'

Rory hung his head. Then he raised it and gave a man-to-man beam. 'I may as well come clean. We had a bit of a fling.'

'For how long?' demanded Carson.

'Oh, can't remember. It was off and on. For a few years.'

'A few years!' explained Carson. 'And yet you didn't tell us?'

'I didn't want the wife to know.'

'Have you any idea who she was going to meet down at the docks when she was killed?'

162

'No, I hadn't seen her for a week or two. I mean, I saw her in the office, of course, but I hadn't visited her at her flat. Things had got a bit out of hand. She'd become a bit clinging and possessive.'

'She must have hated Crystal French,' said Hamish.

'She had no reason to. I mean she didn't know about the fling I'd had with Crystal in Edinburgh.'

'I think Crystal, from what I've learned of her,' Hamish went on, 'would be just the person to tell Felicity. She seemed to like upsetting and humiliating people. Besides, from Felicity's point of view, Crystal had pushed her out of a job.'

'But that's ridiculous. Crystal was brought in as a presenter of a new show. Felicity was the producer of a show with falling ratings.'

'And yet you were going to make Felicity a presenter,' said Hamish. 'And when it came to looks, Felicity was not in the same league as Crystal. She had never presented a programme before, as far as I know. Did Felicity threaten to tell your wife? Did she blackmail you?'

'I want a lawyer,' said Rory sullenly.

'And that pretty much put an end to things for the moment,' said Hamish to Elspeth Grant that evening. 'The lawyer came, Rory clammed up, the lawyer said if we weren't charging him with anything we should allow him to leave.'

Elspeth had knocked at the kitchen door half an hour after he had got home.

'Do you never use your living room?' she asked. 'I would like a comfortable chair.'

'Planning on staying, are you?' asked Hamish. 'I'm tired.'

'Just for a little.'

Hamish and Elspeth went into Hamish's living room. He raked out the fire and lit it while Elspeth settled in an easy chair.

'So the hat,' said Elspeth. 'If it turns out to be worn by Felicity, then that makes her the murderer, and that leaves you with another murderer. Any ideas on that?'

'I think it had to do with stuff she was digging up for Crystal's programme, the behind-the-lace-curtains one. The other researcher, Amy Cornwall, was working on it, but I think Felicity found something out. I'll need to check all the alibis of those that Amy interviewed all over again.'

'Do you think it could be that someone saw Felicity, and that someone was blackmailing her? That someone asked her to meet them at the docks or he or she would tell what they saw?'

Hamish sighed. 'It could be. I've an interview with Amy Cornwall tomorrow. I might get something out of it.'

The phone rang in the police office and then the answering machine took over. 'I couldn't make out what that said.' Elspeth looked at him, her eyes suddenly dark. 'I've got a bad feeling, Hamish. I think you should go and listen to that.'

Hamish shook his head. 'There's a boundary dispute between two crofters going on. Probably one of them. I cannae be coping with them this evening.'

Elspeth crossed her legs. She had very long legs in seven-denier black tights. They might as well be two fence posts, she thought, for all the attention Hamish Macbeth was giving them.

'Aren't you going to offer me anything to drink?' she asked.

'Shh!' Hamish held up a hand. 'Listen!'

In the distance came the faint wail of a siren.

They looked at each other in alarm and then Hamish jumped to his feet. 'Something's wrong,' he said.

He rushed out of the police station with Elspeth following and looked up and down the waterfront. Then he saw Dr Brodie with his black bag running towards the bank manager's house.

'Oh, my God, no,' said Hamish.

He ran along the waterfront to intercept the doctor. 'Out of my way, Hamish,' panted Dr Brodie. 'Suicide.'

Hamish followed him into the bank manager's house. Mr McClellan was there, his face ashen. 'Upstairs,' he said. 'Bedroom.'

Dr Brodie sprinted up the stairs, followed by Hamish. Mrs McClellan lay still and cold in the middle of a double bed. An empty bottle of paracetamol tablets lay on its side on the bedside table. Dr Brodie felt for a pulse and found none. Hamish waited and prayed. 'No life,' he said sadly, straightening up from the body. 'I would say she'd been dead a few hours.'

I hate those television people, thought Hamish. The bastards murdered her just as if they'd stuck a knife in her back.

The ambulance men arrived, and the body was carried out past a silent throng of villagers.

Elspeth was waiting with them. 'Hamish?'

'Not now,' he said.

He turned and went back into the house where Dr Brodie was sitting with Mr McClellan. 'I won't be bothering you now,' said Hamish. 'But I'll need a word with you tomorrow.'

The bank manager looked at Hamish with dazed eyes. 'Why?' he said. 'We were happy here.'

Jimmy Anderson came in. 'A word with you outside, Jimmy,' said Hamish.

They walked out. 'Suicide?' asked Jimmy.

'Yes, she took an overdose. It was that busi-

166

ness about shoplifting that must have been preying on her mind. She'd been done for shoplifting years ago and got treatment. Those television bastards had been after her for their damned programme. It was dropped after Crystal's death, but Felicity was starting the whole business up again.'

'And now Felicity's dead. Think she did it?'

'No. Not in a hundred years. She was a grand lady. This should never have happened. Such a petty little offence, and so many years ago. Those whoring scum over in Strathbane don't know the meaning of decency and respectability. The very idea of putting a bank manager's wife on the rack in front of the cameras must have given them a thrill.'

'Aye, well, I'd best make arrangements to take the husband over to the procurator fiscal tomorrow,' said Jimmy. 'Get a statement?'

'I'll leave it to the morning. Thiss iss a bad business.'

'It is that.'

Hamish sighed. 'One more thing. We'd best go back in and see if she left a note. I wass that upset, I didn't ask.'

Jimmy judged from the thickening of Hamish's accent that he was very disturbed indeed. That was the trouble with village policing, thought Jimmy. You got too close to people.

They walked back in. 'Mr McClellan,' said Hamish gently, 'did your wife leave a note?'

167

His eyes filled with tears and he dug into his pocket and drew out a crumpled sheet of paper and silently handed it over.

Hamish and Jimmy moved a little away and read it. 'Dear John,' it said. 'The old scandal's started again and I can't bear it. I can't take it any more. Please forgive me. All my love, Fiona.'

The paper was blotched with tears. Jimmy took out an envelope and carefully placed the pathetic little note inside.

'I think you should leave things for the moment,' said Dr Brodie. 'I'll give Mr McClellan a sedative.'

Jimmy and Hamish went back outside. The cold and merciless stars shone down on them.

'I'll see you,' said Hamish, and walked back to the police station. He heard the patter of feet, running to catch up with him, and turned round.

'Was it suicide?' asked Elspeth.

Hamish was suddenly consumed with a blinding hatred for the whole of the media.

'Get lost,' he snarled.

Elspeth took a step back as if he had struck her.

Hamish went on to the police station. The dark figure of Mr Patel, the Indian who owned the general stores, detached itself from the shadows.

'I have to talk to ye, Hamish, about poor Mrs McClellan. I feel that guilty.'

Mr Patel had come to Scotland years ago, peddling goods in a suitcase from door to door, saving every penny until he was able to buy a shop. Hamish was always mildly surprised to hear a Scottish accent emerging from his Indian face.

They went into the kitchen. Lugs gave Mr Patel a rapturous welcome, seeing in him a giver of dog biscuits.

'So what's this about?' asked Hamish.

'It wass herself, poor Mrs McClellan. I could not believe my eyes. I have that mirror behind the counter that reflects what's going on in the shop. And then I saw herself sliding things into her shopping basket. I didn't mind. I thought a respectable lady like that would pay for them at the counter. But when she only put one packet of cornflakes on the counter, I told her to come into the back shop.

'I took the stuff she had pinched out of her shopping basket and laid it down. I said. "What's this about?" She began to cry sore and said she meant to pay for it and forgot. It told her I would not be reporting her to the police this time, but I would have a word with her husband. She began to cry harder and said I must not tell her husband. I said I would think about it. And now the poor lady's dead.'

'You weren't to know,' said Hamish heavily. 'She'd been done years ago for shoplifting and got treatment for kleptomania. Somehow those TV people got hold of her past. There was a bit

169

in the Strathbane paper at the time. It came up before. That village dustman, him that was murdered, he ferreted it out and was blackmailing her, and she was so afraid of her husband learning that the old scandal had surfaced that she paid him. I kept it quiet then. You see, she told me that after the scandal, her husband had given up a good job as bank manager in Strathbane and moved here to start a new life. The worry must have brought her old illness up again. Oh, God, what a waste. She wass the fine woman.'

'She wass that,' said Mr Patel, his dark eyes swimming with tears.

'I'll put in my report,' said Hamish, 'and I'll beg them to keep it away from the press.'

When Mr Patel had left, Hamish typed up his report and sent it over to Strathbane. Then he went to bed with Lugs curled against his side. Before he went to sleep, he had a sudden memory of Elspeth's stricken face. He had told her a lot and yet she had not betrayed him by printing one word. He would need to apologize to her. Then he thought of Priscilla. She seemed very distant now. And yet there had been a time when he had imagined her living here with him as his wife, imagined an idyllic married life. He drifted off to sleep.

Chapter Ten

Though the day of my destiny's over,
And the star of my fate has declined.
                    – Lord Byron

Hamish awoke next day with a heavy heart. He dressed and went along to the bank manager's house. Mr McClellan was sitting, white-faced, in his living room with Dr Brodie in attendance beside him. Hamish took a short statement. Dr Brodie said a police car would be arriving soon to take Mr McClellan over to the procurator fiscal in Strathbane.

Returning to the police station, Hamish sent over the statement to Strathbane and then phoned the television station and asked to speak to Amy Cornwall. When she came on the line, he said he would be coming over to see her to ask her a few questions. 'I'll be free at noon,' she said cheerfully. Hamish agreed to see her then, thinking that of all of them, Amy seemed about the only one to have nothing on

171

her conscience – which could be, he calculated, because she hadn't got one.

He was driving out of Lochdubh when he saw the lone figure of Elspeth leaning on the parapet of the humpbacked bridge. He slowed a little, thinking he should apologize to her, and then weakly decided to put it off until later.

When he parked outside the television station, he had to fight down a strong feeling of revulsion towards the building and everyone in it. He walked in and reported at the reception desk and was told Amy would be down in a few minutes.

While he was waiting for her, he suddenly remembered how Rory MacBain had caved in when he had suggested the DNA sample. But he had said he had not seen her for two weeks. He must have done and he must have had intercourse with her shortly before her death, or why else would that have made him confess?

There was a slight cough and Hamish found Amy standing in front of him. 'Can we do the interview somewhere outside?' said Amy. 'This place is giving me the creeps.'

'I know how you feel,' said Hamish. 'There's a café across the road.'

They found a table at the window. It was a busy shopping day and the townspeople of Strathbane surged past: jeans and trainers, bomber jackets, anoraks, walking along slouched, vacant eyes, sour mouths. Well, if I lived here, I'd probably get like that, thought Hamish.

'So what do you want to ask me?' Amy looked at him out of her bright blue eyes.

'Before we start, do you know that Mrs McClellan, the bank manager's wife, one of your research subjects, thanks to you, committed suicide last night?'

'That's a bummer. But those kleptomaniacs are all a bit unbalanced anyway, aren't they?'

'Don't you care?'

She shrugged. 'Nothing to do with me.'

He decided that if he started to argue with her or berate her he wouldn't get much out of her. 'The behind-the-lace-curtains show was to go on with Felicity as presenter. Had you started to interview the same people again?'

'No, I hadn't begun the research. But there was an item in the papers about Felicity doing that show, so I suppose some of them, like Mrs McClellan, might have got rattled.'

Hamish fought down his dislike for her with an effort. 'Would Felicity, when Crystal was presenting that show, do some report for this programme on her own without telling you?'

'She might have done. Crystal treated her badly, and the worse Crystal got, the more Felicity crawled to her like a whipped dog.'

'Did you know that Felicity was having an affair with Rory MacBain?'

'Yes.'

'How?'

173

'Caught them at it in his office one night. Rory had asked me to type out a report and get it to him quick. He must have forgotten asking me, for when I pushed open his office door, they were hard at it on the floor. They didn't see me. I opened the door quietly and then I shut it quietly.'

'The night before she was murdered, was Felicity in the office late?'

'I think so. We were all working late. You see, Callum Bissett likes endless meetings that go on forever and usually never get anything resolved. There's been an offer to buy out Strathbane Television. Jackson's, one of the biggest television companies, have put in a bid. Callum thinks the shareholders will go for it. The meeting ended at nine o'clock. We all went our separate ways. Felicity had been given Crystal's old office. I saw a light under the door before I left.'

So Rory could have had sex with Felicity before he left the office, thought Hamish. He's got to tell us more than he has been doing.

'Do you think Felicity could have killed Crystal?'

'A rabbit like that! Still, now I come to think of it, it was hard to really know Felicity. She was a devious woman, secretive. But you wouldn't want that to be the case. I mean, if Felicity killed Crystal, who killed Felicity?'

'So what happens to the programme, *Highland Life*, with both presenters dead?'

'Nothing. I think we'll cruise along on old movies and old sitcoms until this bid takes place. They're doing a special memorial programme on both Crystal and Felicity this evening. Crystal's body has been released for burial, so the funeral's taking place in Edinburgh today and a team have gone down to film it.'

'Did anyone on your list for the programme actually want to go in front of the camera?'

'Not one. Nothing but threats.'

'And that didn't make you stop?'

'Oh, no, we were just going to swoop on them, and even if we got doors slammed in our faces, Crystal was going to stand in front of their houses and describe what they had done.'

'You are a bunch of right bastards, aren't you?' demanded Hamish.

Amy shrugged again. 'That's show business.'

Carson, passing the detectives' room later, saw Hamish typing busily away and told him to follow him up to his office. 'Any results from the lab on that hair sample?' asked Hamish.

'Not yet. What have you got?'

Hamish described his interview with Amy. 'I'll get Rory MacBain back round here now,' said Carson. 'What is it?' For Hamish suddenly had that struck-by-lightning look.

'The day Crystal was murdered,' said

Hamish slowly. 'That was the day the *Highland Times* came out. She was anxious to see her astrology forecast. Felicity said that Crystal had sent out that morning for a copy of the paper, but how would Felicity know that? I mean, she left at eight. I'm beginning to think that Felicity stopped her on the road to Lochdubh.'

'Could be. But we'll know something as soon as that lab report comes through. I'll get MacBain round. You can sit in on the interview.'

'I'll wait for my lawyer,' said Rory MacBain pompously.

'Then I think we should pass the time by taking a blood sample,' said Carson.

'Why?'

'I think it will prove that you had sex with Felicity Pearson before she died.'

'That's ridiculous!'

'So if you just wait here, I'll get someone . . .'

Rory caved in. 'Okay, okay. It was just a quickie in her office.'

'I must warn you that if you try to impede police inquiries any further by covering up or lying, I will charge you. So go on. At what time did you have intercourse with her?'

'Sometime after the meeting broke up,' said Rory, his face as red as Hamish's hair. 'Say about quarter past nine.'

'And when did you finish?'

'I suppose about nine-thirty.'

'And what was her state of mind?'

'Well, you know.'

'No, I don't, and I'm waiting for you to tell us.'

'Sort of giggly and clingy. She was after me again to get a divorce. I refused. She went off to her office.'

'And was that the last you saw of her?'

'She came back in about ten o'clock. She asked if she found out something that would make the show a nationwide hit, would I marry her? I said I would marry anyone who got us nationwide and she said something like, watch this space, and that's the truth and that is definitely the last time I saw her.'

'So you feel she had learned of some big story?'

'Not really. She was a bit of a fantasist.'

'And she said nothing about a meeting at the docks?'

'Not a word.'

'How late did you stay in the office?'

'Until ten-thirty. Then I went home to the wife. God, she'll kill me if this comes out.'

'At the moment, we will only be asking her to corroborate your statement. You may go, but if you are leaving Strathbane, please inform us of your movements and leave your passport at police headquarters. That will be all . . . for the moment.'

When he had left, Carson turned to Hamish. 'Let us suppose that Felicity killed Crystal. Felicity was going to do that muckraking programme. Mrs McClellan committed suicide over it. Someone else may have been worried enough to murder Felicity. I'm afraid you will need to go back and see them all again, including the crofter and shopkeepers she humiliated. Get on with it, man. What are you waiting for?'

Hamish glanced at Maggie, who had been on duty at the tape machine. She saw him looking and turned her back on him.

For heaven's sake, thought Hamish angrily, as he walked to his Land Rover. You would think I had been having an affair with the girl and jilted her. I only had a business dinner with her. Now I'd better go back and apologize to Elspeth, although thon lassie is weird. There's something about her that's strange.

But when he got back to the police station, he was suddenly filled with heavy inertia. The thought of Priscilla entered his mind and he savagely pushed it away. He was tired and depressed and did not feel like spending the rest of the day in interviews.

He needed something to clear his brain, something to take his mind away from the case. He decided to see if Archie Maclean could lend him a rowing boat.

He walked to the harbour with Lugs trotting along at his heels. He saw the bundled-up figure of Elspeth standing at the harbour and nearly turned back, but then he decided he'd better get the apology out of the way.

Elspeth was wearing her fishing hat and an ankle-length tweed coat that had seen better days and a pair of boots as heavy and clumsy as his own.

'I'm sorry,' said Hamish, going up to her. 'I'm sorry I shouted at you. But I got this hatred for the whole of the media.'

'It's a bad business,' said Elspeth sadly. 'What a waste of a life.'

'It is that.'

'Where are you off to?'

'Fishing. Thought I might catch some mackerel.'

She turned away from him, her shoulders hunched. 'I leave you to it then.'

On impulse, Hamish said, 'Like to come?'

Her odd eyes lit up. 'Love to. I'm off work today.'

'Well, let's see if Archie's awake and can spare the boat.'

They walked to Archie's little cottage beside the harbour and knocked at the door.

Mrs Maclean opened the door. A cloud of steam wreathed itself around her red and angry features. 'Oh, it is yourself,' she said crossly. 'I'm boiling clothes.'

And shrinking them as usual, thought Hamish as her husband appeared behind her in his tight and uncomfortable suit.

Mrs Maclean retreated back into the kitchen. 'I wondered if we could have the loan of your rowing boat, Archie,' said Hamish. 'I'd like to see if I can get some mackerel.'

'Help yourself,' said Archie gloomily. 'I hate wash days.'

'I thought every day in your house was wash day,' said Hamish sympathetically.

'That it is. One o' these days, herself is going to boil me in the copper and hang me on the line. She should ha' married that Willie Lamont and they could ha' scrubbed and cleaned together all the day long. Have you got a spinner for the mackerel?'

'No,' said Hamish. 'I can't find mine. I was hoping . . .'

'Wait there,' said Archie. 'Though it'll be a mercy if she isnae cleaning that as well.'

But he returned with the spinner. Hamish thanked him. Elspeth and he and Lugs walked down the seaweedy steps cut into the harbour wall to the shore of Lochdubh. 'That's Archie's boat,' said Hamish. 'Jump in and I'll give you a push.'

Hamish took off his boots and socks, lifted Lugs in beside Elspeth, and pushed the boat out. Then he climbed in and put his boots and socks on before picking up the oars.

It was a still, calm autumn day without a breath of wind. A light grey sky stretched above them, and the waters of the loch were still and glassy. A scent of pine wafted over from the forest on the far shore. Looking back at Lochdubh, Hamish could see that most of the curtains in the windows of the cottages had been drawn closed as an old-fashioned mark of respect for Mrs McClellan's death.

'Do you believe in the afterlife, Elspeth?' asked Hamish.

'Yes, and if you're worried about poor Mrs McClellan, she's happy now.'

'You believe that?'

'I know it.'

'How?'

'Just a feeling.'

'You and your feelings. I wish you had a feeling about the murderer.'

'You mean Felicity's murderer?'

'Aye.'

'It's someone I haven't met yet.'

'Havers. You mean if you met the murderer, you could tell?'

'Probably.'

They had reached the middle of the loch. Hamish shipped the oars and studied her. 'You really believe that, don't you?'

'Yes, I do.'

'But why? Has it happened before?'

'Not with murder, no.'

Hamish shook his head in bewilderment. 'Why are you so puzzled, Hamish?' she teased. 'Some police forces employ psychics.'

'So you're psychic?'

Elspeth shifted uneasily. She took off her

181

fishing hat and ran her fingers through her thick brown hair. 'I was just joking, Hamish.'

But Hamish thought that she really believed she could tell a murderer if she met one. And she had prophesied Crystal's death.

Hamish unwound the line until the silver spinners drifted out over the water. Then he let the boat move along on the current. 'Do you mind not talking for a bit, Elspeth?' he said. 'I want to be quiet for a bit and think.'

'Okay, Sherlock.'

Lugs put his head on Elspeth's lap and she stroked his ears. Hamish tried to think of the case but found his mind fairly empty. He really didn't want to think of much more than the water and the sky and the peace of the loch around him. The water chuckled around the boat and a heron soared lazily overhead.

He found himself beginning to wish for the first time that he wasn't a policeman. But crofting did not pay these days, he did not want to leave Lochdubh, so what else could he do? If only he had Johnny's talent for making furniture. If he were not a policeman, and had just a little bit of money, then he could let the lazy days drift past like this.

There was a violent tug on the line and he began to reel it in, hand over hand, and then with a sudden jerk, he landed six mackerel. Elspeth quickly removed the hooks and killed the fish, and Hamish threw the line back in again. Another six and Lugs, leaping up and down, nearly fell into the water. 'I think that's enough,' said Hamish. 'More would be greedy. We'll give Archie some.'

'Just in time,' said Elspeth, looking down the loch in the direction of the sea. 'Here comes the rain.'

Grey curtains of rain moved lazily towards them as Hamish began to row back. Soon they were drenched and Lochdubh was blotted from sight.

They were soaking and shivering when Hamish beached the boat and helped Elspeth and Lugs out. 'Back to the station,' he said, 'and we'll get dried out.'

'What about Archie's fish?'

'He can get them later. Come on.'

They scrambled up the beach and then up the steps to the harbour.

When they were in the police station, Hamish said, 'Do you want to run home and get changed? Or there's a dressing gown in the bedroom you can use.'

'I'll use the dressing gown.'

'The water's hot. I'll run a bath for you.'

Hamish returned with a scarlet velvet dressing gown. It had the name Olivia embroidered on one pocket. 'Who's Olivia?' she asked.

'Sad story. Tell you sometime.'

While she was in the bath, Hamish dried himself and changed into clean clothes. He stoked up the stove in the kitchen and began to clean the mackerel. Then he lowered the

183

old-fashioned pulley, as it used to be called, a wooden clothes rack, down from the ceiling and arranged his wet clothes on it. Elspeth emerged from the bathroom, carrying her wet clothes. 'Where's your tumble drier?' she asked.

'I don't have one. Put them on this rack.'

'I've seen one of those in a museum recently,' said Elspeth. 'My mother used to have one. She said all her clothes used to smell of cooking.'

'They are going to smell a bit fishy, but they'll be dry soon,' said Hamish, hoisting the rack up to the ceiling. 'Sit down and I'll cook us some of these mackerel. I feel like a quiet, peaceful evening. No policing.'

Over in Strathbane, Detective Chief Inspector Carson felt weary. The results had come through from the lab. The hair that had been in the hat had belonged to Felicity Pearson. He picked up the phone to call Hamish and tell him the results and then decided to drive over to Lochdubh instead.

As he drove along the heathery single-track roads that led to the village of Lochdubh he felt he was leaving a rather nasty world behind him. The rain had eased off and stars were twinkling through a haze of cloud. As he parked outside the police station, he reflected that he should have phoned first. After all, the police station was also Hamish's home.

But he had driven this far and was reluctant to turn back. He knocked at the door. Hamish opened it. He was wearing a flowery apron.

'It iss yourself,' he said pleasantly. 'Would you like some fish? I was just about to cook some.'

Carson was about to refuse, to say he had come on police business, and then he saw a girl in a scarlet dressing gown. 'I'm sorry,' he said. 'I'm interrupting you.'

'Och, no, the pair of us got drenched. This is Elspeth Grant, our local reporter and astrologer. But she's discreet and won't go publishing anything you say. It's going to be a bad night. Forecast's terrible. Come along in.'

Carson took off his overcoat and hung it on a hook behind the door. He sat down at the kitchen table. Hamish placed a glass of whisky in front of him. 'I'll just be getting dinner,' said Hamish, 'and then you can tell me your news.'

'I thought you would want to hear it right away.'

'I find,' said Hamish, taking down an enormous frying pan, 'that a time away from police work clears the brain wonderfully.'

'You've been fishing,' accused Carson, half-exasperated, half-amused.

'Yes.'

Carson decided to wait until Hamish had finished cooking. The kitchen was warm and comfortable. Elspeth began to ask him how long he would be in Strathbane, and then, learning that he was from Inverness, told him about her upbringing there.

Hamish finally put fish in front of them and a bowl of potatoes, a bowl of oatmeal, and a large pat of butter. 'You dip your potatoes in the oatmeal,' he said, 'and then add a lump of butter. Wait a bit. Wine. I've got some white I won in a raffle. I'll go out and get it.'

'Have you another fridge outside?' asked Elspeth.

'No, it's in the henhouse.'

Hamish went out and reappeared after a few minutes with two bottles of wine.

'What is it?' asked Elspeth.

'That's the pity of it. I've had it so long, the labels have fallen off. There was a leak in the roof of the hen house, right over where the wine was stacked, and by the time I repaired it, the bottles had got soaked.'

He opened one of the bottles. 'It's nice and cold anyway.'

He poured glasses all around. They sipped and guessed Chablis.

'I haven't had fresh mackerel in ages,' said Carson. 'They're not the same fish when you buy them in the shop. Now, why I came is to tell you the lab result is through. That hair did come from Felicity Pearson's head.'

'I thought it might,' said Hamish. 'Listen to that wind. Up here, it rises out of nowhere. One minute it's as calm as anything and the next it's blowing a gale.'

'You don't seem surprised by my news.'

'Och, no,' said Hamish. 'I was sure she had done it. I wonder who did her.'

Carson was about to snap that it was Hamish's job to find out, but the meal was delicious and he was filled with good food and lazy warmth. It was a private visit. Officialdom could wait.

'The thing that bothers me,' went on Hamish, dipping a potato in oatmeal, 'is that not one of those people on the list had done anything really bad. I would have thought a murder not detected would have prompted someone to commit murder. Maisie Gough, her over in Cnothan, now she was accused of pinching the Mothers' Union funds, but she had just forgotten she had given them to her friend for safekeeping. A verra respectable body she is and horrified and terrified by the television programme, but not a murderer. Then there is the woman at Bonar Bridge, accused of murdering her two bairns, but it was cot death, that's all. The chip shop man was a wife beater, but he hasnae got a wife to beat at the moment and there's an awful lot of wife beating goes on. Mrs Harrison's got two nasty sons but they've got alibis. And poor Mrs McClellan, God rest her soul. I can't think one of them did it. The only thing I can think of is checking up on Mrs Swithers, the chip shop man's wife, and see if she's still all right. With your permission, I'll get on to Inverness police station in the morning and find out if they've got an address for her. It'll be a start.'

Hamish smiled at Elspeth. 'Of course our astrologer here might solve the case for us.'

'How's that?' asked Carson.

Elspeth blushed and glared at Hamish.

Had Elspeth not looked so very attractive in that dressing gown, then Hamish would not have gone on. But she disturbed him. He was off women and he wanted to keep her at arm's length.

'Oh, she says if she meets the murderer, she'll be able to tell right away.'

'Do you believe that?' Carson asked seriously. 'I mean, I have heard of psychics helping the police.'

'I was pulling Hamish's leg,' said Elspeth crossly.

'And are you pair an item?' asked Carson.

'Oh, no,' said Elspeth sweetly. 'I am never interested in philanderers. I mean, take this dressing gown and the name on it. Who's Olivia and why do you have her dressing gown, Hamish, *dear*?'

'Olivia Chater was Detective Chief Inspector Chater from Glasgow,' said Hamish sadly. 'She worked with me on a case. I had hoped we could get married but she went back to Glasgow.'

'Oh, I remember,' said Carson. 'The poor woman died of cancer.'

188

Elspeth looked down at the table, suddenly feeling shabby.

'It's difficult to pinpoint the exact time of Crystal's death,' said Carson quickly, changing the subject. 'We feel it could have been early in the morning and that would be before Felicity reached Lochdubh officially. You would think someone would have seen something. I thought in these villages they knew every time you changed your underwear.'

'Normally that's the case,' said Hamish. 'But that back road is not overlooked by any cottages. No one uses it much, except Willie Lamont, who walks his dog there, and that morning he decided not to. But I'm thinking, what if someone did see something and was trying to blackmail her?'

'Possible,' said Carson, pushing his plate away. 'You're a grand cook.'

There came a knock at the door. Hamish opened it and found Archie Maclean there. 'Come in, Archie. Too bad to go out tonight?'

'Aye,' said Archie, 'and it's going to get worse.'

'I've got some mackerel for you.'

'Thanks, Hamish. I didn't come about that.'

'We'll go through to the living room,' said Hamish. 'This is Detective Chief Inspector Carson, Archie, and Elspeth, you know.'

They walked through to the living room. Hamish lit the fire and they settled in chairs around it while the increasing force of the wind beat against the windows.

'I've come because we're planning to give Mrs McClellan the grand send-off,' said Archie.

Again, there was a knock at the door. This time it was Mrs Wellington and the Currie sisters.

Hamish took them into the living room and introduced them to Carson. 'It's about the funeral,' boomed Mrs Wellington. She looked at Carson. 'When will the body be released?'

'I should think next week. It seems a straightforward case of suicide.'

'Mr McClellan is in no state to handle the arrangements, so we thought we would organize the food and drink at the church hall. The whole village will be going,' said Nessie.

'I'll do what I can,' said Hamish.

'You're to read the eulogy,' said Mrs Wellington.

'I wasnae that close to her,' said Hamish, alarmed.

'No one really was,' said Mrs Wellington, 'and as a village policeman, it's your duty. We're all going to do our bit.'

Another knock at the door. This time Dr Brodie and Angela; Willie Lamont and his wife, Lucia; and Mr and Mrs Anderson, Willie's neighbours.

Hamish found more chairs. Carson was relaxed and amused as the villagers promptly seemed to forget the existence of Hamish and began to discuss funeral arrangements. Archie produced a bottle of whisky, the doctor another, and Willie another. Hamish fetched glasses. Drinks were poured all round. The talk moved from Mrs McClellan's suicide to village gossip. Archie went home and came back with his accordion. Soon they were all singing and clapping, and the drinks kept going round.

When at last they decided to go, Carson noticed with a shock that it was two in the morning and that he was unfit to drive. As the guests filed out, the Currie sisters took Elspeth to one side. 'It's a shame,' said Nessie. 'Shame,' echoed Jessie. 'Him parading you like that with hardly a stitch on,' said Nessie. 'Get him to make a decent woman of ye.'

'We were fishing and I got wet,' said Elspeth desperately. 'My clothes are drying in the kitchen.'

Nessie gave her a hug. 'You get them on quick, lassie. No woman is safe with Hamish Macbeth around.'

When they had all left, Elspeth said, 'I'd better change and get home.'

And Carson said, 'I'm afraid I'm not fit to drive. Too much whisky.'

'You can have my bed. There's a bed in the cell I can use.' There was one cell off the police office.

'Do you ever use that cell for criminals?' asked Carson.

'No, just for sobering up the occasional drunk.'

Hamish changed the sheets on his bed and then said to Elspeth, who had changed into her dry clothes, 'I'd better walk you home. It's a bad night.'

They headed out into the scream of the wind. The normally placid loch was full of pounding white horses, crashing on the shingly beach. He took hold of Elspeth's arm as she swayed in a particularly vicious buffet of wind.

Then he stood outside the house where she had a flat. 'I'm sorry I jeered at you in front of the boss,' he said. 'But I'm off women at the moment.'

'And I'm sorry I asked about Olivia. Did you love her very much?'

'I don't know now. Sometimes I think I just wanted to get married. But she was very special.'

'Never mind.' She put her arms round him and hugged him. He could feel the warmth of her body through her clothes. He bent his head to kiss her and then thought angrily, what on earth am I doing? and pulled away.

'Night,' he said gruffly, and, bending his head against the gale, he strode off down the waterfront.

Chapter Eleven

Art thou pale for weariness
Of climbing heaven, and gazing on the earth,
Wandering companionless
Among the stars that have a different birth –
And ever changing, like a joyless eye
That finds no object worth its constancy?
*   – Percy Bysshe Shelley*

Carson awoke the following morning and glanced at the alarm clock beside the bed. Ten o'clock! How could he have slept so long? He got out of bed and found that Hamish had washed and ironed his shirt and also washed and dried his underwear.

He washed and dressed and went through to the kitchen. There was no sign of Hamish. He then went into the police office and phoned headquarters to say that he would be in his office within the hour.

He heard the kitchen door open and went through. Hamish was wearing his flowered apron over his uniform. He grinned sheepishly.

'I just had to fix the roof on the hen house again. Some damage from the wind last night.' He removed his apron and hung it on a hook. 'Did you sleep well?'

'Very well, thank you,' said Carson. 'I must be off. Are you going to Inverness?'

'With your permission, sir. I'll phone first.'

'I'd like to attend that funeral,' said Carson.

'I'll let you know the minute I get the date and time.'

As Carson approached Strathbane, he saw it spread out below him as he crested a hill and felt a sinking of his heart. It was a depressing, awful place. He could understand Hamish Macbeth not wanting to leave Lochdubh. He longed to be able to turn the wheel and go back there himself. But duty was duty. He drove on down into the city.

Hamish obtained an address for Ruby Swithers in Inverness. The police told him that two years ago she had taken an injunction out against her husband. She lived in a council house in an estate off the Beauly Road.

He wondered whether she would be at home or had gone out to work to support herself, but the prim little woman who answered the door confirmed that yes, she was Ruby Swithers and then asked eagerly, 'Is he dead?'

'Your husband? No. Why should you think that?'

'It's the drink. It'll get him one day. Come in.'

He followed her into a pleasant living room. The furniture was old and had seen better days, but the upholstery was clean. The wallpaper was a noisy design of trellised roses and the carpet a screaming mixture of yellow and red, but it had an air of comfort. Cheery, thought Hamish, and what's good taste anyway?

'I came to ask you if he's been bothering you lately.'

She sat down on the edge of an armchair, red workworn hands folded neatly in her lap. She had pale, indeterminate features and grey hair, cut short and permed. 'No,' she said. 'My friend Islay told me to take out an injunction and that I did. Used to come round and throw things at the windows. Drunk, of course.'

'I'll come out and ask you straight, would you consider him capable of murder?'

'You're thinking of them television lassies.' The fact that Felicity had committed the first murder had so far been kept out of the newspapers. 'The one where the suicide was faked? Well, that would take a clear brain. Finlay would sock you on the head with a bottle when he was drunk, but planning something like that, he hasn't got the brains, and what he's got left are addled with drink or hangover.'

'Why did you finally leave him?'

'He tried to kill me,' she said.

'What? There's nothing in the reports about that.'

'I didn't report it at the time. I just wanted to get away.'

'What did he do?'

'It was one night after the shop was closed. He got all lovey-dovey, strange for him, and he says, let's have a dram. Well, I was so relieved he was in a good mood that I agreed. He says, get some of thae cheese things to go with it. Now he hates those cheese things, what d'you call them?'

'Straws?'

'Aye, them. I looked through a crack in the kitchen door and I saw the wee scunner put something in my drink.

'I got the straws and came back. Let's drink it down in one go, he says. Right, says I, and walked to the window. I tipped it into the plant and then raised the empty glass to my lips. He kept watching me and watching me. I pretended to pass out. I watched him under my eyelids. He goes into the kitchen. I hear him lighting the gas and clattering something. Then he runs out the door and I can hear him rattling down the stairs. I ran for the kitchen. He'd set a chip pan on fire. I threw a damp dishcloth over it and managed to get the flames out. I was terrified. I packed my things and went down to the shop and took all the money out of the till. Then I called a cab and went all the way to Inverness to my mother. This is her house. She bought it from the council. She died last year and left it to me. That bugger tried to kill me.'

'Wait a minute,' said Hamish, scratching his head in bewilderment. 'Was he sober when he did all this?'

'He'd had a few but not much.'

'But you said he couldn't plan a murder and then you tell me that he tried to plan yours!'

'I couldn't think he really meant to go through with it,' she said, all mad reason. 'I mean, he liked to give me a fright.'

Hamish sighed. 'You should have reported him. The police would have checked your empty glass and found traces of whatever it was he tried to drug you with. He would have been charged with attempted murder and put away.'

'That's what my friend Islay said. She's such a strong woman. I'd never even have taken out an injunction against him if she hadn't forced me into it. I even thought of going back.'

'WHAT!'

'I mean, he wasn't that bad.'

Hamish had interviewed battered wives before and had heard the same excuses, but never from one who had nearly been murdered.

'I would advise you not to go near Cnothan or to have anything to do with such a man again.'

'No, I won't. Islay wouldn't let me. Oh, that's her now.'

'Is she living with you?'

'Yes, we're great friends.'

Islay came in. She was a squat, powerful woman with tattooed arms. She gave Ruby a kiss and said, 'What now? That bastard been after you again?'

'Oh, no dear. The constable was thinking maybe Finlay murdered those television lassies.'

'Probably did. Did you tell him that Finlay tried to murder you?'

'Yes, though mind you, I think he just meant to give me a fright.'

'You listen here,' said Islay, folding her muscular arms. 'He tried to murder you and you should have told the police at the time. Now run along and make me something to eat.'

Changed one bully for another, thought Hamish. But I'd best go and see Finlay Swithers.

As he drove back towards the west, he wished again that he could just go home and forget about policing. And yet, how could he do that when home was the police station? The gale had blown itself out, and great puffy clouds soared over the mountains on a wind that did not reach the ground. The mountains were blue that day and the air through the open window of the Land Rover seemed full of life and energy. A great day for taking a rod out on the river.

But as he got closer to Cnothan, the sky clouded over and a smear of rain blurred the windscreen, to remind Hamish that the year was dying and soon the long winter nights would set in. It was like travelling in a train that was moving rapidly towards a long dark tunnel.

He parked outside the fish and chip shop. He rang the bell at the side door. Finlay Swithers answered it and his face fell when he saw Hamish. 'What is it now?' he demanded crossly.

'Let's go upstairs,' said Hamish. 'I'm here to talk about an attempted murder.'

'Nothing to do with me,' remarked Swithers, leading the way up the stairs. Hamish wrinkled his nose in disgust as the smell of the man wafted back towards him: a mixture of greasy oil, unwashed clothes, and last night's booze.

Once in the living room, Hamish looked immediately to the window, hoping suddenly that in all this mess, Swithers had kept that flower pot. But the window ledge was empty apart from dust and cobwebs.

'Sit down,' ordered Hamish, taking out his notebook. 'I have been to see your wife.'

'What's she got to say for herself? Usual lies?'

'She says you tried to kill her and make it

look like an accident, that you drugged her whisky and set light to a chip pan in the kitchen so that she would burn with the place.'

'That what she told you? Well, it's a load of rubbish. Where's your proof?'

'Long gone, I suppose.'

'There you are. You've got nothing and neither has she. I'm telling you, man, ever since she hitched up with that dyke, she's been poison. Used to be a nice quiet lassie.'

'One who took a beating without complaint? I'm warning you. You go near her again and I'll have you. I'll be watching you from now on. Come to that, where were you when Felicity Pearson got shot down at the docks?'

'I was here. I closed the shop up at eleven o'clock and went down to the Dandy Duck for a jar. Don't remember much about getting home, but the locals will tell you I was there and when I left I was in no fit state to drive to Strathbane or anywhere else.'

His reddened eyes held a triumphant gleam.

'Cocky wee soul, aren't you?' said Hamish bitterly. 'But this is only the beginning. I'm going to dig into everything to do with you.'

'This is harassment,' said Swithers. 'I'll report you.'

'Do that,' said Hamish, 'but I'll be back.'

He made his way back to Lochdubh after checking Swithers's alibi at the local pub and typed a long report about everything Swithers had told him. The police would not like to think that anyone had got away with attempted murder. Swithers would be pulled in for questioning.

He should really have asked Maisie Gough what she had been doing when Felicity was killed but was fearful that any visit from him might frighten her to death.

He then set out again. It was time to talk to Barry McSween. For some reason he had been on Amy's list. He decided to go to the Tommel Castle Hotel where the manager was a good source of gossip.

The girl at reception told him she would find Mr Johnston for him and to make himself comfortable in the office.

Hamish helped himself to a cup of coffee from the machine in the corner of the office. He remembered when the Tommel Castle Hotel had just been Tommel Castle, home of the Halburton-Smythes. When the colonel fell on hard times, it was Hamish who had suggested the hotel idea, a fact the colonel had conveniently forgotten, bragging to all that would listen that it had been *his* idea. The colonel had always lived in fear that his precious daughter would marry Hamish. No chance of that now, thought Hamish.

Mr Johnston came back. 'So what can I do for you, Hamish?'

'I'm after some gossip about Barry McSween,' said Hamish. 'Now there's this other murder. Do you know what the television people might have found out about him? He'd been humiliated on the crofting show, but they were trying to get him on the local scandals show.'

'There was something a few years back. I think it was when you went on holiday to that health farm out on the island. He was up before the sheriff in Dornoch.'

'What for?'

'Dynamiting salmon.'

'My, I thought only the Glasgow gangs did that.'

'No, he was caught red-handed up at the Crumley estate with sticks of dynamite in his bag and the fish that had been blown up lying belly up in one of the pools and him in his waders hauling them out. The water bailiff caught him. Wee bit in the papers about it. Got a hefty fine but no prison sentence, as it was a first offence.'

'I'd best go and see him.'

'His wife's left him.'

'Jeannie? Why? When was this?'

'Last week. One of the maids told me.'

'And where's she gone?'

'Strathbane to stay with her sister, Elsie.'

'Do you know where the sister lives?'

'I'll find out. Those maids know everything that goes on.'

Hamish helped himself to another cup of coffee. He had a sudden sharp longing for a cigarette. The craving was so intense that he was amazed. He had given up a few years ago.

Mr Johnston came back. 'I wrote it down. It's Barry Road, near the docks, don't know the number.'

'Is it now?' said Hamish slowly. 'Is it indeed?'

He decided to go straight to Strathbane to see Jeannie McSween first and try to learn if Barry had been in Strathbane the night Felicity had been killed. He felt a little pang of guilt. He should really let Strathbane police take over. He was off his beat. But Carson would understand – he hoped.

When he reached Strathbane and Barry Road, he wondered if he would ever find Jeannie, for Barry Road was lined on either side with depressing tower blocks. He should have asked the sister's name and then he would have been able to check the electoral roll. He phoned Mr Johnston on his mobile. Mr Johnston said he would try to find out, but when he returned it was to say that no one knew the sister's second name.

Here goes, thought Hamish wearily, climbing down from the Land Rover. He hoped Lugs wasn't dining out at the kitchen door of the Italian restaurant. He had forgotten to warn Willie not to feed the dog. He had left the dog outside the police station, guessing that it might be a long day.

He started knocking on doors. The people who lived in these tower blocks seemed to have given up on life: tired faces, druggy faces, despairing faces looked out of doorways at him to tell him they hadn't a clue where he would find a woman called Elsie whose sister had just moved in with her. He was beginning to feel silly. If he had started with Barry, he would have had the address. He considered phoning Barry but did to want to alert the man.

Jeannie McSween was a respectable house-wife. What on earth was she doing living in surroundings like this? Perhaps it got more respectable towards the far end. He got back into the Land Rover and drove along, looking to right and left. Sure enough, towards the end, Barry Road curved away from the docks and towards the centre of the town. The tower blocks fell behind and the road ended in neat Victorian villas. He parked the Land Rover again and began to knock at doors.

At the fourth try, he landed lucky. A house-wife told him that there was an Elsie Simms living at number five. Hamish walked along and there it was, nearly at the end of the road.

He knocked at the door. Jeannie McSween herself answered the door, her eyes widening at the sight of him. 'Hamish. It's yourself. What brings you?'

'Can we go in?' asked Hamish. 'Just want to ask you a few questions.'

'Come in. I was just packing.'

'Going away?'

'As far as I can get. Sit yourself down. It's not Barry, is it?'

'I'm checking alibis for the night Felicity Pearson was murdered. Was your husband in Strathbane?'

'Let me see, that would be sometime on the Monday night?'

'That's right.'

'He came round knocking at the door but I shouted through the letter box that if he didn't go away, I would call the police. He shouted back that he would divorce me and I wouldn't get a penny. That's a laugh.'

Hamish sat down and removed his hat. She sat down opposite. She looked very happy, and her brown hair had been styled.

'And why is that a laugh? Have you found a job?'

She leaned forward. 'I'll tell you, but you're not to tell a soul, mind.'

'I cannae promise that, Jeannie, if it's anything to do with the murder.'

'Nothing at all. I won the lottery.'

'Neffer! What did you get? Millions?'

'No, no, it was the second prize. Two hundred and fifty thousand pounds.'

'Barry must have been right sore at you taking off with the money.'

'He didn't know! I always bought a lottery ticket when I visited Elsie in Strathbane. The minute I got the money, I left him. I've been wanting to leave him for years. I'm off to stay with my daughter in the States.'

'Good for you. So when did Barry come round? What time would that be?'

'It must have been about nine o'clock.'

'Was he ever violent?'

'Not with his fists, but he had a right nasty tongue on him. Picking on me from morning till night. I tell you, Hamish, the thought of never having to listen to that voice again makes me feel like a new woman.'

Hamish left her and headed back to Lochdubh and then on to Barry McSween's croft. He heard a frantic bleating from the field closest to the croft house as he climbed down from the Land Rover. He sprinted across the field and found a sheep on its back, and he hoisted the animal upright. Then he wiped his hands on his uniform and headed for the house.

An unkempt and unshaven Barry McSween answered the door to him. 'Barry, one of your beasts was out there up on its back,' admonished Hamish. 'You should be out there, taking care of them.'

'Is that why ye came?' demanded Barry truculently. 'To tell me one o' thae useless beasts was on its back?'

'Let's go inside,' said Hamish. 'I've got more questions to ask you.'

Barry shrugged and led the way in. 'The wife's left me,' he said, sinking down into an armchair.

'That's why I'm here,' said Hamish. 'I've been down to see Jeannie, and she tells me that on the night Felicity Pearson was murdered, you were down in Strathbane, yelling outside her sister's house.'

'Was I?' said Barry wearily. 'I cannae remember. To tell the truth, I had the drink taken. I 'member driving back and then going into a ditch near Sean Fitzpatrick's house. I wanted him to get his tractor and pull me out, but he made me sleep in an armchair.'

'And what time would that be?' asked Hamish.

'Ask him,' said Barry. 'I cannae remember.'

'I will. How did you feel when that television lassie, Amy Cornwall, got on to you about that old business when you were charged with dynamiting the salmon pool on the Crumley estate?'

'How the hell do you think I felt, man? They'd already made a right fool o' me. I told her I would wring her neck if she came round here again.'

'I'll need to take your guns, Barry.'

'It wasnae me.'

'Nonetheless, I need your guns. I'll give you a receipt for them.'

He rose wearily and took a key out of a drawer. 'You'll find the gun cabinet over there on the wall. Help yourself.'

Hamish unlocked the gun cabinet, put on a pair of thin plastic gloves and took out two shotguns and a rifle. 'Got a gun bag?'

'On the floor, over to your left.'

Hamish carefully lifted the guns into the gun bag and hoisted it on his shoulder. 'I'll take these over to headquarters.' He wrote out a receipt and handed it to Barry. 'And I'll be checking with Sean.'

'Do that,' said Barry, sunk in gloom. 'Why did she leave me, Hamish? I was a good husband.'

'It might be a good idea to get cleaned up and go down there sober and ask her.'

Hamish drove straight to Sean Fitzgerald's cottage. 'I heard him go into the ditch about ten o'clock,' said Sean. 'I made him black coffee and told himself to make himself comfortable in the armchair and sleep it off.'

'Have you heard anything else that might be of interest?' asked Hamish.

'Nothing at all. They're not scared in the village. They're convinced it was one of those television people.'

'I hope so,' said Hamish fervently. 'I would hate it to be one of us.'

He drove on to police headquarters in

Strathbane and turned the guns over to be sent to the lab for analysis. Then he went into the detectives' room and asked if he could use a computer.

'Help yourself,' said Jimmy Anderson ungraciously. 'Everything must be done to help Carson's pet.'

'I bet you're wishing Blair was back to keep me in my place,' said Hamish amiably. He sat down and typed out his report on Barry McSween.

When he had finished, Jimmy said, 'That Finlay Swithers has been brought in for questioning, and his wife, too.'

'They can't make anything stick,' said Hamish. 'They've only got her word against his. She even might cave in and deny everything.'

'I doubt it. She turned up with a monster of a woman friend who seems determined to nail Swithers.'

'Doesn't matter. It's all too long ago.'

'So what are you going to do next?'

'Go and see the Harrisons, and I'm not looking forward to it. I don't like her and I don't like her sons. What about Mrs McClellan's body? When is it going to be released for burial?'

'I think in a few days' time.'

'Give me a ring when you find out,' said Hamish. 'The village wants to give her a big send-off.'

'Fat lot o' good that'll do her now,' said Jimmy heartlessly. 'Oh, by the way, police-woman Maggie's right sore at you. Says you took her out to dinner and romanced her and you had a girlfriend all along.'

'That's rubbish,' said Hamish, turning red. 'Where is she?'

'Downstairs in the ops room.'

Hamish clattered down the stairs and went into the ops room. Maggie was just taking off her headphones and saying to a colleague, 'Thank goodness that shift's over.' She stood up and turned round and saw Hamish.

'A word with you, Maggie, in private,' said Hamish sternly.

They walked out to the reception area. The desk sergeant looked at them curiously. 'Outside,' ordered Hamish. 'Just for a minute.'

They walked outside and Hamish turned to face her. 'What's all this rubbish you've been telling folk about me romancing you? I asked you out to find out the details of Felicity Pearson's murder, that's all.'

Maggie tossed her head defiantly. 'You were sending out the vibes.'

'Oh, I was, was I?' demanded Hamish. 'I thought you were an attractive girl, yes, but it was purely business.'

'So you say,' said Maggie.

'Yes, it was.'

'And is she your girlfriend?'

Hamish saw the easy way out and took it. 'Yes, we're going to get married.'

'I hope you'll be very happy,' said Maggie stiffly, and she walked back into the police station.

Women, thought Hamish. I cannae figure them out at all. You want them, they don't want you, you don't want them, they want you. I'm sick of the lot of them.

He drove back through Lochdubh and out to Braikie and on to the Harrison boys' croft.

They were loading feed out of the back of a battered old van when Hamish arrived.

Iain and Jamie Harrison turned to face him, their faces marred by identical scowls. 'You been bothering Ma?' asked Iain.

'Not yet,' said Hamish. 'Where were you on Monday night, the night Felicity Pearson was murdered?'

They looked at each other and then Jamie said, 'We were both down at Strathbane at the ten-pin bowling.'

'Times?'

'We got there about eight and left at eleven and came back here.'

'Witnesses?'

'Ask at the ten-pin bowling alley. It was full. Lots of people saw us.'

'I'll do that. I'll need your guns.'

'Whit for?' asked Jamie.

'I have to check they haven't been fired. I'll give you a receipt.'

211

Once again Hamish had to stack guns in a gun bag, hand out a receipt, and head back to Strathbane. The light was fading and frost was beginning to glitter on the road.

He handed over the guns and put in another report. But he did not go to the ten-pin bowling alley. Let Strathbane police check that out. He was weary and he still had to see Mrs Harrison in the morning.

He raced back to the police station, anxious now about Lugs being out in the cold. But when he got there, the dog's feeding bowl was full and there was no sign of Lugs.

He phoned the Italian restaurant but was told they hadn't seen the dog. He walked along to Elspeth's flat and rang the bell. 'Have you come for Lugs?' she asked when she opened the door. 'I went to the police station to speak to you. I found Lugs looking miserable and the night was getting cold, so I took him home.'

'You might have left a note,' grumbled Hamish.

'I did. I shoved one through the door. You probably walked over it with your great boots. Come in.'

She was wearing a short skirt and black stockings with her usual boots, and a man's shirt under a blue sweater. She led the way upstairs to her flat.

Lugs rushed forward to greet his master. 'Cosy here,' said Hamish, looking around. A fire was burning in an old Victorian tiled fireplace. The furniture looked shabby but comfortable. The bookcase was stuffed with paperbacks and the coffee table covered in magazines.

'Sit down and tell me how you got on,' said Elspeth. 'I was just about to eat. Want some?'

Hamish's stomach rumbled. He had not eaten since breakfast. 'Aye, that would be grand. If you have enough, that is.'

Elspeth smiled at him. She had no intention of telling him that she had been cooking since she got home from work. She set the dining table in the corner of the room and then carried in a casserole and opened a bottle of wine.

'Come and sit down,' she said.

'What is it?' asked Hamish.

'Coq au vin. Lugs isn't having any. He's already had two pieces of liver and three large sausages.'

'If this goes on, he'll never touch dog food again.' Hamish shook out his napkin and tackled his food.

Elspeth waited until he had cleared his plate and asked again. 'How have you been getting on?'

Hamish sighed. 'Interviewing a lot of people and getting nowhere.'

'Tell me about it?'

'You'll keep it to yourself?'

'Haven't I always?'

'Here goes, then.'

He told her about his interviews.

She leaned her elbows on the table. 'I wonder . . .' she said.

'Wonder what?'

'Well, you say that Finlay Swithers is a wife beater and a drunk. But he enjoyed beating his wife. A man like that wouldn't want to kill her, unless . . .' She took a sip of wine.

'Unless what?' demanded Hamish impatiently.

'Unless he had her heavily insured.'

Chapter Twelve

Above thy deep and dreamless sleep
The silent stars go by.
     – Philips Brooks

Hamish stared at her. 'There's a thought. If he had, it would be interesting to find out. I've got to see Mrs Harrison tomorrow and then I've got to go to Bonar Bridge again.'

'I'll phone round the insurance companies for you. Tomorrow's a quiet day,' said Elspeth.

'That's good of you. I must say, Elspeth, you're a right brick the way you've kept everything I've told you out of print.'

She laughed. 'It's easy. We're a weekly family paper. People can get all the hard news from the nationals. What they want from us is the local stories – you know, school sports days, Highland Games, all with as many photographs as possible – and recipes and gossip. If I started to write what you'd told me, I would lose a good friend.'

Her eyes were very large and silver in her

gypsy face. He felt a tug at his heart immediately followed by a cold feeling of distaste. Where had involvements with women ever got him? Better to keep it light and friendly.

He returned to the subject of Swithers. 'Even if he did insure his wife heavily, we still can't get him on it. Still, it would be nice to know. Because if he's still got her heavily insured, he might be daft enough to try again. But hadn't I better contact the insurance companies myself? They would tell a policeman but not you.'

'I have useful friends.'

'I'll leave you to it and if you don't get anywhere, I'll take over.'

'Coffee?'

'No, I'd best be going. Thanks for a grand meal. What about me taking you out to the Italian restaurant tomorrow night?'

'Great. I'll see you there at eight.'

Hamish stood up. 'Come on, Lugs. Time to go home.'

She followed him to the door and then put her hand on his arm and looked up into his face. He ducked his head in an embarrassed motion and said gruffly, 'Aye, well, good night then,' and clattered down the stairs with Lugs pattering after him.

The following morning he bearded Mrs Harrison in her dingy shop. 'Oh, you're back,' she said sourly.

'What were you doing on Monday night, the day Felicity Pearson was killed?'

'I was at home at the croft. The boys were in Strathbane, as you know, at the bowling alley. I was watching the telly with my neighbour, Betty Murray. Go and ask her.'

'I will,' said Hamish. 'Address?'

She gave it to him, her old eyes gleaming with mockery as if amused at his pursuit.

He left and checked with Betty Murray, who confirmed that Mrs Harrison had been with her up until nearly midnight and added that Mrs Harrison could not drive.

Hamish then drove across country to Bonar Bridge to see Jessie Gordon. But the house had a dead, empty look and no one answered the door. He was turning away when a woman next door called to him. 'Are you looking for Jessie?'

'Aye.'

'She's in hospital in Inverness. I found her lying in her garden and called the ambulance. I phoned the hospital. They said she might pull through. Bad case of alcohol poisoning.'

'When was this?' asked Hamish.

'I found her last Sunday morning. She must have been lying there all night, they said. It's a wonder she's still alive.'

Hamish thanked her and walked back to the Land Rover. Lugs gave a bark of welcome from the front seat. Hamish had decided to take him along for company.

When he got back to the police station, he sat at his desk and began to make notes. The Harrison boys' alibi was not foolproof. They could have left the bowling alley, gone to the docks, and shot Felicity. He would need to wait for a report from the lab on the guns.

The day dragged on. He made notes and then studied his reports on the computer. Perhaps there was something in there that might give him a clue.

By evening, he was glad to leave his work and get dressed and go to meet Elspeth. Instead of his best suit, he put on a shirt and cords and an old and comfortable Harris tweed sports jacket. Elspeth had made him feel overdressed the last time.

But when he entered the restaurant, he saw she was wearing the cherry red dress, black sheer tights and high heels.

'You're looking very grand,' he said. 'What was the occasion?'

'This. I thought I'd dress up.'

He wished she hadn't. The dress revealed her excellent figure.

'So how did you get on?' he asked, sitting down opposite her.

'Got it first time.'

'Good girl. What?'

'The Strong Insurance Company in Inverness. A friend of mine told me that Finlay Swithers insured his wife's life for one hundred thousand pounds.'

Hamish's eyes gleamed. 'He did, did he? I'd better report it, and warn his wife.'

'Sorry, he fell behind on the payments right after she left him, so the policy was cancelled.'

'Well, it's another dead end like all the dead ends I keep running into.'

They ordered their food, each having the same, veal escalopes with marsala sauce. 'I suppose it's wicked to eat veal,' said Elspeth.

'Not here. It's actually pork fillet beaten thin. Not thinking of becoming a vegetarian, are you?'

'Sometimes. It's all right in the city when you buy the meat at the supermarket in packages, but around here, you see it on the hoof.'

'Usually it's the other way round. It's the townies who get sentimental about animals and go on about the darling foxes. Anyway, it's been a dreary day. I keep going over and over my reports. I keep hoping there's something concrete there but all I get are a lot of perhaps and maybes.'

Hamish's mobile phone rang. 'I thought I'd switched this thing off,' he said, pulling it out of his pocket.

It was Carson. 'Just to let you know that Mrs McClellan's body is being released tomorrow. Mr McClellan has been told. Let me know when the funeral is to be held.'

'Will do.'

'How have you been getting on?'

'A lot of dead ends. I've gone round them all again. Only one thing. Finlay Swithers insured his wife for one hundred thousand pounds, but stopped paying after she left, so the policy was cancelled.'

'I wish we could get that man on something. What's that music in the background?'

'I'm in the local Italian restaurant.'

'Food good?'

'Excellent.'

'I wish I could join you.'

'I'm with Elspeth Grant. We could wait for you, sir.'

'If you don't mind.'

'Not at all.'

'I'm on my way,' said Carson cheerfully.

'That's the boss,' said Hamish to Elspeth. 'I'll tell Willie to hold our food. We could have a starter while we're waiting.'

'As you've already invited him,' said Elspeth coldly, 'I can hardly object.'

'Elspeth, he's my boss and he's lonely, I think.'

'Tough.'

Hamish went off to the kitchen. Willie followed him back, carrying menus.

'Choose a starter, Elspeth,' begged Hamish, 'and stop sitting there making me feel guilty.'

She suddenly smiled at him. 'You're not very romantic, are you?'

'No, he's not,' said Willie. 'Waste of space, if you ask me.'

'No one asked you,' snapped Hamish. 'For heaven's sake, order something, Elspeth, so we can send him on his way.'

They both ordered Parma ham and melon.

Mrs Wellington then came up to their table. 'When is Mrs McClellan's body being released?'

'I've just learned it's tomorrow.'

'Good. The sooner that poor woman has a Christian burial the better.' She pulled up a chair and sat down and pulled a notebook out of her capacious bag.

'We thought that instead of sandwiches and canapés, we would have a buffet lunch after the funeral. Roast chicken. Potatoes. Salad. Green peas. Trifle as dessert. Now what will your contribution be?'

'I'm doing the eulogy,' said Hamish.

'But everyone is to help with the catering. Do you think we should have wine?'

'Definitely not,' said Hamish. 'Whisky is what will be expected.'

'I'll put you down for a couple of bottles. Miss Grant?'

'I'll give you a couple of roast chickens,' said Elspeth.

'Good girl. I'll make a note of that. Angela Brodie is doing a giant trifle.'

'Is that wise?' asked Hamish. 'Angela's cooking is not of the best.'

'You can't make a mistake with trifle,' said Mrs Wellington.

They were then joined by the Currie sisters, and discussions of the arrangements went on right up until Carson arrived. So much for buying a new lipstick and French perfume and putting my best dress on, thought Elspeth gloomily, as Carson sat down when the others had left and immediately plunged into discussing the two murder cases with Hamish. To Elspeth's relief, Carson only had one glass of wine and said he had to keep a clear head to drive back to Strathbane. Maybe Hamish would ask her back to the police station for a nightcap.

But when they all stood outside the restaurant, Carson thanked Hamish for the meal and drove off.

'That was a waste of time,' said Elspeth crossly. 'You both went over and over everything and got nowhere.'

'Well, that's policing,' said Hamish vaguely. 'Good night and thanks for finding out about that insurance policy for me.' He waved his hand and strolled off down the waterfront.

That waiter was right, thought Elspeth angrily. He is a waste of space and if he wants any more help from me, he can *beg* for it.

The day of Mrs McClellan's funeral dawned cold and still. Hamish put on his best suit and a black armband on his sleeve.

He walked to the Church of Scotland and joined the other mourners who were streaming in the same direction. He was suddenly nervous. He hadn't prepared anything for the eulogy, but surely a few words would do.

He was stopped before the church by two American tourists. 'Excuse me, sir,' said the man politely, 'do you think it would be considered rude if me and the wife attended the service?'

'No, not at all. Everyone welcome.'

'Thank you, sir. I am Brad Kirk and this here's my lady, Jo Ellen. We are from Baton Rouge.' He was a serious-looking little man with thinning hair and gold-rimmed glasses. His wife was equally small, but plump and wearing a long blue fun fur.

'What is the denomination of this church?' asked Mr Kirk.

'Church of Scotland.'

'Ah, that should be inneresting. We are Southern Baptist ourselves. But Jo Ellen and me are innerested in all sorts of religions.'

'I am Hamish Macbeth, the local policeman. Are you staying in Lochdubh?'

'Yes, at the Tommel Castle Hotel.'

'And what brings you so far north out of season?'

'The weather never bothers us, sir. We like quiet places. We are by way of being Scottish ourselves. My great-grandfather, I believe, was Scottish, and that makes Jo Ellen Scottish by marriage.'

'We'd best go in,' said Hamish, glancing at his watch. 'The service will be about to start.'

Mrs Wellington rushed Hamish to the front of the church. The coffin stood before the altar table with a bunch of white heather on top of it.

Mr Wellington, the minister, started the service. Soon the church was filled by the sound of weeping. Hamish had quite forgotten he was to read the eulogy until Mr Wellington called him up.

'Mrs McClellan was a good woman, a quiet woman, who enjoyed her garden,' began Hamish. 'She wass verra much a part of our daily lives.' He saw the church door at the back open and Callum Bisset come in. Hamish felt a blinding surge of anger. He hung on to the brass eagle and stared down the aisle in the direction of the television managing director.

'And Mrs McClellan would still be part of our community had not Strathbane Television set out to ruin her life.'

'That iss the truth!' shouted someone.

'She had committed a small transgression away in the past due to a minor mental illness. She had received treatment for it. But the television people decided to muckrake. Having no sense of common decency themselves, they did not know what effect such exposure would have on a God-fearing woman. They were going to expose her on national television, hold her up to ridicule, and so she took her own life.'

Hamish pointed down the church at Callum Bissett. 'I wonder you dare show your face in here, for you killed that woman as surely as if you had poisoned her.'

Callum Bissett shot to his feet and hurried out.

'But I suggest we remember the charming lady we knew,' said Hamish, 'and remember her in our prayers.'

He regained his seat.

Carson shifted uneasily in his pew. He wondered if Hamish Macbeth were a trifle mad. But round about him, villagers were murmuring their approval of his eulogy.

At the end of the service, the coffin was raised on the shoulders of six villagers. A piper led the way, playing a lament.

And then behind the coffin, the congregation walked out of the church and along the waterfront and over the humpbacked bridge to the cemetery. Hamish saw Elspeth a little way in front of him. He felt he had behaved badly last night, walking off like that. He could at least have given her a kiss on the cheek. But the wail of the pipe lament was being echoed back by the mountains and he felt a great sadness.

They huddled around the graveside while the minister committed the body to the ground. Then he read the famous passage from Corinthians. 'A time to love and a time to die.'

Villagers were weeping openly as Mr McClellan threw the first handful of earth on the coffin.

Then they all walked to the church hall, sniffling and drying their eyes.

He found the Americans beside him. 'That was very affecting,' said Mr Kirk.

'You'd best come along to the church hall,' said Hamish. 'There's going to be hot food.'

'I am by way of being in the same business as yourself, sir,' said Mr Kirk.

'Police?'

'No, insurance investigator.'

'Ah, same sort of work.'

'Sometimes it can be very frustrating,' said Mr Kirk. 'There was a case in New Orleans. I was sure the husband had killed his wife but I couldn't prove it and neither could the police.'

'Why was that?'

'This man had been out rowing with his wife. The boat capsized, she couldn't swim and drowned. He said he made heroic efforts to save her. Trouble was, he had insured her life heavily. It had been a calm day. He said she was fooling around and had stood up in the boat and that's what made it capsize. I checked around and found she wasn't the sort of lady to fool around, she had never gone out with her husband before in the boat, and everyone including her husband knew she couldn't swim. That was a mighty powerful speech you made in the church.'

They were nearly at the church hall. Elspeth hovered for a moment by the entrance but Hamish was now engrossed in describing the

226

murders to Mr Kirk. She gave a slight shrug and walked into the hall.

At first it was all very decorous and sad. People collected plates of food and sat at long tables talking in hushed whispers. At last, Dr Brodie said something to Mr McClellan and led him out of the hall.

Whisky bottles were passed around. The talk became livelier. 'How long does this go on?' asked Mr Kirk, who was sitting next to Hamish.

'It'll go on until late. Ways have changed up here. Not so long ago, it would have gone on all week.'

By evening, people were singing ballads and people were reciting poems. Mr Kirk took out a large notebook and began to make notes as if reporting of some weird aboriginal tribe.

Hamish noticed with surprise that his boss was still there, his tie loosened, chatting to the villagers.

At last, when he saw an empty seat beside Elspeth, he rose and went to join her.

'Everyone's here,' he said. 'Met your murderer yet?'

'I told you, I was just joking, Hamish. I've got to leave shortly and write this up.'

Her manner was cold, her silver eyes veiled.

'I haven't been reading my horoscope,' said Hamish. 'Any more messages for me?'

Elspeth got to her feet. 'Not worth the effort, Hamish,' she said, and walked away.

* * *

Elspeth went back to the office. 'I took a load of photos,' said Sam Wills. 'I'll have them shortly and then you can do the captions. You know everyone in the village now, so it shouldn't be a problem.'

Sitting down at her computer, Elspeth began to write her report slowly and carefully, for she had drunk too much whisky and Angela's trifle had been swimming in sherry.

Sam appeared with the photographs. She drank strong black coffee, numbered the photographs, and then began to write the captions. At one point she frowned. They couldn't use all the photographs in the newspaper, so she discarded a pile of them after looking at them. There was one face missing, she was sure of it. She picked up the photographs again and studied them and then shook her head. She must have been mistaken.

By midnight, she had finished.

She switched off the computer and went out on to the waterfront. The lights were still blazing from the church hall. But what was the point in going back?

Elspeth went home to her flat, glad she didn't have to bother cooking, for she had eaten a lot at the reception.

She washed and went to bed, and just before she closed her eyes, she vowed never to think of Hamish Macbeth again.

* * *

'Yes, you can have my bed again, sir,' Hamish was saying patiently as he supported a very drunk Carson back to the police station.

'I could live here,' said Carson, waving a drunken arm in the direction of the loch.

'You might find it a bit boring,' said Hamish soothingly.

He got his boss to bed and then took Lugs for a walk. 'I'll need to buy a good mattress and a duvet for that cell, Lugs,' said Hamish, 'for I think I might be using it a lot.'

He returned to the police station and wearily undressed and washed and got into the hard bed in the cell. Loud snores were coming from the bedroom. I feel just like a married man who's had a tiff with the wife, thought Hamish.

Elspeth sat bolt upright in bed. She could smell smoke, still hear the crackling of flames and the howl of a dog. What a dream! But so real!

'I'm about to make a fool of myself,' she muttered. She got out of bed and went to the phone and phoned the police station.

Hamish would not have bothered answering it had Lugs not already woken him by barking sharply. Lugs's bark had risen to a howl as Hamish picked up the phone.

'It's Elspeth,' he heard. 'Hamish, I'm probably mad, but take a look outside and make sure no one's trying to set fire to the police station.'

'Right.' He slammed down the phone. 'Shhh,' he commanded Lugs. He crept through to the kitchen and, without switching on the light, peered through the window. To his left, he saw a sort of darker blackness and he smelled petrol.

He took a powerful torch down from a shelf and gently unlocked the kitchen door and moved softly out into the blackness. Lugs had fallen silent but was right behind him.

Suddenly Lugs hurtled off into the blackness. There was an oath and a sharp cry of pain.

Hamish shone his torch. Finlay Swithers stood there, a petrol can beside him, trying to beat off Lugs, who had sunk his teeth into his leg.

'Get the dog off me!' shouted Swithers. 'My leg. Oh, my leg.'

Hamish went swiftly up to him and twisted his arm up his back and only then did he command Lugs to let him go. He marched Swithers into the police station, into the cell, and locked him in.

Then he roused Carson. 'You'd best get up,' said Hamish. 'It's Finlay Swithers. He's just tried to set fire to us.'

Carson jumped out of bed and grabbed his trousers and pulled them on. 'Here,' said Hamish, throwing him a pullover. 'Your shirt's in the wash.'

'Where is he?'

'In the cell.'

'Charged him yet?'

'No, we'll have a look at the evidence.'

He gave Carson another torch and they went outside. Underneath the kitchen window, they found bales of straw soaked in petrol and at the front door of the police station as well. Carson phoned Strathbane and ordered them to send men over.

Then he went to the cell, and while Hamish took notes, he charged Finlay Swithers with attempted murder and arson.

'Why did you do it?' Carson demanded.

'I wanted rid of that bastard,' said Swithers, glaring at Hamish. He stank of booze.

'Right. This'll put you away for a long time.'

They had to wait until a team arrived from Strathbane. The petrol-soaked bales of straw had to be photographed and taken away for evidence, along with the can of petrol Hamish had found Swithers with and the empty cans of petrol that were found in his truck outside.

'How did he hope to get away with it?' marvelled Carson.

'He knew about the funeral,' said Hamish. 'He knew everyone would be in the church. He picked his moment.'

'I think I'm sober enough to get back to Strathbane,' said Carson wearily. 'Just put my clothes in a bag. They won't be dry yet. It's a good thing you woke when you did.'

Hamish wondered whether to tell him about Elspeth. She must have seen something, or was she psychic? He decided to leave it for the moment.

'The cheek of the man,' said Carson as they walked out to his car. 'He left threatening to sue you because that dog of yours bit his leg.'

'At least he'll be in prison where he should have been all along,' said Hamish. 'Good night, sir.'

'Did I make a fool of myself last night? I can't remember getting to bed.'

'Och, no, you were the perfect gentleman.'

'See you, Hamish. By the way, my name's Pat, short for Patrick.'

'Go carefully, Pat.'

'That I will. Take care.'

Carson drove off. Hamish grinned. Blair would go ape if he knew he was on first-name terms with his superior officer.

He went into the police station and phoned Elspeth. Her sleepy voice answered. 'I suppose you've rung me at dawn to tell me what a fool I am.'

'No, you were right. How did you know?'

'I had a dream. It was so real. The flames, the smoke, the dog howling. I thought of Lugs and then I thought of you.'

'So you are psychic, you have the second sight, just like the seer said. Has it happened before?'

'Twice. But it always makes me feel sick and frightened. I don't want to talk about it.'

'I'm right grateful to you, Elspeth. I'm sorry I've been a bit ... well ... cold at times, but I don't want another involvement. I don't want anyone getting close.'

'Who's getting close?' demanded Elspeth crossly.

'I mean, I would like it if we could be friends.'

'Okay. Now can I get back to sleep?'

Chapter Thirteen

Oh, thievish Night,
Why shouldst thou, but for some felonious end,
In thy dark lantern thus close up the stars,
That nature hung in heaven, and filled their
    lamps
With everlasting oil, to give due light
To the misled and lonely traveller?
                                        – John Milton

Any impetus there had been in solving the
murder of Felicity Pearson had ebbed away.
Hamish covered his local beat, attended to his
crofting chores, and occasionally went over
and over his notes, looking to see if there was
anything he might have missed.

On his day off, two weeks after the funeral,
on impulse he phoned Grace Witherington
and asked if he could have another chat with
her. She told him to come over for coffee at
three in the afternoon.

He took Lugs with him, telling the dog to be
on his best behaviour. The mobile van had

gone from outside the flats. What the police in Strathbane were doing about solving the murder, Hamish did not know. Jimmy had been avoiding his phone calls and Carson had not made another visit to the police station in Lochdubh.

'Come in,' said Grace, opening the door of the flats to him. 'I'm upstairs.'

'Is it all right if I bring my dog?'

'Certainly. I like dogs. I don't have one myself any more,' she said, mounting the stairs. 'My old dog, Queenie, died ten years ago and I couldn't bear to get another. They need such a lot of love and attention and I wasn't free to travel. Of course, I could have put Queenie in kennels like everyone else who goes abroad, but then, I knew I wouldn't enjoy my holiday. I'd always have been worrying about how she was getting on. Here we are.'

She led the way through a small hall and into a book-lined living room. 'Make yourself comfortable and I'll get the coffee.'

Lugs stretched out in front of the fire. Hamish suddenly found he was fumbling in his pocket for a cigarette packet. How odd that after all this time, he should still automatically go through the motions of looking for a cigarette.

Grace came in carrying a laden tray, which she set down on a low table in front of him. 'Help yourself to sugar and milk and tell me why you have come. I'm intrigued.'

'It's Felicity Pearson,' said Hamish. 'I get a

picture of a vain, weak, not likeable woman, and yet you were a friend of hers. I'm trying to get a better picture of her.'

'Now you're making me feel guilty,' said Grace. 'I wasn't ever a friend of hers, I told you that. The fact is that the television programme she produced brought me in some welcome money. I wanted to keep her on my side. I am afraid she was in fact all the things you said about her. But I began to think even the television programme wasn't worth the hours I spent listening to her talk about herself. Have you heard the actor's joke? That's enough about me. Let's talk about my performance.'

'So there was no one she was really close to?'

'Have you tried Rory MacBain?'

'I think that one didn't care what she was like and what she looked like. All he was after was a quickie on the office floor when it suited him.'

'Dear me. I should feel sorry for her but I can't. I had really begun to dislike her so much, you see. I read in the papers this morning that she has been found guilty of the murder of Crystal French.'

'So they've released that bit of news at last. How did you feel when you read it?' asked Hamish.

'Do you know, I wasn't surprised, and yet I should be. I mean, when she was here talking to me, I didn't think, oh, here's a murderer. But if that murder's solved, why do you want to know about her?'

'Because her own murder isn't solved.'

'She was killed down at the old docks. No one saw or heard anything?'

'I don't know what headquarters have got, but I don't think they've found any witnesses.'

'Wait a minute. Drink your coffee. It's getting cold. There's something. We were doing a discussion programme on drugs and the menace of crack and heroin in Strathbane. Professor Tully said something like the old docks should be pulled down to make way for waterfront housing because they were only a marketplace for drug dealing. I mean, it's a long shot. But someone might have been there that night who didn't want to have anything to do with the police.'

'You might have something there,' said Hamish slowly. 'I'd better have a word with Professor Tully first. He might just have thrown that in to pretend to an inside knowledge he doesn't have.'

'How cynical of you and how well you know him!'

'I don't know him, but he's a Highlander.'

'And it takes one to know one?'

'Exactly.'

Hamish drove over to Bonar Bridge. The light was already fading fast and cold little stars twinkled above in the Sutherland sky.

Professor Tully lived in an old Georgian house, just outside the town. It was Scottish

Georgian, eighteenth century, square and without ornament. The garden was a wilderness of weeds.

To Hamish's relief, the professor was at home. He invited Hamish in but insisted Lugs be left outside. 'I have cats,' he explained.

'Lugs is very kind to cats,' said Hamish.

'No dog is kind to cats,' replied the professor, so Hamish had to take Lugs back and shut him in the Land Rover.

Hamish went back into the house. The professor ushered him through to a dark and grimy kitchen where not much seemed to have been changed since the eighteenth century. There were two old stone sinks and enormous wooden dressers, their once-white paint yellow with age. Light came from a dingy forty-watt bulb high up in the ceiling.

'So how can I help you?' asked Professor Tully.

'On one of your discussion programmes, you said that the old docks at Strathbane should be pulled down because they had become a market for drug dealing.'

The professor leaned back in his chair and stared at the ceiling. 'I can remember those docks when they were thriving. I can even remember Strathbane when it wasn't a sink of iniquity, a monstrous carbuncle on the face of the Highlands.'

'But about the drugs?'

'I wouldn't want to be getting anyone in trouble.'

'I'm only interested in finding out a possible witness to the murder of Felicity Pearson.'

The professor lowered his gaze to the battered kitchen table, which still held the remains of his lunch.

'You see,' he said at last, 'there's this lad lives in Bonar Bridge. He's clean now. But I got talking to him one day when I was shopping in town. He said he used to buy his stuff down at the docks, said it was a sort of marketplace at night. He said it was safer than the clubs because the police hardly ever went around the docks at night.'

'What's his name?'

'I don't think . . .'

'If he's clean, then he won't be getting into trouble and any information he gives me, well, I'll protect the source.'

'It's Barry Williams, a young English fellow. Family moved up here some years ago.'

'And where does he live?'

'Somewhere up at the council houses.'

Hamish thanked him and left. He did not want to ask the local police for the address and maybe scare the boy into silence. He asked for the address at the shops and finally found that Barry lived near Mrs Gordon.

A woman answered the door to him and looked shocked when he asked to speak to Barry. 'My son's a good boy,' she said defiantly.

'I'm sure he is,' said Hamish patiently. 'I just want a wee word with him.'

She turned and called, 'Barry!'

A thin youth came down the stairs behind her, dressed in torn jeans and a bomber jacket. 'I was just going out,' he said sulkily.

'Come on, then,' said Hamish. 'We'll just walk along the road a bit.'

'I haven't been doing anything,' said Barry, hunching his thin shoulders against the cold.

'I know. Look, Barry, you once told Professor Tully that they dealt drugs down at the docks. I know it's all behind you now, but I want a name of your supplier.'

'I can't be doing that!'

'Barry, I have to know. A murder was committed at the docks and I'm looking for witnesses. No one will know it was you that told me. But if you don't tell me, I'll need to get all official and take you into Strathbane for questioning.'

Barry moodily kicked a Coke can. 'You're sure?'

'You have my word.'

'It was the Big Drip.'

'Come on. A name?'

'I'm telling you. That's what he was called.' Hamish sighed. 'What did he look like?'

'Sort of tall, as tall as you, and with bleached hair in spikes and a nose ring. Dealt heroin.'

'And you only know his nickname?'

'Yes. That's all anybody knew.'

Back at the police station, Hamish phoned Carson. Not so long ago, he would have

241

phoned Jimmy, but he knew now that Jimmy would pretend that the information was his own.

Carson listened carefully and then said, 'I'll look into it. Stay by the phone.'

Hamish cooked dinner for himself and Lugs. He wondered what Elspeth was doing. She had not called at the police station for a good few days now.

He was just getting ready for bed when the phone rang. It was Carson. 'Got him,' he said cheerfully. 'Hughie Fraser, otherwise known as the Big Drip because he's six feet tall.'

'Any chance of finding him?'

'Every chance. He's just started doing time in Strathbane prison for pushing. We'll see him in the morning.'

'*We*, sir?'

'Yes, you can come as well. I'll meet you outside the prison at nine-thirty in the morning.'

Carson was waiting outside the prison when Hamish drove up. 'What's this?' snapped Carson, looking at his watch. 'Highland time?'

Hamish glanced at his own watch. It was nine-thirty-one. 'I am sorry I am a minute late, sir,' he said. 'The traffic was awful.'

Carson knew that as the prison lay on the outskirts of the town, there had probably been no traffic except an occasional sheep, so he knew Hamish was mocking him. He also knew he deserved it. But he was beginning to want to put a distance between himself and this odd constable. He knew he was not following procedure by inviting Hamish along. He should have had a detective with him, not a local bobby.

The prison was a Victorian one, made of shiny red brick. Inside, the walls were painted institutional green. They were led along bleak corridors and up an iron staircase. A warder opened a door to a dark room furnished only with a table and three chairs. 'I'll go and get him, sir,' he said.

Carson and Hamish waited in silence, side by side at one end of the table, looking at the empty chair opposite. Prison noises filtered in through the thick door from outside; clanging of gates, raucous shouts, curses.

Then the door opened. A tall man in prison overalls came in with the warder. He had a long white face and a very red mouth and weak, watery eyes. The warder took up a position at the door.

'Sit down, Hughie,' ordered Carson.

Hughie sat down and looked at them. His eyes had that peculiar faraway stare of someone who had served time before.

'Got any cigarettes?' he asked.

Hamish took out a packet and a box of matches but kept them on his side of the table. 'In a minute,' said Hamish. 'Let's see if you can help us first.'

Carson leaned forwards. 'We believe you were in the habit of peddling drugs down at the docks. Did you ever go to Dock Number Two at night?'

Hughie eyed the cigarettes hungrily but said nothing.

To Carson's surprise, Hamish shouted angrily, 'We know you did, man, so give us a bit of help.'

He inched the packet of cigarettes nearer Hughie.

'What if I did?' asked Hughie.

'We're interested in the night Felicity Pearson was killed,' said Carson.

'I'd nothing to do with that. Give me a cigarette.'

Hamish drew the packet back towards him and put his hand over it. 'You saw something,' he said. 'And you'd better tell us what it was. We'll take your fingerprints and casts of every shoe in your digs and we'll prove you were there.' Hamish gambled on the prisoner's almost superstitious fear of forensic work. 'And if you sit there silent, we'll assume you did the murder because she wandered on to your patch. We're anxious to clear the murder up.'

'I didnae do it,' said Hughie, becomingly visibly alarmed. 'You can't pin it on me.'

Hamish gave him a slow smile. 'Oh, no? Try me.'

Hughie hunched forwards. 'Give me a cigarette and I'll tell you.'

Hamish took one cigarette out of the packet and handed it to him and then struck a match and lit it.

Hughie took a hungry draw, blew out smoke, and then said sulkily, 'I was there. I heard the blast, that's all. I went out and saw a body lying on the ground. I was in the warehouse. Man, I ran like hell.'

'But did you see the murderer?' asked Hamish.

'I got a glimpse of a figure walking away. It was dark, man. Light footsteps. Could have been a man or a woman.'

'Which way did this person run?'

'Out on to the road. Whoever it was went left and I ran right and didn't look back.'

'Skirt or trousers?'

'Trousers and a jacket of some kind.'

'So it was a man?'

'Funny thing. I thought it was a woman. I don't know why. Just a figure with a gun held down at the side. Something in the walk. Light, quick steps.'

Hamish pushed the packet of cigarettes and matches over to Hughie. 'Can you think of anything else? Were you waiting for a customer?'

Hughie looked shifty. 'Just hanging around in the hope someone turned up.'

Hamish studied him narrowly. 'You weren't waiting for a customer. You were waiting for *your* supplier. You're only the street man. Who was it?'

'No, no,' said Hughie desperately. 'I cannae be telling you that. I tell you that and I'll be found strung up in my cell.'

Carson took over the questioning but could get no further information. Hughie would not reveal his supplier, nor could he add any more about the murder than he had done.

When they were outside the prison, Carson said abruptly, 'There's a café round the corner. We'll go there and talk this over.'

The café was full of tired-looking women and squalling children. They had obviously been waiting for the official visiting hour, because at exactly ten o'clock, they all rose and filed out. Carson and Hamish found a table.

'So,' said Carson. 'Did you believe anything he said?'

'Yes, he was there. Yes, he heard the blast and saw the body. Yes, he thought it was a woman.'

'So we have to start looking at female suspects? Who?'

'I'd start with Amy Cornwall. Where was she the night of the murder?'

'We interviewed them all. I think she said she had gone home late and washed her hair, watched a bit of television, and went to bed. Why her? And there's no shotgun registered to any of them.'

'They're easy to come by,' said Hamish.

'So why Amy Cornwall?'

'Crystal French drove Felicity into murdering her. Felicity might have given Amy a rough time as well.'

'But Amy Cornwall is just a pretty wee lassie.'

'She doesn't have a conscience.'

'Come on. We all have one.'

'No, some are born without one. It's always everyone else's fault.'

'I'll get Jimmy Anderson on to it. Thank you for coming over, but I am sure you have enough on your own beat to keep you busy.'

Hamish looked hurt.

'Look here,' said Carson. 'It's like this. You've chosen to be a village constable over in Lochdubh. Proper procedure must be followed. I cannot go on ignoring the talents of your seniors. This is work for the CID. Now, if you wish promotion, I will do everything to help you. But as long as you decide to remain a village constable I cannot work with you and leave the CID out of it. I warn you. They are closing village police stations down all over the country. It's got so bad in the south that the farmers are complaining that whole combine harvesters are being stolen out of their fields and they are threatening to form vigilante societies. If Lochdubh is closed down, you have no option but to get transferred to Strathbane. Start now getting promoted, or you could end up on the beat down here.'

'I'll keep that in mind,' said Hamish with all the haughtiness of the truly offended Highlander, 'and get back to my beat.'

'Think about it,' said Carson.

'So I'm off the case?'

Carson made an impatient noise. 'You haven't been listening to me.'

But as he drove home, Hamish still felt cross. One minute Carson was saying, Call me Pat, the next he was behaving like God Almighty.

He climbed down from the Land Rover outside the police station and sniffed the air. It was one of those odd, balmy autumn days when soft winds blow in off the gulf stream.

He fed Lugs and told the dog what a shite Carson was, and Lugs wagged his tail in agreement and shoved his face in his food bowl.

He decided to relax and have a lazy day, maybe get out his rod and poach one of the colonel's salmon. Hamish did not regard his own occasional poaching exploits as criminal. It was every Highlander's right to take a deer from the hill and a fish from the stream.

Hamish was just getting out his rod when he heard the wail of a siren and stiffened in alarm. Lugs barked sharply.

He ran out to the waterfront. An ambulance was standing outside Patel's. Hamish rushed along. He pushed his way through the crowd into the shop. Two ambulance men were bending over Elspeth, who was looking sick and white-faced.

'What happened?' asked Hamish.

'The poor girl screamed and fainted right in the shop,' said Mrs Wellington.

'I'm all right. I just fainted,' said Elspeth feebly. 'I don't need to go to hospital.'

'I think you should go and get a checkup,' said Mrs Wellington. 'You young girls are always up to something these days. I read about it. Either starving yourselves or vomiting.'

'No, nothing like that.' Elspeth stood up. She looked at Hamish. 'Could you take me home? I'll be all right if I get to bed.'

'If you're sure you shouldn't be in the hospital,' said Hamish doubtfully.

She gave him a weak smile. 'Mrs Wellington kept me captive here for nearly an hour, waiting for the ambulance. I've had plenty of time to recover.'

Hamish took her arm and led her out. 'If she's pregnant,' he heard Nessie Currie say as they walked off, 'then he'd better make an honest woman of her.'

Hamish took Elspeth's keys and unlocked the door of her flat. Lugs, who had followed Hamish to the shop, trotted in after them.

Colour had returned to Elspeth's face. 'Do you want me to run a hot bath for you?' asked Hamish.

'No, just make us some tea.'

Hamish went into the kitchen and made tea, and collected milk, sugar and biscuits along with the teapot on a tray, and carried the lot into the living room.

'So,' he said, setting the tray down, 'what brought it on?'

'I'm frightened, Hamish. I think I must be mad.'

He took her hand in a warm clasp and squeezed it. 'You're not mad.' He released her hand. 'Here, let me pour you some tea. Lots of sugar. You seem to have had some sort of shock.'

He handed her a cup of tea and poured one for himself. 'What frightened you?'

'You won't tell anyone?'

'I promise.'

'My friend Sally is coming up from Inverness to stay with me for a few days. I hadn't much food in the house. Oh, I've left all my groceries in Patel's.'

'You can get them later or I'll get them for you.'

'I hadn't paid for them. He'll probably just put them back on the shelves.'

'Never mind the groceries. Drink some tea. Nice and hot. Good girl. Now, go on.'

'The shop was very full. I was just putting a packet of cereal in my basket when suddenly everything was dark and there was a blast, like a gun blast. I felt it hit my chest and the pain was awful. That's all I remember. Oh, Hamish, I've had a fit.'

'There now.' He put an arm around her. 'I don't want to distress you, Elspeth. You said that if you ever came across the murderer, you'd know.'

'Oh, you're as mad as I am.'

'Let's chust take a flight of fancy. Somewhere in that shop was the murderer of Felicity Pearson, so for one split second, you *were* Felicity Pearson and you felt the shotgun blast in your chest. Who was in the shop?'

'Half the village seemed to be milling around. I'm scared. I don't want a turn like that again. Funnily enough, I was playing a sort of game after the funeral. I was captioning the photographs and putting aside a great pile that weren't to be used. Sam always goes in for overkill. Sometimes he publishes so many photographs, there's hardly room for print. I remember thinking someone was missing and that intrigued me, because even old Mrs Syme who's half blind and can't walk was there in her wheelchair.'

'And you thought if you could find out who the missing person was then you might get the vibes about a murderer?'

'Something like that. It seems silly now. I mean, although my mother left the gypsies, she was fey and superstitious, too, and she filled my head with a lot of stuff.'

'I'm prepared to try anything,' said Hamish. 'I've got the electoral roll back at the police station. After you've relaxed and had a sleep, I could take it along to your office and go through the photos and find the missing person.'

'I'm all right now,' said Elspeth. 'I'll come with you.'

'Are you sure?'

'Yes,' said Elspeth reluctantly, although she felt it would be nicer to sit there forever with his arm about her shoulders.

'Have some more tea first. Do you need aspirin or anything?'

'No, Hamish. I'm just the same as I was before the attack.'

'I'll just use your phone and call Mr Patel and ask him to make a list for me of everyone he can remember who was in the shop when you were there.'

'He was so busy at the counter, Hamish, he mightn't remember.'

'Worth a try.'

He phoned Patel and then came back and held out his hand. 'Up you come and let's see if you're fit to walk.'

Chapter Fourteen

He reached a middle height, and at the stars,
Which are the brain of heaven, he looked, and
*   sank.*
Around the ancient track marched, rank on rank,
The army of unalterable law.

– George Meredith

Hamish went to the police station first to collect the electoral roll and then along to join Elspeth at the newspaper office.

She had a room, more of a ribbed-glass, open-topped excuse for a room, and was sitting with piles of photographs from the funeral in front of her.

'I've got the list,' said Hamish, sitting down next to her. 'I'll read out the names and you tick them off.'

'I've been thinking,' said Elspeth, 'there might be a few of the staff at the Tommel Castle Hotel. They would be on duty at the time of the funeral and some of them came in from other parts and might not be listed.'

'Let's try anyway,' said Hamish.

And so they began. The day dragged on. Sam looked in and asked what they were doing and Elspeth said vaguely she was helping him identify someone.

'If there's a story in it, let me know,' said Sam. 'We may only be a local paper but I could flog a good story to one of the nationals' – all of which made Hamish realize how much he owed to Elspeth for keeping silent about what he had told her.

'How far have we got?' asked Elspeth after several hours. 'I'm hungry.'

'We're three-quarters of the way down,' said Hamish. 'Let's just finish it and then we'll get a bite to eat.'

'I can't wait. Hamish, see if Willie at the restaurant can make us some sandwiches.'

'Right,' said Hamish, 'and I'll pick up that list from Mr Patel.' He left, followed by Lugs.

Elspeth ploughed on. The light had faded outside. She came to yet another name and began to go through the photographs. Not one single picture. She sat back and frowned. Of course Sam might have missed someone. But at the reception in the church hall he had taken sections of views of the room, capturing everyone present. She checked carefully again.

Hamish came back in carrying a thermos of coffee and a plate of sandwiches. 'Lugs has stayed behind,' said Hamish. 'I've told Willie Lugs can have something to eat just this once. Don't want the dog to die of obesity.'

'Hamish, I've found something. Or rather, I haven't found something.'

He sat down beside her. 'What? Who?'

'Mary Hendry.'

'What! Her at the craft shop?'

'That's the one.'

Hamish stood up and collected a couple of mugs from a shelf and poured coffee. 'Eat,' he commanded. 'We've got to think.'

He took a bite of sandwich and then said, his voice muffled by ham, egg and bread, 'I should have looked at her more closely.'

'Don't speak with your mouth full. I can hardly hear you.'

Hamish chewed and swallowed. 'Felicity Pearson spent a full hour with her. They got on. People did not get on with Felicity Pearson or want her company. I wonder what they really talked about.'

'Say Felicity was crawling to Crystal and had found something out about Mary Hendry,' said Elspeth. 'Say she *was* working on background for the behind-the-lace-curtains show. But what was there about Mary Hendry to find out?'

'Her husband died a couple of years ago,' said Hamish. 'I was away on holiday at the time.'

'How did he die?'

'He was out fishing on the Anstey above the falls. He was drunk and fell over to his death.'

They both sat eating in silence.

At last Elspeth said, 'And she had money enough to set up the shop?'

'Yes, but her husband, Frank, had a reputation for being a skinflint so it was assumed he'd left her pretty well off.'

'Was he usually drunk?'

'Quite often. I had to take his car keys away from him a few times.'

'Hamish, drinkers aren't famous for saving money.'

'What are you getting at?'

'I don't know. Just thinking.'

Lugs came panting in and slumped down on the floor and began to snore.

'Good night, you two,' called Sam from the outer office. 'Lock up when you go.'

Hamish sat with his eyes half-closed. Lugs snored and a rising wind blew along the waterfront outside.

He opened his eyes. 'How about this? Unless Felicity had something on Mary Hendry, then Mary Hendry wouldn't have talked to her amicably for an hour.'

'She might have pleaded with her to leave her alone,' suggested Elspeth.

'I can't see that cutting any ice with Felicity if she thought she was on to something. What if – just what if – Mary Hendry had seen something that incriminated Felicity and they did a deal? You leave me alone and I'll leave you alone, that sort of thing. And then when there's a paragraph in the papers about Felicity being presenter and doing the lace-curtains thing, Mary begins to think that silencing her might be a good idea. So she phones up and says something about how she can't stand the guilt any more. Mary says she'll meet Felicity at the docks to tell all. Felicity is too excited to wonder why she should choose the docks. Her vanity makes her feel immune from danger. All she can think of is what a scoop it would be to have a real live murderess confess in front of the camera.'

'But when you came back from holiday, wouldn't the village be buzzing if there had been a murder inquiry?'

'That's true. But say it seemed a straightforward accident and that Frank Hendry was proved at the autopsy to be full of booze.'

He checked the list Mr Patel had given him. 'She was in the store when you fainted, Elspeth.'

'That must have been the first time she crossed my path,' said Elspeth. 'I'd never gone to the craft shop. I was going to go nearer Christmas to get suggestions for Christmas presents. Do you want me to go and see her? I'll do it if you want, but I'm frightened.'

'No, don't do that. We need hard evidence against her, not psychic evidence. Let me think a bit more. There's something running around in the back of my brain.'

Elspeth stifled a yawn. She was suddenly feeling weary and all she wanted to do was sleep.

Hamish suddenly heard the voice of that American, Mr Kirk, saying that his work was like Hamish's own in that he was an insurance investigator.

He sat up straight. 'I wonder whether Frank Hendry was insured. I mean, look at it this way, Elspeth. The police have got so much work, they'd jump at the chance of it being a straightforward accident. But an insurance company would be reluctant to accept things just like that. What about that friend of yours at Strong Insurance? Do you think you could phone him up? Oh, it's late. The office will be closed.'

Elspeth took a thick book out of her desk drawer. 'I have his home phone number.'

'Old boyfriend?'

'You could say that. I'll fix up an appointment for you tomorrow. What time?'

'When he can manage. But it's a long drive to Inverness. Make it about ten in the morning if you can.'

Elspeth dialled. Hamish heard her say, 'George, it's me, Elspeth. Yes, I'm fine. No, I won't be down in Inverness for a bit. Our local policeman would like to have a word with you. I'll let him explain. Could you see him at ten in the morning? No, I have to work, but I'll fix up a date with you soon. His name's Hamish Macbeth.' She said goodbye and rang off and stretched and yawned.

'Well, that's that.'

'Don't you want to come with me?'

Elspeth smiled. 'No. George – his name is George Earle – he's very clinging.'

'All right. Thanks, Elspeth. Keep away from Mary Hendry.'

'Oh, I will. I'm covering a school concert over in Braikie, so that'll keep me out of the village tomorrow. It's going to be hard to prove anything after all this time, Hamish.'

'Maybe George can help.'

'Frank Hendry's life may not have been insured with Strong Insurance. But George might have heard something from one of the other insurance agencies. If you like, I'll take Lugs to Braikie with me tomorrow.'

'That would be grand. The key to the police station is up in the gutter above the kitchen door.'

George Earle was not what Hamish had expected. He had expected to confront a clerk-type person, maybe with receding hair and glasses. George Earle was tanned and fit and handsome, with thick blond hair and blue eyes.

'I was interested in finding out if someone from the village of Lochdubh, Mary Hendry, had her husband's life insured with you. He died about two years ago.'

'Right.' George switched on the computer. 'Is Elspeth well?'

'Yes, very well.'

'I don't know why she has to go and lose herself up there. Has she got a boyfriend?'

'No.'

'Well, that's something at least. Let me see. Yes, a Frank Hendry was insured by us.'

'How much?'

'One hundred and fifty thousand pounds.'

Hamish let out a whistle. 'So your insurance investigator would be looking into that death. Any chance of having a word with him?'

'I'll get my secretary to see if he's in the office. His name's Matthew Thorne.'

Hamish waited patiently. After about fifteen minutes, George came back with a small, dapper man. Everything about him was neat, from his well-brushed, thinning hair to the knife-edge creases in his trousers and the glassy polish on his shoes. 'I'll leave you to it,' said George. 'You can use my office.'

'So,' said Thorne, sitting down and carefully hitching up the creases of his trousers, 'you want to know about the Hendry business?'

'Yes, please.'

'It's like this. When a wee woman in a Highland village insures her husband for a whack and then said husband plunges over a waterfall, I naturally get suspicious. Yes, he had

gone out fishing in the pools above the waterfall. Yes, he was drunk. But I gather from the
locals that he often went out fishing when
drunk. And he wasn't that drunk, not for a big
man like that. He was over the limit for driving, but to my mind he was far from the
staggering stage. Now, do you know the top of
the falls?'

'Yes.'

'Well, the way the water rushes through the
rocks, it might just possibly pull a man over,
and yet the water is shallow. Mrs Hendry suggested that her husband may have been playing a salmon that plunged over the falls and
took him with it. The police recovered his rod.
It had been in the pool at the bottom. No fish
had been on that line. Then there was something else. By the side of the pool above the
falls, there was the remains of a half-eaten
lunch. Half a cup of coffee and half an eaten
sandwich with two sandwiches left to go.'

'If he was eating his lunch, how could a wee
woman like Mary Hendry get him to his feet
and shove him over?'

'I know. It seems impossible. But what about
this? She appears at the top of the falls. There
are a few flat rocks. She walks to the middle
and then calls out she's got her foot stuck in
the rocks, or that she's afraid. He gets up and
wades over to her. She gives him an almighty
push. He goes over. She knows what she's
doing, for there's sharp rocks at the bottom.

She gets his fishing rod and throws it over after him. I think something must have disturbed her and that's why she left the remains of the lunch.'

'Two years ago. I suppose the police combed every rock, every bit o' heather, and searched the water.'

'As a matter of fact they didn't,' said Thorne. 'I was up against Detective Chief Inspector Blair. Know him?'

'Oh, yes,' said Hamish gloomily.

'He berated me and said us insurance investigators were all the same, do anything not to pay out. In their opinion, it was an accident, and so we had to pay.'

'And what did you make of Mary Hendry?'

'Not much. She burst into tears every time she saw me. I couldn't tell whether she was acting or not. I don't see what you can do.'

'I hope I think of something,' said Hamish. 'If there's anything at all, I'll let you know.'

'Here's my card with my home phone number and mobile phone number.'

Hamish rose and made for the door. Then he turned. 'I was away on holiday at the time. Who was with Mary Hendry? I mean, who in the village was there to comfort her?'

'The minister's wife, Mrs Wellington.'

Hamish went out. 'Oh, Mr Macbeth,' said the secretary. 'Just a minute.' She handed him a large bunch of red roses. 'Mr Earle says, Would you give these to Miss Elspeth Grant?'

'Yes, I'll be seeing her later.' Hamish took the flowers.

Back in the village, he left the flowers at the newspaper office for Elspeth and then went up to the manse to speak to Mrs Wellington.

'What brings you, Hamish?' demanded the minister's wife. 'I'm going out shortly, so I haven't time to make you tea.'

'I wanted to ask you about Mary Hendry. Are you close to her?'

'Not close, no.'

'But you spent time with her after her husband died?'

'That is part of my duties as minister's wife.'

'Would you say she was in a bad state of shock?'

'Yes, I would. And very frightened, too.'

'Why frightened?'

'Those dreadful insurance people sent a man to hound her. I told him that Frank Hendry was dead drunk and had an accident and that they should be fulfilling their obligations instead of making a poor widow's life a misery. I'm glad she set up that shop soon after. Took her mind off the tragedy. I thought at one point she might lose her mind.'

'Oh, really? Why?'

'I couldn't sleep one night and I thought I would go downstairs and make myself some hot milk. I took it into the living room and looked out. It was a clear starry night and there was a phosphorescent glow from the loch. I saw Mary, walking along the waterfront. I went right out, nightgown and dressing gown and all. I said, "Mary, where are you going? It's two in the morning." She was muttering, "I must find it. I must find it." I asked her what it was, very gently you know, because I feared her mind might be going. She said she had lost a Celtic cross that she wore on a chain round her neck. I took her arm and guided her back to her home, got her into bed and gave her a sleeping pill. Poor woman. I blame that insurance company. They nearly turned her mind.'

Hamish drove to the Tommel Castle Hotel, past the hotel entrance and down a bumpy track that led through the estate. He stopped at the water bailiff's cottage. Joe Kennedy, the water bailiff, was at home. 'What d'ye want?' he demanded with a scowl. He had been trying to catch Hamish poaching for years.

'I want to search up at the top of the falls and I don't want you charging at me, messing up the ground.'

'Go ahead,' said Joe, 'but if I catch you with a rod, I'll have you this time.'

Hamish climbed up to the top of the falls and put on his waders, which he had fetched from the Land Rover. The peaty brown water of the

River Anstey swirled around the rocks. Curlews piped dismally from the heather. He moved slowly through the water. How on earth could he hope to find anything after all this time? And it was a beauty spot. Hotel visitors came here to fish or just to admire the view. The strong flow of water tugged at his feet and ankles, but it was not powerful enough to drag a man over.

Right, thought Hamish, let's suppose the scenario that the investigator conjured up was true. If I were a small woman who wanted to get a large man off balance, where would I stand? He moved to the centre of the river right above the falls. Yes, I think right here. The riverbed dips right here.

He bent down and began to search in the water, feeling round and under stones until his hands were numbed by the icy water.

Wait a bit, he thought. It wouldn't come off just like that. Say he grabbed at her and caught the chain. It would be wrenched off. It might be down in the pool below.

He made his way down the side of the falls. The water plunged with a roar into the pool below. Hamish looked at it helplessly.

Then he suddenly remembered that Ian Chisholm went scuba diving. He went back to the Land Rover and then drove quickly to Ian's garage in Lochdubh.

Hamish explained what he wanted and said eagerly, 'I'll pay you for your time, Ian.'

265

'Och, I'll do it for the fun, Hamish. I owe you something for catching those schoolboys. So you're looking for a silver Celtic cross on a chain? It's a long shot.'

'The light's fading, Ian.'

'Doesn't matter. It'll be dark anyway. I've got one of those underwater lamps.'

'Fine, how long will it take you to get ready?'

'I'll get my gear now.'

Elspeth stood on the waterfront with Lugs. She had just got back from Braikie. She watched with interest as Hamish and Ian loaded scuba-diving equipment into the Land Rover. 'What's happening?' she called.

'I'm thinking it's better you don't know,' said Hamish, frightened that if he told Elspeth any more, she might take it upon herself to confront Mary Hendry.

Elspeth watched him drive off and then ran to her own car, got in with Lugs, and set off in pursuit.

Hamish waited patiently beside the pool below the waterfall while Ian suited up and plunged in. He could see flickers of light from Ian's lamp dancing on the surface.

Suddenly a voice in his ear said. 'What's he looking for?'

Hamish started and turned around. Elspeth was standing over him, Lugs panting beside her. 'If you must know,' he said, 'Mary Hendry lost a silver Celtic cross on a chain and it's a slim chance she might have dropped it here.'

Elspeth sat down beside him and hugged her knees. 'So why didn't you tell me that before?'

'I was frightened you would rush off and see Mary Hendry and have another of your turns. Get the flowers from lover-boy?'

'Yes, thanks. So Frank Hendry was insured?'

'Heavily.'

'Didn't the police divers search the river at the time?'

'No, Blair wrote "accident" on the case and that was that.'

'But you think Frank might have grabbed at his wife's chain before he went over?'

'Something like that.'

Mary Hendry was standing patiently in Patel's store behind Joe Kennedy, who was buying a bottle of whisky. 'I'd better get back up the river,' Joe was saying. 'I feel that lang drip of a policeman is up to something.'

'Our Hamish?' Mr Patel's dark face broke into a grin. 'What's he up to?'

'I took a look before I came here. He's got Ian Chisholm in scuba-diving gear searching the pool under the falls. I bet he's got that diver picking out the salmon with his hands and throwing them out to him.'

'I should think that's an impossibility,' said Mr Patel. 'Here's your whisky. Why, Mrs Hendry! You've dropped your groceries. Wait a minute and I'll be round there to help you pick them up.'

'When he surfaces again, I'll get him to quit,' said Hamish gloomily. 'Either he's going to freeze or we are.'

'Look at the stars!' said Elspeth. 'How bright they are! And there's a new moon.'

'Bugger the stars,' said Hamish rudely. 'This iss the wild goose chase if effer there was one.'

Elspeth clutched his arm.

'Look!'

A hand rose out of the dark waters of the pool and the starlight shone down and glinted on a silver Celtic cross.

Chapter Fifteen

A pair of star-cross'd lovers.
— William Shakespeare

When the cross had been safely stowed away in one of the forensic envelopes and Ian was getting changed, Elspeth said eagerly, 'What now? Do we go and confront her?'

'Procedure, procedure, Elspeth. I phone Strathbane. Carson and detectives will arrive.'

'But you ought to get the credit!'

'Too much credit'll get me a posting to Strathbane. There's method in my duty.'

They drove back to the police station. 'You'd better be ready to make a statement, Ian,' said Hamish.

He phoned Strathbane and spoke urgently to Carson.

'Good work,' said Carson. 'Don't move. We'll be right over.'

'What will we do until they get here?' asked Elspeth. 'Eat something?'

'I think for this one, they'll probably take the

police helicopter. They'll be here right soon. But I can fry us some eggs and bacon.'

'I'll do that.'

'No, it's my kitchen and I'll do it.' Hamish somehow didn't want any woman taking over his kitchen. That would be a start to some woman taking over his life and breaking his heart.

They had just finished eating when Hamish heard the whirr of a helicopter. 'That's them,' he said.

They walked outside. A police helicopter was landing on the waterfront. Carson got out with Jimmy Anderson and Detective Harry MacNab and a policewoman. 'Backup's on its way,' he said. 'Where does she live?'

'Over there. The flat above the craft shop.'

'Right. You go back to the police station, Macbeth, and leave this to us.'

'But I'm the one who's found out everything,' protested Hamish.

'I'll call round afterwards and let you know what happens,' said Carson, not meeting his eyes.

'This is outrageous!' shouted Elspeth, who had followed Hamish out to meet the helicopter.

Hamish pulled her away. 'It's no use,' he said. 'Let's stand here and watch.'

Carson and the detectives and policewoman marched to the craft shop and climbed the stairs at the side that led to the flat above. The detective chief inspector rang the bell. Then he hammered on the door. No reply. He stood back and nodded to Jimmy. Both Jimmy and Harry threw their shoulders against the door, to no effect.

'Try opening it,' said the policewoman.

Carson turned the handle and the door swung open. They rushed inside. In the bedroom, two suitcases full of clothes lay open on the bed, but of Mary Hendry, there was no sign.

Hamish and Elspeth were joined by Ian. 'She's gone,' said Hamish. 'I know it.'

'I know where she might be if she thought the game was up. You could hear that helicopter for miles,' said Elspeth.

Hamish swung round. 'Where?'

'It's a long shot. The falls.'

'Let's get in the Land Rover,' said Hamish. 'It's worth a try.'

Carson came out on the steps of Mary Hendry's flat in time to see Hamish speeding off. He felt angry because he knew he should have taken Hamish with them, he should never have listened to complaints from CID.

Hamish, Ian, and Elspeth were soon climbing up towards the falls, their torches sending yellow beams of light across the heather. They stopped by the pool at the bottom of the falls to catch their breath.

Hamish shone his torch up at the top of the falls. 'There she is,' he cried. 'Don't do it, Mary.'

She was standing in the water at the very edge of the falls, just where Hamish had guessed she had pushed her husband over.

Hamish scrabbled up the side of the falls with Elspeth and Ian behind him.

He began to edge his way towards her through the swirling water.

'Don't come any nearer,' shouted Mary.

They were only about two feet apart now.

'I knew the game was up when Joe Kennedy told me you were diving up at the falls,' she said. 'There's no way I'm spending the rest of my life in prison.'

'Why did you do it?' asked Hamish.

'He was a bastard, that's why. Kept me practically in rags so that he could drink and drink and use his fists on me.'

'But why kill Felicity?'

'That bitch had it coming. I went up the back road for a walk to clear my head and I saw her. I knew she was coming to see me because she'd phoned me the day before. So when she called round, I told her I'd seen her. If she kept quiet about me, I'd keep quiet about her. She seemed glad to talk.'

Elspeth crouched on the bank, listening to every word. Despite the roar of the falls, every word that Mary said reached her clearly.

'She said she'd taken enough. She said she'd been planning it since Crystal arrived. I told her that I'd killed Frank. We were sisters in crime. But when I read she was going to do that programme, I got frightened. I had nothing on her, but she could bring the police and the insurance company down on my back. I phoned her and said I was prepared to talk about it on camera because it was weighing on my conscience. She was so vain, I think she even forgot that I had witnessed her murdering someone. So she got it, right in the chest. Frank had a shotgun he'd never bothered registering.'

'Mary, if you can prove Frank was a nasty husband, they'll go easy on you. Don't be silly. I'll get you a good lawyer.'

'I had years of it,' said Mary bitterly. 'Years! He made my life a hell.'

'Look, come on, Mary. Don't jump. It's a nasty death. Here, take my hand.'

Hamish held out his hand.

'Did you find it?' she asked.

'What? The cross? Yes.'

'I knew things would go wrong for me ever since I lost that cross.'

'Mary,' coaxed Hamish. 'It's a cold, cold night and the water's freezing. If you're in prison, at least you'll be alive. Come, now. Take my hand.'

He leaned nearer while Elspeth and Ian held their breaths.

Suddenly a great beam of light shone up and on Mary and Hamish. A stentorian voice through a megaphone shouted, 'Mary Hendry. You are under arrest.'

'*NO!*' shouted Hamish.

And Mary jumped.

Her body hurtled down into the falls and on to the jagged rocks below. The cascading water tore at her body, which slowly dislodged itself from the rocks and sank into the swirling waters of the pool and disappeared from sight.

Hamish slowly picked his way back to the bank and slumped beside Elspeth. 'The fools,' he said. 'The bloody fools.'

Back at the police station, Hamish grimly typed his report and then placed it with the little cross on his desk. The police divers were recovering Mary Hendry's body. He knew Carson would be with him presently. He had typed up statements from Elspeth and Ian, who were waiting in the kitchen.

He walked through. 'Thanks,' he said curtly. 'You can both go home. I've no doubt our famous CID will be calling on you tomorrow.'

'Don't you want me to stay?' asked Elspeth plaintively. 'As moral backup?'

Hamish's face softened. 'No, you've done your bit, lassie. Go home and get a good night's sleep.'

Elspeth rose and shivered. 'I don't think I'll ever forget the sight of her going over the falls. If only they had left you alone.'

Carson walked in. Elspeth and Ian stood up to leave. 'You,' said Elspeth, facing Carson, 'are a stupid bastard.'

They both walked out.

'I have your report, sir,' said Hamish, 'and the cross as evidence.'

'You should have told us where you were going,' said Carson, sitting down.

'I wish you'd never come,' said Hamish, sitting down as well. 'I nearly had her.'

'At least it saves the state a court case,' said Carson. 'How did you guess it was her?'

'At Mrs McClellan's funeral, there was an insurance investigator from America. That got me thinking about insurance, and when I found out she'd insured her husband for a lot of money, I started asking around. Mrs Wellington said that right after Frank's death, Mary was going mad with worry over a Celtic cross she had lost, so I got Ian to dive in the pool. Och, it's all in the report,' said Hamish wearily. 'I'll get it for you.'

He came back and placed the report in front of Carson. 'That's your copy. I've sent a copy to police headquarters.'

'Thank you. Fine bit of detecting.'

'So why did you keep me off the case? If you had not, I would have told you about my guess that she was at the falls and suggested you leave it to me.'

'I was following procedure,' said Carson heavily. 'CID were complaining that I was keeping them off the case. It's your fault for wanting to stay a village constable.'

'It's because I'm a village constable that I solved your murders for you. I know people better than I know police procedure. With your permission, sir, I'd like to go to bed. It's been a long day.'

'Certainly. We'll meet again tomorrow. I'll need to stay here for the night.'

'I believe they have rooms at the Tommel Castle Hotel, sir.'

Carson rose and looked at Hamish awkwardly, but Hamish, who had risen as well, stood there, ramrod stiff, his blank eyes staring at Carson's left shoulder.

Lugs, sensing his master's anger, let out a low growl.

'Right. I'll be off then.' Carson walked to the door. Hamish glared at his retreating back and experienced a spurt of rage.

Lugs leapt from his corner and bit the retreating detective chief inspector on the backside.

Carson swung round, his eyes blazing. Hamish looked at him steadily.

'Good night, sir,' he said.

Carson went off.

'Come here, Lugs,' said Hamish, stooping down and picking up his dog. 'You shouldnae hae done that but I'm right glad you did. Let's go to bed.'

Carson was a churchgoing man and had a healthy conscience, and that conscience was bothering him. He had to admit to himself that it was not only complaints from CID that had made him keep Hamish away, but vanity on his part. He wanted the solution to the case to be all his own.

He knew that Hamish could probably have talked Mary Hendry out of jumping over the falls. He remembered the good times he had enjoyed at the police station and felt he had lost a friend.

Jimmy Anderson was subdued as he took statements from Elspeth and Ian the following day. Both of them let him know what they thought about heavyhanded interference in a case that Hamish had solved for them.

The normal place for himself and Carson and the rest of the police force to meet in such circumstances would have been at the police station. But by tacit consent, they agreed to meet at the Tommel Castle Hotel, where they were conscious of sour looks from the staff, for the news of what had happened had been spread by Elspeth and Ian.

Frank Hendry's shotgun had been found under Mary's bed. They had no doubt that the lab would prove it had been used to kill Felicity.

For his part, Hamish went about his usual crofting chores, not at all surprised that none of them had called on him. He had to admit that he had brought things on himself. He should have challenged and charged Mary and then sent in his report. It was no use blaming Carson for her death when he felt he was as much to blame. Did ever a man have such dread of promotion?

He was just washing his hands at an outside tap at the back of the police station when Elspeth appeared.

'Feeling all right?' asked Hamish.

'Bit shaky. To tell the truth, I'll see that body going over the falls until the day I die.'

'Come inside. I'll make coffee.'

'I thought they'd all be here.'

'No, their guilty consciences are keeping them away. But I'm as much to blame.'

'Why?' she asked, following him into the kitchen. Hamish took the cleat and lifted the top off the stove and threw some peat inside.

'If I hadn't been so anxious not to leave Lochdubh, not to get promotion, I'd have charged her myself. I could have talked her away from the edge of the falls.'

278

'Maybe you could. But you're forgetting one thing. She'd killed two people. If her husband treated her so badly, then maybe that turned her mind. But to plan cold-bloodedly to kill Felicity! I mean, when she saw Felicity, all she had to do was tell you. Felicity would have been arrested. But she'd still be alive. No one would have been any the wiser about Mary. On the other hand, I don't think anyone should go unpunished for taking a life.'

Hamish put a kettle on the stove. 'You're a comfort, Elspeth. That's a rare gift you've got. It was you fainting in Patel's that put me on to her.'

'Don't tell anyone about it, Hamish. It's not in your report, is it?'

'Not a word.'

'Thanks. Heavens! Is that the time? My friend Sally will be arriving on the bus any moment. I'll get coffee another time.'

Hamish walked her to the kitchen door. 'Thanks again.'

She suddenly put her arms around him and held him close. She closed her eyes and raised her lips for his kiss.

Nothing happened. She opened her eyes. Hamish was looking down at her with an expressionless face.

She released him and backed away, her face flaming. 'Got to go,' she said, ducking her head. She hurried out.

* * *

Friend Sally listened fascinated to Elspeth's tale. Then she said, 'You seem keen on this Hamish Macbeth.'

'I was. In fact I made a pass at him today. Got rejected.'

'Well, it's your fault when you've got a gorgeous man like George Earle panting after you.'

'Oh, George is just George.'

'And George is just what you need. Show that village copper you don't care. Tell George to drive up here after work. Go on. You phone him or I will.'

'All right,' said Elspeth reluctantly. 'May as well.'

Later that day, Carson stood awkwardly in the police station. 'Blair will be back next week, so I'll be leaving for Inverness.'

'Right,' said Hamish, fiddling with a pot on the stove.

'I didn't want to leave without saying goodbye and thanking you for your hospitality.'

'Right.'

'Hamish, come and sit down and listen to me!'

Hamish sat down at the kitchen table opposite him. 'It was like this,' said Carson heavily. 'I'll be honest with you. Yes, I didn't want to keep the CID out of it, but I should have taken you along. Mary Hendry's death is on my conscience.'

Hamish rose and took a bottle of whisky and two glasses down from the cupboard. He sat down again and screwed the top off the bottle. 'I am as much to blame as you,' he said. 'If I hadn't been so anxious to avoid promotion, I would have handled it all myself. But Elspeth pointed out that we're forgetting Mary Hendry killed two people. All she had to do was report Felicity. Felicity would have been banged up and we'd never even have looked at Mary. Have a dram.'

'Thanks. So we'll never really know quite how the murder of Crystal was done.'

'I think Felicity had it well planned. I think she was waiting on the Lochdubh road, on a quiet stretch, not far outside Strathbane. I think maybe she left her own car in Lochdubh, say the evening before, and took the bus back. There's a bus leaves at seven in the evening. I can check that, just out of curiosity. So, she waits until she sees the green BMW coming along. Maybe she phoned from a call box and asked Crystal when she was leaving. She sees Crystal coming along and flags her down. Says something like her car's broken down and she had started to walk. Then maybe she says something like, your tyre's flat at the front. Crystal gets out to have a look. Felicity stuns her with a wheel brace or something. Crystal may have staggered a bit before collapsing in the heather at the side of the road. Felicity heaves her into the backseat, puts on the hat and glasses, and drives like hell. First she thinks of the Glenanstey road, but remembers the back road at Lochdubh and how it's never used. During that Gaelic programme of hers, she must have picked up a lot of local knowledge.

'She drags Crystal out and pushes her into the front seat and then arranges the suicide and goes about her interviewing. She must have got a shock when Mary Hendry told her she had seen her. Mary must have found it a relief after all this time to be able to confide in a fellow murderer. We'll never know exactly, but to my mind, that's probably the way it happened.'

Carson surveyed him. 'I went through all your notes again, Hamish. Before, I could understand you wanting to live here. Nice, simple life. But there's a nasty picture comes out, of brutal marriage, petty crime, and nasty little secrets. It's no different from Strathbane, really.'

'There are right nice people here,' said Hamish defensively.

Carson gave him a sly smile. 'Your girl-friend's a fine lassie.'

'She's not my girlfriend.'

'Why not? Taken a vow of celibacy?'

'Och, I'm off women at the moment.'

'The trouble about being off women,' said Carson, 'is that when a stunner comes along, you never even notice her.'

'You speak from experience?'

'I was getting over an affair away back when. I said I'd never look at another woman again. But I had to take someone to the police ball in Inverness, so I asked a neighbour's daughter, Anna. I didn't really notice her, until all the other fellows at the ball seemed fair taken with her. That opened my eyes. She's now my wife and we've been happily married for twenty years. Imagine if I had let such a chance slip!'

'So you're going back to Inverness.'

'Yes.' He drew out a card. 'That's my home address and telephone number. If you ever feel like coming down to see us, you'd get a right welcome.'

'Thanks.'

'So am I forgiven?'

'Och, yes. We just have to forgive ourselves.'

Carson drained his glass and stood up. 'Take my advice and don't let that lassie get away.'

When he had gone, Hamish pulled forward a copy of the *Highland Times*. He wondered how Elspeth's horoscopes were getting on. 'Libra,' he read. 'There are none so blind as cannot see. You are at a crossroads in your life. One road leads to romance and companionship, the other to solitary loneliness. Which will you take?'

The trouble was, thought Hamish, that he had been pushing Elspeth away because he kept imagining commitment and marriage.

There had been no reason to be so heavy. Nothing to stop him having a light and enjoyable romance and seeing where it led.

He went through to the bedroom and laid out his best suit. Then he had a long hot bath and washed and dried his red hair until it shone with purple lights. He dressed carefully, patted Lugs, and went along to Patel's where he bought a large box of chocolates.

He then headed for Elspeth's flat. He was nearly there when under the greenish pools of light cast by the lamps on the waterfront, he saw her walking toward him. She was on the arm of George Earle. They were laughing together. George's face was radiant. They had not seen him.

Hamish leapt over the nearest garden hedge and crouched down. 'Come on, Elspeth,' he heard George say. 'What about coming back to Inverness? You could maybe get a job on the *Courier*.'

'I might at that,' Elspeth replied. 'This is a bit of a dead-alive hole. Nothing ever happens here.'

Except two murders, thought Hamish bitterly.

A voice behind him made him jump. 'What are you doing in my garden, Hamish Macbeth!'

Nessie Currie stood looking down at him, her arms folded across her aproned chest.

Hamish straightened up and handed her the large box of chocolates. 'I wanted to surprise you. These are for you.'

'Oh, Hamish. Thank you. I never guessed. I mean, an old woman like me. Mind you, there was this interesting article in *Elle* magazine about summer-winter relationships . . .'

'Nessie!' called her sister. 'What is happening out there, out there?'

'Nothing,' called Nessie. She winked at Hamish and smiled roguishly. 'Let it be our secret.'

Hamish let out a squawk of alarm and jumped back over the hedge and headed away as fast as he could.

He went straight to the Brodies' cottage. Angela let him in. 'What's up, Hamish? You're all flustered. Come in.'

'You've got to help me, Angela. I'm in a right mess.'

He followed her into the kitchen and told her about his meeting with Nessie Currie. Angela laughed until the tears streamed down her cheeks.

When she had finished laughing, Hamish said, 'How do I get out of it?'

'I don't think this Elspeth is having a romance with this George person. Yes, he's staying with her, but she's got a female friend staying there as well. I would watch until he leaves and then go and tell Elspeth what happened. Ask her to look like your girlfriend to help you out. That way Nessie will feel she's been jilted for a young woman, and as she thinks you're a Lothario anyway, she'll only be nasty for a bit. Then with Elspeth playing at your girlfriend, you'll get to know her better and it might turn into the real thing.'

'I'll try.'

'His car's a Volvo, parked outside her flat. I'll let you know if I see him leave.'

Angela phoned at lunchtime the following day to say that she had just seen George loading an overnight bag into the Volvo and drive off. He had Elspeth's girlfriend with him.

Hamish was about to leave the police station when he saw Nessie heading purposefully in his direction. He ran up the back way, vaulting over dry stone walls, across muddy fields, and so in a large circle and then back down into the village again.

He ran to the newspaper office. Sam said that Elspeth was over in Drim, covering a concert, but was expected back at any moment.

Hamish waited and waited. The light was fading fast. The sun went down about two in the afternoon, now the winter nights had set in.

At last he saw her car driving up outside and rushed out to meet her.

'Hamish,' said Elspeth. 'Are you waiting for me?'

'Yes, I need to talk to you.'

'Can it wait until I've typed out my report?'

'Yes, I'll wait for you. Don't be long.'

Hamish sat down in the reception area of the newspaper office. It was great to finally take action. Time to go on living. After an hour, she came out. 'Now what is it?'

'Let's walk a bit and I'll explain.'

They went outside. There was a full moon, and the black sky was thick with stars.

'It's like this, Elspeth,' said Hamish, stopping and looking down at her.

'You're so serious. Not another murder?'

'God forbid. No, I've done something daft. You see . . .'

'Hamish!' cooed a voice.

He stiffened. There was Nessie Currie leering up at him. 'I left a casserole for you on the kitchen step . . . darling,' she said. 'Come along.'

Elspeth stared at Hamish.

'Can't it wait, Nessie?' he said desperately.

'No, come quickly before Jessie sees us.' She hooked a surprisingly powerful arm in his and began to drag him away.

Hamish twisted his head back and looked at Elspeth.

'Hamish Macbeth,' she said clearly, 'you're *weird*.'

If you enjoyed *Death of a Celebrity*, read on for
the first chapter of the next book in the *Hamish
Macbeth* series . . .

DEATH OF A
VILLAGE

Chapter One

In all my travels I never met with any one Scotchman but what was a man of sense. I believe everybody of that country that has any, leaves it as fast as they can.

– Francis Lockier

The way propaganda works, as every schoolboy knows, is that if you say the same thing over and over again, lie or not, people begin to believe it.

Hamish Macbeth, police constable of the village of Lochdubh and its surroundings, had been until recently a happy, contented, unambitious man. This was always regarded, by even the housebound and unsuccessful, as a sort of mental aberration. And he had been under fire for a number of years and from a number of people to pull his socks up, get a life, move on, get a promotion, and forsake his lazy ways. Until lately, all comments had slid off him. That was, until Elspeth Grant, local reporter, joined the chorus. It was the way she

291

laughed at him with a sort of affectionate contempt as he mooched around the village that got under his skin. Her mild amazement that he did not want to 'better himself', added on to all the other years of similar comments, finally worked on him like the end result of a propaganda war and he began to feel restless and discontented.

Had he had any work to do apart from filing sheep-dip papers and ticking off the occasional poacher, Elspeth's comments might not have troubled him. And Elspeth was attractive, although he would not admit it to himself. He felt he had endured enough trouble from women to last him a lifetime.

He began to watch travel shows on television and to imagine himself walking on coral beaches or on high mountains in the Himalayas. He fretted over the fact that he had even taken all his holidays in Scotland.

One sunny morning, he decided it was time he got back on his beat, which covered a large area of Sutherland. He decided to visit the village of Stoyre up on the west coast. It was more of a hamlet than a village. No crime ever happened there. But, he reminded himself, a good copper ought to check up on the place from time to time.

After a winter of driving rain and a miserable spring, a rare period of idyllic weather had arrived in the Highlands. Tall twisted mountains swam in a heat haze. The air through the open window of the police Land

Rover was redolent with smells of wild thyme, salt, bell heather, and peat smoke. He took a deep breath and felt all his black discontentment ebb away. Damn Elspeth! This was the life. He drove steadily down a winding single-track road to Stoyre.

Tourists hardly ever visited Stoyre. This seemed amazing on such a perfect day, when the village's cluster of whitewashed houses lay beside the deep blue waters of the Atlantic. There was a little stone harbour where three fishing boats bobbed lazily at anchor. Hamish parked in front of the pub, called the Fisherman's Arms. He stepped down from the Land Rover. His odd-looking dog, Lugs, scrambled down as well.

Hamish looked to right and left. The village seemed deserted. It was very still, unnaturally so. No children cried, no snatches of radio music drifted out from the cottages, no one came or went from the small general stores next to the pub.

Lugs bristled and let out a low growl. 'Easy, boy,' said Hamish. He looked up the hill beyond the village to where the graveyard lay behind a small stone church. Perhaps there was a funeral. But he could see no sign of anyone moving about.

'Come on, boy,' he said to his dog. He pushed open the door of the pub and went inside. The pub consisted of a small white-washed room with low beams on the ceiling. A few wooden tables scarred with cigarette burns were dotted about. There was no one behind the bar.

'Anyone home?' called Hamish loudly.

To his relief there came the sound of someone moving in the back premises. A thickset man entered through a door at the back of the bar. Hamish recognized Andy Crummack, the landlord and owner.

'How's it going, Andy?' asked Hamish. 'Everybody dead?'

'It iss yourself, Hamish. What will you be having?'

'Just a tonic water.' Hamish looked round the deserted bar. 'Where is everyone?'

'It's aye quiet this time o' day.' Andy poured a bottle of tonic water into a glass.

'Slainte!' said Hamish. 'Are you having one?'

'Too early. If ye don't mind, I've got stock to check.' Andy made for the door behind the bar.

'Hey, wait a minute, Andy. I havenae been in Stoyre for a while but I've never seen the place so dead.'

'We're quiet folks, Hamish.'

'And nothing's going on?'

'Nothing. Now, if ye don't mind . . .'

The landlord disappeared through the door.

Hamish drank the tonic water and then pushed back his peaked cap and scratched his fiery hair. Maybe he was imagining things. He hadn't visited Stoyre for months. The last time had been in March when he'd made a routine call. He remembered people chatting on the waterfront and this pub full of locals.

He put his glass on the bar and went out into the sunlight. The houses shone white in the glare and the gently heaving blue water had an oily surface.

He went into the general store. 'Morning, Mrs MacBean,' he said to the elderly woman behind the counter. 'Quiet today. Where is everyone?'

'They'll maybe be up at the kirk.'

'What! On a Monday? Is it someone's funeral?'

'No. Can I get you anything, Mr Macbeth?'

Hamish leaned on the counter. 'Come on. You can tell me,' he coaxed. 'What's everyone doing at the church on a Monday?'

'We are God-fearing folk in Stoyre,' she said primly, 'and I'll ask you to remember that.'

Baffled, Hamish walked out of the shop and was starting to set off up the hill when the church doors opened and people started streaming out. Most were dressed in black as if for a funeral.

He stood in the centre of the path as they walked down towards him. He hailed people he knew. 'Morning, Jock ... grand day, Mrs Nisbett,' and so on. But the crowd parted as they reached him and silently continued on their way until he was left standing alone.

He walked on towards the church and round to the manse at the side with Lugs at his heels. The minister had just reached his front door.

He was a new appointment, Hamish noticed, a thin nervous man with a prominent Adam's apple, and his black robes were worn and dusty. He had sparse ginger hair, weak eyes and a small pursed mouth.

'Morning,' said Hamish. 'I am Hamish Macbeth, constable at Lochdubh. You are new to here?'

The minister reluctantly faced him. 'I am Fergus Mackenzie,' he said in a lilting Highland voice.

'You seem to be doing well,' remarked Hamish. 'Church full on a Monday morning.'

'There is a strong religious revival here,' said Fergus. 'Now, if you don't mind . . .'

'I do mind,' said Hamish crossly. 'This village has changed.'

'It has changed for the better. A more God-fearing community does not exist anywhere else in the Highlands.' And with that the minister went into the manse and slammed the door in Hamish's face.

Becoming increasingly irritated, Hamish retreated back to the waterfront. It was deserted again. He thought of knocking on some doors to find out if there was any other answer to this strange behaviour apart from a religious revival and then decided against it. He looked back up the hill to where a cottage stood near the top. It was the holiday home of a retired army man, Major Jennings, an Englishman. Perhaps he might be more forthcoming. He plodded back up the hill, past the church, and knocked on the major's door. Silence greeted him. He knew the major lived most of the year in the south of England. Probably not arrived yet. Hamish remembered he usually came north for a part of the summer.

When he came back down from the hill, he saw that people were once more moving about. There were villagers in the shop and villagers on the waterfront. This time they gave him a polite greeting. He stopped one of them, Mrs Lyle. 'Is anything funny going on here?' he asked.

She was a small, round woman with tight grey curls and glasses perched on the end of her nose. 'What do you mean?' she asked.

'There's an odd atmosphere and then you've all been at the kirk and it isn't even Sunday.'

'It is difficult to explain to such as you, Hamish Macbeth,' she said. 'But in this village we take our worship of the Lord seriously and don't keep it for just the one day.'

I'm a cynic, thought Hamish as he drove off. Why should I find it all so odd? He knew that in some of the remote villages a good preacher was still a bigger draw than anything on television. Mr Mackenzie must be a powerful speaker.

When he returned to Lochdubh, Hamish found all the same that the trip to Stoyre had cheered him up. The restlessness that had plagued him had gone. He whistled as he prepared food for himself and his dog, and then carried his meal on a tray out to the front garden, where he had placed a table with an umbrella over it. Why dream of cafés in France when he had everything here in Lochdubh?

He had just finished a meal of fried haggis, sausage and eggs when a voice hailed him. 'Lazing around again, Hamish?'

The gate to the front garden opened and Elspeth Grant came in. She was wearing a brief tube top which showed her midriff, a small pair of denim shorts, and her hair had been tinted aubergine. She pulled up a chair and sat down next to him.

'The trouble with aubergine,' said Hamish, 'is that it chust doesnae do.'

'Doesn't do what?' demanded Elspeth.

'Anything for anyone. It's like the purple lipstick or the black nail varnish. Anything that's far from an original colour isn't sexy.'

'And what would you know about anything sexy?'

'I am a man and I assume you mean to attract the opposite sex.'

'Women dress and do their hair for themselves these days.'

'Havers.'

'It's true, Hamish. You've been living in this time warp for so long that you just don't know what's what. Anyway, I'm bored. There's really nothing to report until the Highland Games over at Braikie and that's a week away.'

'I might have a wee something for you. I've just been over at Stoyre. There's a religious revival there. They were all at the kirk this morning. Seems they've got a new minister, a Mr Mackenzie. I was thinking he must be a pretty powerful preacher.'

'Not much, but something,' said Elspeth. 'I'll try next Sunday.'

'The way they're going on, you may not need to wait that long. They've probably got a service every day.'

'Want to come with me?'

Hamish stretched out his long legs. 'I've just been. Have the Currie sisters seen you in that outfit?'

The Currie sisters were middle-aged twins, spinsters, and the upholders of morals in Lochdubh.

'Yes. Jessie Currie told me that I should go home and put on a skirt and Nessie Currie defended me.'

'Really! What did she say?'

'She said my boots were so ugly that they made everything else I had on look respectable.'

Hamish looked down at the heavy pair of hiking boots Elspeth was wearing. 'I see what she means.'

Elspeth flushed up to the roots of her frizzy aubergine hair with anger. 'I don't know why I bother even talking to you, Hamish Macbeth. I'm off.'

When she had gone, Hamish lay back in his chair, clasped his hands behind his head. He shouldn't have been so rude to her but he blamed her remarks about him being unambitious for having recently upset the lazy comfort of his summer days.

The telephone in the police station rang, the noise cutting shrilly through the peace of the day.

He sighed, got to his feet, and went to answer it. The voice of his pet hate, Detective Chief Inspector Blair, boomed down the line. 'Get yoursel' over to Braikie, laddie. Teller's grocery in the High Street has been burgled. Anderson will be there soon.'

'On my way,' said Hamish.

He took his peaked cap down from a peg on the kitchen door and put it on his head. 'No, Lugs,' he said to his dog, who was looking up at him out of his strange blue eyes. 'You stay.'

He went out and got into the police Land Rover and drove off, turning over in his mind what he knew of Teller's grocery. It was a licensed shop and sold more upmarket groceries than its two rivals. He was relieved that he would be working with Detective Sergeant Jimmy Anderson rather than Blair.

He parked outside the shop and went in. Mr Teller was a small, severe-faced man with gold-rimmed glasses. 'You took your time,' he said crossly. 'They've taken all my wine and spirits, the whole lot. I found the lot gone when I opened up this morning, and phoned the police.'

300

'I was out on another call,' said Hamish. 'How did they get in?'

'Round the back.' Mr Teller raised a flap on the counter and Hamish walked through.

A pane of glass on the back door had been smashed. 'The forensic people'll be along soon.' said Hamish. 'I can't touch anything at the moment.'

'Well, let's hope you hurry up. I've got to put a claim into the insurance company.'

'How much for?'

'I'll need to total it up. Thousands of pounds.'

Hamish looked blankly down at the shopkeeper. He had been in the shop before. He could not remember seeing any great supply of wine or spirits. There had been three shelves, near the till, that was all.

He focused on Mr Teller. 'I haven't been in your shop for a bit. Had you expanded the liquor side?'

'No, why?'

'I remember only about three shelves of bottles.'

'They took all the stuff out of the cellar as well.'

'You'd better show me.'

Mr Teller led the way to a door at the side of the back shop. The lock was splintered. Hamish took out a handkerchief and put it over the light switch at the top of the stairs and pressed. He stood on the top step and looked down. The cellar was certainly empty. And dusty.

He returned to the front to find that Jimmy Anderson had arrived.

'Hullo, Hamish,' said the detective. 'Crime, isn't it? A real crime. All that lovely booze. Taken a statement yet?'

'Not yet. Could I be having a wee word with you outside?'

'Sure. I could do with a dram. There's a pub across the road.'

'Not yet. Outside.'

Under the suspicious eyes of Mr Teller, they walked out into the street.

'What?' demanded Jimmy.

'He is saying that thousands of pounds of booze have been nicked. But when I pointed out to him that he only kept about three shelves of the stuff, he said they had cleared out the cellar as well.'

'So?'

'The cellar floor is dusty. Even dust. No marks of boxes and, what's more to the point, no drag marks. It is my belief he had nothing in that cellar. He could have been after the insurance.'

'But the insurance will want to see the books, check the orders.'

'True. Well, we'd best take a statement and then talk to his supplier.'

They returned to the shop. Hamish took out a notebook. 'Now, Mr Teller, you found the shop had been burgled when you opened up. That would be at nine o'clock?'

'Eight-thirty.'

'You didn't touch anything?'

'I went down to the cellar and found everything gone from there.'

'We'll check around and see if anyone heard or saw anything. What is the name of your supplier?'

'Frog's of Strathbane. Why?'

'The insurance company will want to see your books to check the amount of the lost stores against your record of deliveries.'

'They're welcome to look at them anytime.'

'Have you seen anyone suspicious about the town?'

'Now, there's a thing. There were two rough-looking men came into the shop two days ago. I hadn't seen them before. They asked for cigarettes and I served them but they were looking all around the place.'

'Descriptions?'

'One was a big ape of a man. He had black hair, foreign-looking. Big nose and thick lips. He was wearing a checked shirt and jeans.'

'Did he sound foreign?'

'I can't remember.'

Two men in white overalls came into the shop carrying cases of equipment. 'We'll stop for a moment while you take the forensic boys through the back to check the break-in,' said Hamish.

'What do you think?' Hamish asked Jimmy when the shopkeeper had gone through to the back shop with the forensic team.

'Seems a respectable body. Still, we'll check with Frog's. If he'd had the stuff delivered, then he must be telling the truth.'

'I don't like the look o' that cellar floor.'

'Well, if there's anything fishy, the forensic boys will find it.'

They waited until Mr Teller came back. 'Now,' said Hamish, 'what did the other fellow look like?'

'He was small, ferrety. I remember,' said Mr Teller, excited. 'He was wearing a short-sleeved shirt and he had a snake tattooed on his left arm.'

'Hair colour?'

'Maybe dark but his head was shaved. He had a thin face, black eyes, and a long nose.'

'Clothes?'

'Like a told you, he had a short-sleeved shirt on, blue it was, and grey trousers.'

Hamish surveyed the shopkeeper with a shrewd look in his hazel eyes. 'I'm puzzled by the state of your cellar floor.'

'How's that?'

'There were no marks in the dust. No signs of dragging.'

'Well, maybe they just lifted the stuff up.'

Jimmy Anderson was exuding the impatient vibes of a man dying for a drink.

'Come on, Hamish,' he said impatiently. 'Let forensics get on with it while we go over what we've got.'

Hamish reluctantly followed him over to the

pub. 'Maybe I'll nip back and tell those chaps from forensic about that cellar floor.'

'Och, leave them. They know their job.' Jimmy ordered two double whiskies.

'Just the one, then,' said Hamish. 'I don't trust that man Teller one bit.'

Finally he dragged a reluctant Jimmy away from the bar. Mr Teller was serving a woman with groceries.

'I think you should close up for the day,' said Hamish.

Mr Teller jerked a thumb towards the back shop. 'They said it was all right.'

'Let us through,' said Hamish.

Mr Teller lifted the flap on the counter.

Hamish and Jimmy walked through to the back shop.

'How's it going?' Jimmy asked one of the men.

'Nothing much,' he said. 'Looks like a straightforward break-in. Can't get much outside. There's gravel there. Nothing but a pair of size eleven footprints at the top of the cellar stairs.'

'Those are mine,' said Hamish. 'But what about the cellar itself, and the stairs? When I looked down, there seemed to be nothing but undisturbed dust.'

'Then you need your eyes tested, laddie. The thieves swept the place clean and the stairs.'

'What?' Hamish had a sinking feeling in his stomach.

'Have a look. We're finished down there.'

Hamish went to the cellar door, switched on the light, and walked down the steps. He could see sweeping brush marks in the dust.

'Those weren't there before,' he said angrily. 'Teller must have done it when you pair were out the back.'

Hamish retreated wrathfully to the shop, followed by Jimmy. 'Why did you sweep the cellar?' he demanded angrily.

Mr Teller looked the picture of outraged innocence. 'I never did. I went back outside to ask them if they wanted a cup of tea. I am a respectable tradesman and a member of the Rotary club and the Freemasons. I shall be speaking to your superior officer.'

'Speak all you want,' shouted Hamish. 'I'll have you!'

'Come on, Hamish.' Jimmy drew him outside the shop. 'Back to the bar, Hamish. A dram'll soothe you down.'

'I've had enough and you'd better not have any more. You're driving.'

'One more won't hurt,' coaxed Jimmy, urging Hamish into the dark interior of the bar. When he had got their drinks, he led Hamish to a corner table. 'Now, Hamish, couldn't you be mistaken? When anyone mentions Freemasons, my heart sinks. The big cheese is a member.' The big cheese was the chief superintendent, Peter Daviot.

'I'm sure as sure,' said Hamish.

'So what do you suggest we do if the wee

man's books are in order and tie in with Frog's records of deliveries?'

'I don't know,' fretted Hamish.

'It's your word against his.'

'You'd think the word of a policeman would count for something these days.'

'Not against a Freemason and a member of the Rotary,' said Jimmy cynically.

Hamish made up his mind. 'I'm off to Frog's. You can have my drink.'

Jimmy eyed the whisky longingly. 'I should report what you're doing to Blair.'

'Leave it a bit.'

'Okay. But keep in touch. I'll see if I can sweat Teller a bit. The wonders o' forensic science, eh?'

'There's something up with that lot from Strathbane. It seems to me they're aye skimping the job because they've got a football match to go to or something.'

Hamish drove to Strathbane after looking up Frog's in a copy of the Highland and Islands phone book he kept in the Land Rover. Their offices were situated down at the docks, an area of Strathbane that Hamish loathed. The rare summer sunshine might bring out the beauty of the Highland countryside but all it did was make the docks smell worse: a combination of stale fish, rotting vegetables, and what Victorian ladies used to describe as something 'much worse'.

The offices had a weather-faded sign above the door: FROG'S WHISKY AND WINE DISTRIBUTORS. He pushed open the door and went in. 'Why, Mary,' he exclaimed, recognizing the small girl behind the desk, 'what are you doing here?'

Mary Bisset was a resident of Lochdubh, small and pert. Her normally cheeky face, however, wore a harassed look. 'I'm a temp, Hamish,' she said. 'I cannae get the hang o' this computer.'

'Where's the boss?'

'Out in the town at some meeting.'

'Who is he?'

'Mr Dunblane.'

'Not Mr Frog?'

'I think there was a Mr Frog one time or another. Oh, Hamish, what am I to do?'

'Let me see. Move over.'

Hamish sat down at the computer and switched it on. Nothing happened. He twisted his lanky form around and looked down. 'Mary, Mary, you havenae got the damn thing plugged in.'

She giggled. Hamish plugged in the computer. 'What do you want?'

'The word processing thingy. I've got letters to write.'

'Before I do that, do you know where he keeps the account books?'

'In the safe.'

Hamish's face fell.

'But you're the polis. I suppose it would be all right to open it up for you.'

'Do you know the combination?'

'It's one of thae old-fashioned things. The key's on the wall with the other keys in the inner office.'

Hamish went into the inner office. 'Where is everyone?' he asked over his shoulder.

'Tam and Jerry – they work here – they've gone into town with Mr Dunblane.'

Hamish grinned. There on a board with other keys and neatly labelled 'Safe' was the key he wanted. 'Come in, Mary,' he said. 'You'd better be a witness to this.'

Hamish opened the safe. There was a large quantity of banknotes on the lower shelf. On the upper shelf were two large ledgers marked 'Accounts'. He took them out and relocked the safe. He sat down at a desk and began to go through them. 'Keep a lookout, Mary,' he said, 'and scream if you see anyone.'

'What's this all about?'

He grinned at her. 'If this works out, I'll take you out for dinner one evening and tell you.'

Chief Superintendent Peter Daviot had finished his speech to the Strathbane Businessmen's Association. He enjoyed being a guest speaker at affairs such as these. But his enjoyment was not to last for long. He had just regained his seat to gratifying applause when his mobile phone rang. He excused himself from the table and went outside to answer it. It was Detective Chief Inspector Blair. 'Macbeth's landed us in the shit,' growled Blair.

'Moderate your language,' snapped Daviot. 'What's up?'

'Teller's shop up in Braikie was broken into and all his booze stolen. Macbeth's accusing Teller of covering up evidence and Teller is threatening to sue.'

'Dear me, you'd better get up there and diffuse the situation.'

'Anderson's up there.'

'Go yourself. This requires the attention of a senior officer. And tell Macbeth to report to me immediately.'

When Daviot returned to police headquarters, he was told to his surprise that Hamish Macbeth was waiting to see him. 'That was quick,' he said to his secretary, Helen. 'Where is he?'

'In your office,' said Helen sourly. She loathed Hamish.

Daviot pushed open the door and went in. Hamish got to his feet clutching a sheaf of photocopied papers.

'What's this all about, Macbeth? I hear there has been a complaint about you.'

'It's about Teller's grocery,' said Hamish. 'He claims to have had all his booze stolen, booze that was supplied by Frog's. These are photocopies of the account books at Frog's. They are an eye-opener. The last delivery to Teller is recorded in one set of books. But this other set shows five more shopkeepers from all over who claimed insurance and were paid fifty per cent of the insurance money.'

'How did you come by this?'

'Dunblane, the boss, and two others were out. I know the temp. She let me into the safe.'

'Macbeth! You cannot do that without a search warrant!'

'So I need one now. The temp won't talk. We'd better move fast.'

'I sent Blair up to Braikie because Teller was threatening to sue. I'll issue that search warrant and we'll take Detective MacNab and two police officers and get round there.'

It was late evening by the time Hamish Macbeth drove back to Lochdubh. He was a happy, contented man. Blair had returned from Braikie in time to hear about the success of the operation. The five other shopkeepers were being rounded up. They had claimed on supposedly stolen stock, taken it themselves and hidden it. So they gained half the insurance money and still had their stock after they had paid Dunblane.

That strange half-light of a northern Scottish summer where it never really gets dark bathed the countryside: the gloaming, where, as some of the older people still believed, the fairies lay in wait for the unwary traveller.

As Hamish opened the police station door, Lugs barked a reproachful welcome. Hamish took the dog out for a walk and then returned to prepare them both some supper. There came a furious knocking at the kitchen door just as he had put Lugs's food bowl on the floor and was sitting down at the table to enjoy his own supper.

He opened the door and found himself confronted with the angry figure of Mary Bisset's mother.

'You leave my daughter alone, d'ye hear?' she shouted. 'She's only twenty. Find someone your own age.'

Hamish blinked at her. 'Your daughter was of great help in our inquiries into an insurance fraud,' he said. 'I couldn't tell her what it was about but promised to take her out for dinner by way of thanks and tell her then.'

'Oh, yeah,' she sneered. 'Well, romance someone of your own age. You ought to be ashamed of yourself. Casanova!'

And with that she stormed off.

Hamish slammed the door. Women, he thought. I'm only in my thirties and I've just been made to feel like a dirty old man.

JOIN
M.C. Beaton
ONLINE

www.mcbeaton.com/uk

Keep up with her latest news, views, wit & wisdom
And sign up to the M. C. Beaton newsletter

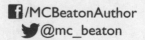

f /MCBeatonAuthor
🐦 @mc_beaton